THE KEEPER OF T

Lior Rei

Production by eBookPro Publishing
www.ebook-pro.com

The Keeper of the Glass House
Lior Reitblatt

Copyright © 2024 Lior Reitblatt

All rights reserved; no parts of this book may be reproduced or transmitted in any form or by any means, electronic or mechanical, including photocopying, recording, taping, or by any information retrieval system, without the permission, in writing, of the author.

The publisher has done everything in its power to locate the copyright holders of all the material taken from external sources. We apologize for any omission or error, and if they are brought to our attention, we will act to remedy the error in subsequent editions.

Translation from Hebrew: Esther Frumkin
Editing: Nancy Alroy

Contact: lrreitblatt@gmail.com

ISBN 9798303802315

THE KEEPER
OF THE
GLASS HOUSE

*A WWII Historical Fiction Novel
Based on a True Story
of a Holocaust Survivor*

LIOR REITBLATT

Chapter 1

January 2022

The classical melody wafting from the Voice of Music channel melded with the pastoral scenery as I whizzed by the Neveh Ilan exit on Highway 1. Pleasant winter morning sunlight lit up the carpets of green on either side of the four-lane road connecting Tel Aviv to Jerusalem. The Waze app surprised me once again by calculating that I would arrive in the center of Jerusalem in a mere 17 minutes. It seemed as though the tranquil mood I'd woken up with this morning had worked its magic on the universe. It started with the fruit smoothie that my partner Sigali left for me in the fridge, then a phone call with Ze'evik in which he sang me a loud, out-of-tune 'Happy Birthday' (once again he got the date wrong and called me a week early), and on to the surprise notification waiting for me on my cell phone that the travel time from Tel Aviv to Jerusalem would be only 50 minutes. Given Waze's deceptive predictions during the Coronavirus era (as though in addition to losing its sense of smell, the app had lost its sense of time), I had allowed myself a 30-minute safety margin. The warm coat I chose, preparing for the frigid cold of Jerusalem in January, was making me sweat. I was performing acrobatic contortions to free myself of it without taking off my seatbelt (while also trying not to endanger the cars around me) when I got a phone call from my daughter, Rona.

"Hi Rona'leh."

"Hi Daddy. Are you coming today?"

"Certainly. I might be early. It seems that the recent Omicron variant of the Coronavirus has left a lot of drivers stuck at home."

"What time do you think you'll get here?"

"My meeting is supposed to end around two-thirty, but I think I'll try to make it earlier."

"I won't be home before three."

"Then I'll walk around Rehavia for a bit. Is the weather there as nice as here?"

"Lovely. Gentle winter sun. Clear sky, but still cold for Tel Avivians." I couldn't tell if she was teasing me or if she meant both of us.

"It's okay, I have a warm coat."

"I can leave you a key with Ruthy."

"Ruthy, Ruthy," I sighed.

"What's that nostalgic tone? Do you know her?"

"No, no," I answered defensively.

"OK. So Ruthy lives in the building across from me, on the ground floor."

"Where? On Ben Maimon Street?"

"Yes. 52."

"I don't believe it."

"What?"

"In which apartment? The front or the rear?"

"The rear one. Why?"

"You're not going to believe this, but I spent a week there one summer almost 50 years ago."

"There in the apartment?"

"No. Grandma lived in the building opposite; I was visiting her the summer before high school and took English lessons from Mrs. Kraus who lived on the ground floor... in the rear apartment... her name was Gusta." I fell silent, lost in memory.

"Wow. Ruthy did tell me something about the Kraus family who once lived in her apartment. He... the husband of that Gusta, served in an important position in the Budapest Jewish community. She told me that he raised a huge ruckus in Israel in the 1950s and went head-to-head with the authorities. Do you know that story?"

"Yes, you're right. I spent a lot of time with him during that unforgettable week. I didn't realize then that I was witnessing such a huge story that so many would try to hide. I was just a boy then. Only later, looking back on it, did I understand the consequences."

"Here in Israel?"

"Yes, Rona'leh. I think that, to this day, part of this story was never publicized."

"It fits," confirmed Rona. "Ruthy told me that he was a special man, very controversial, and that there was something mysterious going on there. She has lots of stories about this building. Did you know Bibi[1] also lived there? On the third floor."

"She's a little confused. That was his first wife's parents' apartment, and he spent a lot of time there."

"Okay, Daddy, I have to run. So I'm leaving you the key with Ruthy, agreed? It says Ruthy Shor on the door."

---

1. Israeli Prime Minister Binyamin Netanyahu

"Ruthy Shor?" I asked in astonishment. "How old is she?"

"Maybe five years older than me, why?"

"Is she from a kibbutz?"

"Yes, she's a kibbutznik. How did you know?"

"From the North? From Bar'am?"

"No, the opposite. From the South. From Yotvata. What's wrong? Why all these questions?"

"No... Nothing... She was Rutha Shorin back then."

"When was that?"

"In 1972."

"Maybe her grandmother."

"Ruthy? A grandmother? Maybe... what does she look like?"

"Daddy... I'm going. So, the Shor family, number 52, ground floor. Rear apartment. Bye."

"Bye..." the conversation with my youngest daughter was disconnected, and I was left trying to digest all this information and the surge of memories that followed in its wake.

• • •

My business meeting was cut slightly short and thus I found myself heading to Ben Maimon Street at two o'clock, happy to find a legal parking space in front of the Levi Eshkol[2] House.

The phone rang while I was busy with the parking app.

"Daddy?"

---

2. Israeli Prime Minister from 1963-1969.

"Yes."

"Ruthy had to go out, so she left the key for you underneath the doormat."

"Rona. That's irresponsible."

"Oh come on, Dad, forget it. In Jerusalem, be a Jerusalemite," she said and hung up.

"Well," I grumbled, apparently to myself, "it's still irresponsible."

I hurried to the apartment, still hoping to run into that Ruthy Shor. The first thing I noticed was the overgrown yard with its tangle of weeds in front of the house. I entered the stairwell and found the key under the mat. With a sense of relief mingled with some disappointment, I knocked on the door, hoping that perhaps she hadn't left yet. There was no sound from the apartment. I went back outside the building and circled it, making my way between the vines and the weeds until I reached the back porch that belonged to the apartment. "Ruthy Shor suffers from overconfidence," I remarked to myself, noticing that all the blinds were up. I moved closer and peeked in, hoping that none of the residents in the neighboring apartments would see me. The sight that met my eyes was familiar. The old walls and floors took me back 50 years. Except for the disappearance of the magnificent furniture that once graced the Kraus's tiny apartment, everything remained unchanged.

I left the overgrown yard, crossed the road, and entered the building opposite, taking the steps three at a time like I used to do as a child. The apartment that my grandmother, Tsipora, had bequeathed to us was on the second floor and, unlike Kraus's apartment, it had undergone a complete transformation since 1972. In her will,

Grandma Tsipora left the apartment to me and my younger sister, Efrat. For years, the apartment had been rented out to Jerusalem students until the summer of 2018 when Rona returned from a post-army trip to India and started to prepare for a degree in sociology at the Hebrew University. With the help of my partner Sigal, the architect, and a Jerusalem contractor, a three-room apartment was turned into a loft with one bedroom and a huge living room connected to the kitchen. The cost of the renovation doubled and tripled during the process, but the end result was spectacularly beautiful.

Grandma Tsipora's famous storage crawl space, where she kept the family archives, was hidden behind a heavy oak door, the lower part of the door hiding the electricity box and telephone/internet connections. After the conversation with Rona which had stirred up so many memories, I decided to use the time while I was waiting to look for my notebooks from the summer of 1972, the summer when I met Moshe Kraus, although I wasn't sure that Grandma had kept them. I pulled over a chair from the dining area and climbed up into the crawl space. That part of the apartment hadn't been touched during renovations. Six cartons were stacked in two layers, side by side, marked with black marker in a clear hand. I brought them down and placed them on the dining table. One box contained Grandma's and Grandpa's legal documents. A second box contained photo albums, most of them in black and white. I opened the third and fourth boxes marked 'Efrat and Uri' and found drawings that my sister and I had made as children, reports about our family history, and yellowing elementary school report cards. The fifth box was devoted to my father, Binyamin, and included various press clippings in which he appeared. The sixth box was marked 'Uri 1972.'

After skimming quickly through the first five boxes, I carried them back up to the storage space and turned my attention to the sixth box. My heart began to pound as I lifted the lid. An old Sanyo tape recorder lay on its side in one part of the box. I remembered Grandma's portable tape recorder, the hours I spent listening to recordings of pop music and hit parades, and I wondered if there was any trace of those tapes. Next to the tape player were some old Dafron notebooks bound in thin blue rubber bands. The top notebook bore the title, in Grandma's handwriting, 'Session #1, Sunday 6 August 1972.' I pulled out the notebook, excited to encounter my own childish handwriting, scribbled in large letters across many pages.

I was thrilled. Grandma Tsipora saved all this... unbelievable. I slid the notebook back into the box together with the others. Next I found 12 audio tapes bundled together with a rubber band and wrapped in a note that read 'Music and Uri's sessions.' I took out the tape player, plugged it in, inserted a tape and, to my delight, strains of George Harrison's 'My Sweet Lord' emanated from the machine. Leaving the tape playing, I went to turn on the espresso machine, enjoying the music and the memories associated with it.

I returned to the box and pulled out a small photo album. I flipped through it quickly, hoping to find pictures of me with the neighbors' children, and maybe also a picture of Rutha Shorin but, unfortunately, it only included photos of me and my grandmother in the Old City, in the Israel Museum and the new neighborhoods that were built in Jerusalem after the glorious victory of 1967. Disappointed, I turned my attention to a small cardboard box in one corner of the carton. Meanwhile, the tape recorder was playing the beloved voice of Boaz Sharabi singing the English version of the love song 'Pamela.' I smiled when I heard a knock on the door. I opened it and my Rona'leh jumped into my arms for a bear hug.

"Rona'leh! How are things, my love? I've missed you."

"Me too, Daddy. Everything is great, but there is a change in plans. Danny is getting out on leave from the army and I'm picking him up in half an hour at the central bus station. But stay, Dad, we'll come back and make lunch. Danny must be hungry. What about you? Did you eat anything?"

"No, but there's really no need. I need to get back to Tel Aviv."

"Relax, Daddy. Where are you rushing off to? I thought you were taking a break from business."

"Yes, but Sigali..."

"Sigali what? I talked to her earlier, she's going out with friends this evening anyway, don't bother her. I'll be back soon, I expect to see you here," she wagged her finger and vanished as quickly as she had appeared.

I returned to the tape recorder on the table. I pushed the 'eject' button, removed the music cassette and put in the tape of the second session. I recognized the elderly man's voice immediately, gentle and soft. It was Moshe Kraus telling me, in English, about Rudolf Vrba's escape from Auschwitz in 1944. I listened to the tape for five minutes before turning the machine off. The curiosity that had been stirred by the conversation with Rona increased. Kraus's voice from a distance of 50 years brought up fragments of memories that I had filed somewhere deep in the recesses of my mind and forgotten about, probably during the time when I had difficulty appreciating the full significance of the deeply hidden secrets revealed to me then.

Rona sent me a WhatsApp message, "Danny missed his bus; I'm waiting for him at the central bus station. We'll probably be there in another hour." My stomach was beginning to rumble. I left all the mess on the table and went outside. Google showed me that the nearest café, Rachel on the Boulevard, was 240 meters away, so I started walking along Ben Maimon Street. To my right was a sign marking 'Jason's Tomb,' with Aviad Garden spread out behind it. I was reminded of the many hours I spent with the neighborhood children playing games in that park, including the frightening séances we once held near the triangular pyramid of the tomb. I debated whether to stop and go down the stairs leading to the park, but I decided to satisfy my hunger first. Rachel on the Boulevard turned out to be a kiosk and, in front of it, several scattered benches and tables. I sat at one of the tables and sated my hunger with a roast beef and red tuna sandwich, washed down with a glass of lemonade. The roll was excellent and the truffle butter with avocado and lemon cream made the sandwich a treat. Contrary to my usual custom, I let the sandwich leak onto my hands and drip onto the small table.

The winter dusk fell early and it began to grow dark along the boulevard. I walked back towards the apartment, passing Aviad Garden again on my way. Twilight lent it an air of mystery. I walked down the stairs and sat on a park bench. I knew that Jason's Tomb at the edge of the park was part of Jerusalem's necropolis during the Second Temple period. This scrap of history, like the nights of terror I spent in this park, began to flood my mind. It was on this bench that I experienced my first 'French kiss' with Ruthy – the same Rutha Shorin who was a year older than me – and transformed that summer from a boy to a teenager. I sat there for a few more minutes savoring the bitter-sweet memory before getting up and starting back to the apartment. When I reached the entrance of the building, my legs carried me to the right, and I found myself crossing the street towards Moshe Kraus's apartment. I stood in front of the door, embarrassed. I could hear the sounds of water running in the apartment, and I waited a few minutes until the sound stopped. I pressed the doorbell. It didn't work. I knocked gently on the door.

"Who is it?" I heard a girl's voice.

"Uri. Rona's father."

"You didn't find the key?"

"I found it, but I wanted... ummm... to see Moshe Kraus's apartment."

"Huh. Kraus. Rona told you?"

"Yes."

"I'm sorry, I'm not dressed yet," she said from behind the closed door, "and I have to go out now. How long are you staying in Jerusalem?"

I didn't know what to answer. "I... I'm staying until tomorrow afternoon," I said impulsively.

"Great. So can you come tomorrow at eight in the morning? I promise you an excellent espresso."

"Okay. Eight. I'll be there. Bye."

I returned to my grandmother's apartment. Rona and Danny came in five minutes later but we didn't get to see each other for longer than a few minutes. It turned out that Danny had surprised Rona by reserving two nights at a hotel at the Dead Sea, and they would be leaving soon.

Swallowing my disappointment, I let them know that I had decided to stay the night in Jerusalem and go through Kraus's tapes.

"Excellent! Finally relaxing the pace a bit," Rona praised me as she packed some clothes in a backpack.

"I'm trying."

"You got hit by a wave of nostalgia, huh?" Rona nodded towards the stack of tapes.

"It seems so," I grinned like someone caught red-handed. "The truth is that I wasn't ready for this."

As Sigal didn't answer the phone, I sent her a text message informing her of my intention to spend the night in Jerusalem. Surprised by my uncharacteristic spontaneity, I wandered towards the bathroom, catching a towel Danny threw at me.

"Okay, Daddy, we're off. Leave the key with Ruthy, okay?" Rona shouted.

"Gladly... I mean fine," I responded to their backs as they were already headed down the stairwell.

I came out of the bathroom, trailing a cloud of steam that followed me into the chill of the living room. I sat down on the armchair, trying to get my thoughts in order, still flitting between the Ruthy of 1972 and the Ruthy of 2022, between a business lunch meeting and Moshe Kraus, and between my Grandma Tsipora and Rona'leh. I turned on the TV but, after briefly flipping through the channels, I turned it off again. I got up, made a cup of coffee and sat down at the dining table. I pulled out the first notebook and the first tape of the meetings with Kraus, turned on the tape recorder, and drifted 50 years into the past.

Chapter 2

August 1972

The summer of 1972 found me in a period of transition. A few weeks earlier I had completed junior high school and, from the results of the survey test that were published, I learned that unlike my classmates I was going on alone to Municipal High School No. 1. My mother, Hayuta, who thought that my level of English was not good enough to start high school, sat me down for a talk.

"We have to do something about your English level," she said.

"What's wrong with my English?" I asked innocently.

"You should take some lessons to improve it before starting high school."

"My English is very good," I protested.

My mother ignored my comment. "There's an excellent English teacher who lives across from Grandma."

"So?"

"So instead of lying around, going to the beach, and fighting with your sister, go visit Grandma and you can get yourself ready for high school."

"Are you serious? All my friends are on summer break and I'm going to sit and study?"

"Your friends are already sorting themselves into groups of those going on to high school together. You said yourself that you hardly see them."

"Right, but still... to Jerusalem?"

"Jerusalem is quite the developing city... would you rather go to Germany?" she suddenly changed direction.

"What? Are we going?" I jumped up.

"Anat Granit is going. There is a youth delegation from the Lions Club doing an exchange with the German branch. We may be able to get you into the group, but it will require work on your part."

Anat Granit was in the same grade, but a different class; I had a crush on her in sixth grade. My mother knew that even though Anat had transferred to the Herzliya Gymnasium for junior high school, I was still under her spell.

"What work?"

"You have to write a history paper on the subject of the Holocaust."

"When will I have time to do it?"

"You have all of August. And Grandma Tsipora said that the English teacher's husband was a prominent Jewish leader during the Holocaust. You can kill two birds with one stone."

"So I will still have to go to Jerusalem... when is the trip to Germany?"

"At the end of the school year. Next summer."

"What? It's another whole year! I don't understand."

"Time flies, and I don't think you'll have time for the project during your first year of high school."

"Then I'll work on it during Passover vacation."

"Uri'leh... you know you're Grandma's favorite grandchild." My mother pulled out the ultimate weapon, glancing towards the bedrooms to make sure my sister didn't hear. "And she is so lonely, and needs help..."

I tried a few more failed arguments but, in the end, Mama Hayuta achieved her goal as usual and, the following Saturday, at the end of a family tour of greater Jerusalem, I remained behind to stay with Grandma Tsipora.

• • •

The next day, Sunday, my grandmother woke me up about twelve o'clock in the morning (or afternoon, according to Grandma Tsipora's clock).

"Ingal'eh, you remember that you have an English lesson with Gusta Kraus at two o'clock?"

"I remember. There's still time, isn't there?"

"She asked that you come at one thirty, so you can meet her husband too."

"Did you ask her about the possibility of her husband helping me with the research for the paper I have to write?"

"Of course, Uri'leh. The truth is, she wasn't very enthusiastic. She said you should see how things go."

"What does that mean?"

"I don't know, Uri'leh. You'll find out when you get there. Get up now, your breakfast is already waiting."

The table in the dining nook was set with all sorts of delicacies. Cheeses, salad, hardboiled eggs and an omelette, salted fish, rolls, sour cream and apricot cake.

"Didn't you go a little overboard, Grandma?"

"It's almost noon and anyway, at the rate you're growing, you need five meals a day."

"I'm not growing so much..."

"What are you talking about? You grew fifteen centimeters taller this past year. I bet all the girls are after you."

"Grandma..."

"Aaah, Uri'leh, I have a surprise for you."

"What?"

"Nurit, Mrs. Zilber's granddaughter, is coming this week." Grandma's face took on a crafty look. "I saw her at Passover, she's also grown a lot..."

It began to dawn on me that my mother and grandmother were in cahoots to get me a girlfriend.

"Great," I said, trying to look nonchalant, but my heart started beating faster.

"You made friends nicely last summer."

"Yes," I said carelessly, remembering my failed attempts to flirt with her. "When is she coming?"

"On Tuesday."

I left the table in high spirits. Full from the hearty breakfast and excited by the latest news, I crossed the road, Grandma's new tape recorder in hand, and knocked softly on the door of the rear apartment on the ground floor of the building across the street.

A elderly, diminutive woman opened the door with a smile on her face.

"Hello, my name is Uri," I said hesitantly, extending my hand.

As she went to shake my hand, it stopped in mid-air and the smile on her face froze.

"Miklós ..." she let out an astonished cry before continuing the sentence in a language that I did not understand, ending with the word "Bela."

From the living room on the left, a man's voice answered in the same incomprehensible language, with the word

"Bela" also featured in his response. He approached the door with an energetic stride.

I found myself facing a kind older man, short and bespectacled, with a searching, curious look. He stopped in front of me and gazed at me for a long time.

"Ori," I said, embarrassed, extending my hand towards him.

Recovering faster than his wife, he returned my handshake and the smile to his face.

"Hello, my name is Moshe Kraus. I apologize for the strange welcome, but you reminded Gusta and me of someone from our distant past. Come in please." I followed him as he walked into the small living room. Gusta, who had regained her bearings by that time, addressed me in heavily accented Hebrew:

"I apologize. My name is Gusta. Welcome. Please have a seat. I'll bring something to drink." Both of them left the room and headed towards the kitchen, continuing a lively conversation in that same foreign language. Again, the word "Bela" came up several more times.

I tried to recover my composure from what had indeed been a strange welcome. I stood and gazed around the room. The furniture was dark and heavy. On the far side of the table where they had seated me, a board was laid out with chess pieces arranged in what looked like the middle of a game.

Mr. Kraus returned first, carrying a glass of red soda pop. "Again I apologize, but such a resemblance... really... it took us by surprise."

"Resemblance to who?" I asked.

"To someone from 'there'..."

"From where?"

"From Mezőladány in Hungary. Sit, sit, have a drink. Gusta will be here a minute."

"Mezőladány..." I tried out the name in my mouth, and remained standing. A head shorter than me, he caught my glance going over his head, directed at the table.

"Do you play chess?" he asked.

"I used to be on the school chess team, but I haven't played in a while. Are you in the middle of a game?" I asked, glad of a chance to break the embarrassing silence.

"No. I'm reconstructing the last game between Spassky and Fischer. Are you following it?"

"Yes, they post the updated game board in the window of the Yafet Bank branch next to my house in Tel Aviv. Yesterday I missed it because I spent the night at my grandmother's in Jerusalem."

"Bobby Fischer won. He was three points ahead," Mr. Kraus said dryly.

"Wow. What a comeback!" I exclaimed. "He started out two points behind."

"Yes, I understand that you're a fan of his."

"Of course. He's a Jew... you're not a fan of his?"

"Ahhhh," Kraus cleared his throat. "He's a tough case. A Jew who's also a bit anti-Semitic," he answered, glancing at me again with that same strange look.

"Is everything okay, Mr. Kraus?" I asked. "If it's not convenient for you, I can come back another day."

"No, no, today is fine, it's convenient. Do you have any relatives from Hungary?"

"No, Mr. Kraus; that is, not that I know of. It's really okay, I can come back tomorrow."

"Come, sit," Kraus collected himself. "Sit. So what do you say about Bobby Fischer?"

"You said that he's a little anti-Semitic."

"That's right," said Kraus, settling his glasses on his nose. "That Fischer is a strange man, he's certainly alienated himself from his origins."

"But he's American," I protested. "And he's fighting the Russians."

"He is indeed fighting the Russians."

His wife came into the living room. Her face was glowing as if she had just washed away the astonishment. "Hello Uri. Again, I apologize... and I'm very happy you came," she smiled and held out her hand.

I was struck by her handsome face and regal demeanor. Her expression once again beamed tranquility. "Everything's okay, Mrs. Gusta. I suggested to Mr. Kraus that if it is not convenient for you now, I can come back another day."

"No, no, Uri," she continued in her heavily-accented Hebrew. "It's very convenient. I see that you found a common interest," she added, waving a hand to indicate the chessboard.

"Yes," Kraus answered. "Uri is a chess enthusiast and a fan of Bobby Fischer."

"Excellent," said Gusta. "So, with your permission, while you two are swapping stories I'll run to the store for a few minutes," she said, turning to the door.

"She'll be back soon." Kraus apparently noticed my surprise at her sudden exit, and went on: "So, you see Fischer as the representative of the forces of light in their war against the forces of darkness?"

"I didn't think of it that way. But yes, maybe. A kind of war," I said.

"It's not so black and white," he smiled. "And, in general, it's more of a game of brains than of power."

"The Munich Olympics start in a few days, and we'll show them too, right?"

"*We'll* show them? Who? We, the Jews?"

"Yes. Mark Spitz is a proud Jew. He's likely to win seven gold medals in swimming."

"Oh-ho. Do you know that Spitz's great-grandfather is from Hungary?"

"I didn't know that."

"Are you a sports fan? A swimmer?"

"No, I'm more into soccer. A fan of Maccabi Tel Aviv. And you?"

"I'm more interested in bridge and chess, brain games."

"We've always been strong with our brains," I replied. "But it didn't help us in exile, right?" I said and then stopped, feeling that I might have crossed some red line, recalling a dim memory from my grandmother's stories about Kraus going through the Holocaust in Hungary. Kraus also stopped for a moment before answering me, gazing at me deeply and, to my relief, I saw that he was not angry nor hurt. I even thought I saw a look of admiration on his face.

"You're a Sabra,[3] aren't you? Your parents?"

"Both my parents are Sabras too," I boasted. "Unlike most of my classmates' parents," I added, and immediately thought that I might have offended him again.

"You are indeed fortunate," he said after a long silence.

---

3. Literally the name of a type of Israeli cactus with soft, sweet fruits that are covered in a prickly skin, the term refers to native-born Israelis (who are said to be "soft on the inside and prickly on the outside").

"Soccer you said... Do you think Israel will ever win the World Cup?"

"Not in the near future, unfortunately. Genetics."

At this point, the palpable tension that had accompanied my entrance dissipated, and we both drifted into a relaxed conversation.

"Do you know that I know the coach who got to the World Cup final?" For a moment he had the expression of a child.

"Wow, who?" I marveled.

"And I also know another coach who won the European Champion Cup twice," Kraus continued with a mischievous look.

"In soccer? Really? What team?"

"Benfica Lisbon."

"Wow, that's right, 1961, 1962. Where do you know them from?"

"Hungary was a soccer power."

"You really know them? What were their names?"

"What *are* their names – they're still alive."

"Can I meet them?"

"I promise that if they come to Israel, I will arrange it," he smiled at me.

The door opened and Gusta entered, unloaded her baskets in the kitchen and came to join us.

"I see you still haven't sat down yet. Chess talk?" she asked with a broad, pleasant smile.

"We moved on to soccer," I smiled.

"Good. With your permission," she emphasized the R with her heavy accent, "we will start our English lesson," she said and switched to English, also with a heavy accent.

"Okay… but…" I turned to Kraus, "You still haven't given me their names."

"Uri. First we'll have a lesson, and then you can continue talking with Mr. Kraus," Gusta said before her husband could answer. I nodded affirmatively, and she emphasized, "provided you speak in English."

"But then Mr. Kraus will probably be at work," I said, fearing that he would leave us.

"Dear Uri," Kraus said, patting my head, pleased with the interest he had aroused in me. "I'm presently enjoying summer vacation. In the coming weeks I will do my work at this table," he said and sat back down in his chair, collecting the chess pieces and returning them to the box.

I sat down with Gusta on the other side of the table. I inserted a tape into the recorder, opened a brown Daphron notebook, and we spent a whole hour going over nouns and pronouns.

Kraus sat not far from us, in front of three books and four open binders, scribbling non-stop in a large notebook. I noticed that every few minutes he would glance at me. He also caught my gaze several times and responded with a ready smile. He got up twice and went out to smoke on the small balcony adjacent to the living room, each such foray accompanied by Gusta's reproachful looks. The third time he went out towards the kitchen. I heard the striking of a match, followed by a prolonged rattle of a spoon on glass. He returned after ten minutes bearing the fruit of his labor, a cup of coffee with magnificent foam. He dropped the cigarette butt from his left hand into the ashtray while using his right to place the mug before Gusta with a flourish.

"My fair lady," he addressed her in English with a graceful turn of his palm.

"Thank you, Miklós," Gusta answered him with a loving look. I diverted my eyes, trying to avoid the intimacy that was taking place in front of me, and surveyed the small, densely furnished room.

"Would you like a drink, Uri?" Krauss asked me.

"I would like to use the bathroom." I got up and followed him as he walked me to the toilet door. When I left the bathroom I stopped to survey the bedroom, the shower and the tiny kitchen. 'A petite apartment for two petite people,' I smiled to myself, 'cute and well-groomed, like both of them.' My entrance interrupted their quiet conversation, causing Gusta to withdraw her hand from Kraus's gentle grip. When we finished the lesson, Gusta directed me to the crowded bookshelves, pointing out the section of books in English.

"I want you to pick one book to read that we can discuss, or that we'll read together if you'd like."

I took my time looking through the books, trying to find a thin book, but most of them were enormously thick. There were books by great writers like James Joyce, Geoffrey Chaucer and Charles Dickens. I paged through a few of them and returned all of them to the shelf in disappointment.

"Do you want me to help you choose a book?" Mr. Kraus addressed me, suddenly appearing at my side. "Do you know these writers?"

"I know the names, but I haven't read any of them, except for this... by Churchill," I said, pointing to a thick volume.

"Memoirs of World War II. You actually read that? Where did you get it from?"

"It was just sitting on our living room bookshelf," I said proudly, noticing that Gusta was again backing away, leaving us to discuss this between ourselves.

"What else is on your bookshelves?" he asked curiously.

"Everything else is in Hebrew. All of Jabotinsky's works, and the books from the Mered Publishing House."[4]

"Ho ho!" he said, looking at me in amazement. "A revisionist family?"

"Yes. My grandfather was a student of Jabotinsky. He immigrated with my grandmother from Odessa in 1918 to Tel Aviv. My uncles were fighters in Etzel."[5]

"You don't say. And your father?"

"My father studied medicine in Switzerland but, in the fifties, he ran for the Knesset on the Herut[6] list."

"A family after my own heart," Kraus said. "You said you read Churchill's book."

"Yes. I like reading about World War II," I said, hoping that this might open up the possibility of help on the paper.

---

4. Hamered [The Rebellion] was a publishing house that promoted books written by supporters of the right wing-revisionist parties in Israel during the 1950s and the early 60s, publishing the stories of the Etzel and the Lechi, two underground organizations active in the 40s before the founding of the state.

5. An acronym for the Hebrew words "National Military Organization in the Land of Israel,' also known as the Irgun ("organization"). It was a Zionist paramilitary organization operating in Mandatory Palestine from 1931-1948.

6. A right-wing party that merged with the Likud in the 1970s.

"Excellent. So I think I have a book you'll enjoy reading," he said, walking over to the third shelf and pulling out a white book with a photo of a soldier on its cover.

As he opened the cover, a photograph kept between the pages of the book fell out and landed on the floor.

"A war book?"

"Not exactly. This is the story of Rudolf Vrba and takes place during the war. 'I Cannot Forgive,'" Kraus replied as I bent down to pick up the picture.

"Is he a soldier? A Jew?"

"Yes. A really heroic Jew. He escaped from Auschwitz and saved hundreds of thousands of Jews."

"Hundreds of thousands?? How? During the war?"

"He ended the war as a Slovak partisan, but the rescue enterprise, in which I also participated, was helped by his actions before he became a partisan – to be more exact, after his escape from Auschwitz."

"And what is the picture that fell out of the book?"

"A picture of Vrba and his daughters; he sent it to me from London."

"I heard about Mordechai Anilevich, about Hannah Szenes. How have I not heard about him?"

"Ask your father or your uncles, they'll explain it to you. A whole Mapai[7] machine worked behind the scenes to make sure that the name Rudolf Vrba and the secrets involving him would remain buried deep underground. Few have heard his name. Maybe your generation will publish these stories…" he said, and stopped himself from saying any more.

---

7. The predecessor of the Israeli Labor party, in power from 1930 -1968.

"I'll ask my dad, but I'd like to hear it from you," I added hopefully, the figure of Anat Granit flashing before my eyes.

"Okay..."

"And also the soccer coaches that you promised to tell me about?" I remembered.

Kraus looked at me for a few seconds and then headed towards the kitchen, where he and Gusta conversed again in that unfamiliar language. At this point I could already guess that it was Hungarian. At the end he came back into the living room and addressed me in English.

"If you want we can continue, but in English, as per Gusta's request. I will give you some background on Vrba and how he was brought up. I'll tell you about the Jewish-Hungarian soccer heroes and how they passed the war years, and also... why your Maccabi Tel Aviv plays in blue and yellow uniforms. But, before that, you must be hungry."

"No. I had a late breakfast."

"Excellent. So let's get started."

"What, now? But Grandma will be worried about me."

Gusta peeked through the door as if eavesdropping on the conversation and said, "I will stop by Mrs. Tsipora's. Anyway I have to bring her the puddings I bought her at the grocery store. I'll tell her you'll be staying a while longer," she said, opening the front door. Children's happy shouts could be heard from the stairwell.

"Hello, Dina," I heard Gusta call. "I see you invited friends over. Will you come over later for cake? It will be ready in an hour."

I was intrigued and walked towards the door where

I spotted two girls and a boy skipping up the stairs. The blonde one stopped for a moment and fixed her gaze on me before running on.

"Uri, Uri," Kraus called me twice, noticing that I was rooted in place.

I shrugged and returned to the table.

"They're cute," said Kraus. "They're Sabras like you."

"What language do you and Mrs. Gusta speak?" I asked to divert the conversation away from potentially awkward areas.

"We mostly speak in Hungarian and German, and sometimes in English and Hebrew. Do you understand some of it?"

"No. That is, only English... and Hebrew, of course."

"Good. So who was this secret hero?" Kraus began solemnly. "Well, Uri, Rudolf Vrba was born in 1924 in the Slovak part of Czechoslovakia, not very far from my own birthplace."

"What... you were also born in Slovakia?" I asked, hoping to solve the riddle of the name 'Bela.'

"No. I was born in a small village ten kilometers from the Slovakian border."

"So, where is this Mazaldani?" I asked.

"Mezőladány," Kraus corrected me, "or, as we sometimes called it, Mezold."

"This Mezold... is this the village where you were born?"

"Yes, but it has nothing to do with Vrba. Vrba was born in Topol'čany in Slovakia and moved with his mother to Trnava, which is 50 kilometers from the Hungarian border."

"So you grew up 60 kilometers apart," I bounced up and down enthusiastically, showing off my rapid calculation.

"No, Uri. The border between Hungary and Slovakia stretches from east to west for almost 500 kilometers and, although we both grew up near the border, the distance between us was like the distance between East and West," he said with a smile and continued, "what's more, Vrba was only born in 1924, so he is 16 years younger than me." He fell silent for a moment, letting me do the math.

"So there was no connection between your communities?"

"Until the fall of the Hungarian Empire in World War I, and for centuries, Slovakia and Hungary were one country and, therefore, the Jewish communities were in close contact even after Slovakia was torn from Hungary. But the truth is that what determined the level of connection was more the affiliation to the same religious stream in Judaism. Most of the Jews in both countries belonged to one of two religious streams. There were the ultra-Orthodox, who are like the 'Haredim'[8] you know, and there were the Neologists, who were... how shall I explain it to you... a hybrid between the Conservative movement and the Reform movement in the United States. I was born to a religious family, which, unlike our neighbors in the shtetl,[9] was open to academic education and to Western culture. When my brother went away to study at Vienna University, the rabbi called my father in for a talk, and many of the shtetl's residents looked upon us with skep-

---

8. *Haredim* ["God-fearing"] is the Hebrew term for the ultra-Orthodox community in Israel.

9. A small Jewish village in Eastern Europe.

ticism. But after my brother paved the way, it was already easier for me to go away to school."

"That was very unusual at the time, wasn't it?" I asked.

"Unusual among us Orthodox, not among Neologs. It's important to me that you know that, like us, two-thirds of Hungarian Jews were open to the Enlightenment movement and were integrated into cultural and scientific life. Most of them lived in Budapest. Even though we were only six percent of the Hungarian population, we represented over 60 percent of those engaged in commerce and banking, law and, most important of all, medicine."

"Were the Neologists Zionists? Was Vrba a Zionist?"

"In general, the Zionist movement was extremely small in both countries. Only about three percent of the Jewish population identified with the movement, and only 3,500 were active in a Zionist organization. I was a Zionist activist from an early age."

"Where, in Mezőladány?" I asked, trying again to crack the Bela riddle.

"The roots of my Zionism came from my father's home in Mezőladány and in the nearby Kisvárda community, but my real Zionist activity was during my yeshiva studies. So, in 1925, together with my friend Bela, I founded the Zionist Youth Group of Miskolc," he said proudly.

"But you said I remind you of Bela from Mezőladány."

"True. Although Bela is a common Hungarian name, the friend who started the youth group with me was Laslo Balak and he got the nickname 'Bela' as an abbreviation of his last name."

"So he's the one I reminded you of?"

"No. His son, Max Balak, who was nicknamed 'Little Bela.'"

"Got it," I nodded, although I had not yet managed to solve the riddle of the shocked looks that had greeted me when I arrived. "So, he was your partner in the Zionist activities?"

"Unfortunately, no. He married a wonderful girl, Margit, whom we had met in Miskolc, and returned with her to Mezőladány to care for his mother who had fallen ill. I started the Miskolc Hachshara movement, in preparation for Aliyah[10] to Israel, without him," he finished sadly, adjusting his shirt collar. "Can we go on?"

"Yes, Mr. Kraus," I answered obediently, even though he had not solved my riddles.

"Good. Then I'll continue. Vrba was born into a secular family with few connections to any Jewish community, and he was certainly cut off from the Zionist movement ... at least until 1942. The connections he made with Zionist organizations during the war years and after his escape from Auschwitz brought him only bitter disappointment and pushed him away from them." Kraus stopped at this point, noticing my sudden embarrassment.

"They pushed him away from the Zionist movement?"

"Yes, well. I jumped ahead to the end of the story a bit but, as you'll see later, the line between good and bad was blurred in those years, especially against the background of the horrific events of World War II. When the Nazis invaded the Czech Republic, after annexing the Sudetenland to Germany, they gave Slovakia autonomy and it joined Hungary, which made an alliance with Hitler.

---

10. The Hachshara [Training] movement was specifically to prepare Eastern European Jews to move to Israel. Moving to Israel for a Jew is known in Hebrew as *Aliyah* [ascent].

Both countries were under heavy Nazi pressure to round up all the Jews and send them to extermination camps. My Hungary managed to hold off the disaster until 1944. Vrba's Slovakia began to round up Jews two years earlier."

"Where were you in those years? And where was Vrba?" I asked.

"When Vrba was first captured in 1942 on the Slovakian border, I was running the Eretz Israel[11] office in Budapest. We were still living peacefully then, confident that our strong standing in Hungarian society would protect us. In Slovakia, on the other hand, as I said, they began to send Jews to extermination camps in 1942. In the first stage, a long list of Jews had exemptions."

"Exemptions? Who gave the exemptions? The Nazis?"

"Since Slovakia could not afford to lose most of its doctors, engineers, etc., a list of exemptions was prepared. The list included all those who had converted to Christianity or married Christians before September 1941, doctors, engineers, managers and essential workers, as well as members of the Jewish Center and their families."

"What is the Jewish Center?" I asked.

"In every country that the Nazis invaded, they appointed a Jewish center – *Judenrat* – and used it to conduct all communication with the community. In 1942, Vrba was an unskilled worker and had no ties or connections to people in any Jewish institutions so, of course, he was not on the exemptions list and was designated to be sent to the labor camps."

"So someone could be saved from extermination by having connections to the right people?" I was shocked.

---

11. Eretz Israel [the Land of Israel] was the Jewish organization in Budapest responsible for immigration to Israel.

"Oh, absolutely," replied Kraus. "At least in the first stages of the extermination in every country, a person could buy his freedom with either connections or money."

"I thought that anyone caught as a Jew was taken to the camps," I said thoughtfully.

Kraus smirked. "There were even cases where deportees were already standing in line by the gate, and those who had been saved by their relatives were pulled out of it and completely random victims were put in their place."

"That's not fair," I declared.

"Your innocence is right, Uri. But the boundaries of morality became very blurred in those times, as you probably know. I'll give you an example," he said, fixing his gaze on me. "Isaac Klein, the one who has the little grocery store next to the synagogue, stood in the Novaky camp with his wife and children; they were sadly watching the column of deportees that the Nazis had lined up by the exit gate when an official German vehicle stopped by the gate and a Nazi officer got out, together with a tall Jew dressed in an expensive fur coat and top hat. The officer exchanged a few words with the Hlinka[12] guards who were organizing the convoy, and they pulled a Jewish family with four children out of the line. The Hlinka guards seized Isaac Klein and his wife and daughters, and dragged them into the line to complete the quota of deportees. All the Klein girls were murdered in Auschwitz. Isaac was the only one to survive.

"You may have heard in the news that, a month ago, the Jerusalem police arrested Isaac Klein on charges of assault. It turns out that at lunchtime an unfamiliar cus-

---

12. A Slovakian fascist movement

tomer came in to the store wearing a top hat; Klein recognized the tall Jew who got out of the German car – and savagely attacked him."

"That makes sense!" I burst out.

"It makes sense? Depends from which side you look at it. That man saved his brother. Who can be blamed here? We must understand that the situation was horrific, and people were fighting for their lives."

"But they didn't fight for their lives, they just replaced victims with other victims."

Kraus nodded without answering.

"And Vrba?" I asked.

"He didn't intend to wait around until the day he was picked up by the Nazis or the anti-Semitic Hlinka guards helping them. He decided to cross the border and make his way to England, where he planned to join the free Czech forces fighting against Germany."

"That was brave," I said.

"Yes. Vrba always was, or rather is..."

"What, he's still alive?"

"Yes. I met him in Israel, and we are in touch to this day, but let's keep going and I'll get there. In short, Vrba crossed the border into Hungary and arrived in Budapest. He went to the center of the Zionist organization, but there they told him that he had to leave, or else they would be forced to turn him in."

"And you didn't intervene?" I was amazed.

"It's not that simple, Uri. I didn't know anything about it. There were several Zionist organizations in Budapest. As I said, I was running the Eretz Israel office of the Jewish Agency, but there was also the office of the Zionist Federation led by Ottó Komoly and Rezső Kasztner."

"Rezső Kasztner?"

"In Israel he was called Israel Kastner. In 1942 he was vice president of the Zionist Federation in Budapest, but I don't know who it was who sent Vrba back to Slovakia. That year I was busy helping illegal Jewish refugees who were flooding into safe Hungary from Poland, Yugoslavia, Slovakia, Austria and other places."

"And you didn't have any influence with the Zionist Federation? Why didn't Vrba contact you?"

"I assume that Vrba did not know of me, and was not referred to me by the Zionist Federation in Hungary because they saw me as a kind of enemy. I was a representative of the Mizrahi movement,[13] what is today called the Mafdal. Ben Gurion's[14] emissaries tried over the years to remove me from my position and transfer control of the office to representatives of Mapai."

I was starting to like the old man. He didn't try to sugarcoat things or describe himself as a hero, like Vrba, but he was turning out to be an honest, decent man who sought justice. "I see. So what happened with Vrba?" I asked.

"He returned to the Slovakian border, where he was captured by the Hlinka guards and transferred to the Novaky camp. He managed to escape from the camp together with another prisoner, Alfréd Wetzler, but they were captured in the adjacent city."

"And that's it?" I asked in disappointment.

"You can imagine that this is not the end. Otherwise, what would the book be about? Vrba is an entrepreneur,

---

13. Mizrahi [Eastern] was a Jewish religious political movement.
14. David Ben Gurion, head of the Labor party (Mapai), head of the Jewish Agency, and later the first Prime Minister of Israel

he's clever, he recognizes opportunities and he's fearless. And, with these qualities, he arrived in Auschwitz after a long journey that also included two weeks in the Majdanek camp in German-occupied Poland."

From the direction of the stairwell came sounds of quick skipping and giggling. Gusta hurried towards the door and Kraus followed, but not before turning around and handing me the book.

"Here. We're here," he pointed to the open page – "and this is your first reading assignment. Up to page 204."

"What? That's a lot!" I protested, but he was already walking towards the door. I packed up the tape recorder and headed towards the door as well, hoping to meet the girls again that I had seen about an hour ago.

"Girls, meet Uri," said Gusta. I smiled shyly. The younger one fixed her mesmerizing gaze on me again, but it was the older one who spoke up and said, "Nice to meet you, my name is Dina, and this is my cousin Rutha and her brother Gideon."

"Nice to meet you," I said. I couldn't take my eyes off Rutha. She was gorgeous. Her blue eyes sparkled. She looked to be my age, shorter than me but, as they say, 'developed.'

"I'm Rutha Shorin," she took a step forward. "You can call me Ruthy."

I blushed and looked down.

"Children, come into the kitchen, Gusta made you a Hungarian walnut cake," Kraus called from the kitchen doorway.

"We have to go," said Dina. "We made plans to meet up with Sima on Ben Yehuda Street, but we'll be back in a few hours."

"Well, we'll be here. Maybe Uri will still be here, right Uri?" asked Gusta, looking to me for confirmation.

"Yes, maybe…" I stuttered as I returned to the table, "I have a lot more to read." The girls hurried out and Gusta smoothed my hair fondly, saying she would let Grandma know. Silence fell. I immersed myself in the book. Descriptions of the Auschwitz extermination camp were difficult to read. Despite the English and Vrba's understated writing style, the precise details hit me hard. Together with Vrba I experienced the backbreaking labor, the carting away of the shriveled bodies, but also all the survival stunts that caused me to immediately admire the man. Kraus returned from his smoking corner on the balcony and came over to me.

"How's it going?"

"Not easy. The English is fine, but…"

"The descriptions are difficult, yes."

"I just finished the part where Vrba makes friends with the Kapo[15] and gets transferred to a job in the food warehouses."

"Very resourceful."

"Unbelievable. I never imagined there were people inside the horrific camps who managed to keep a kind of reasonable standard of living, if you can call it that."

"Yes. There definitely were."

"Now I'm reading about his role in the Canada Commando.[16] I didn't understand why they called it Canada."

"Canada… yes. In the camp inmates' imagination, Canada was the land of dreams, the crown jewel of North

---

15. A kapo was a Jewish leader appointed by the Nazis to be in charge of his or her fellow camp inmates.

16. A commando was a slave labor unit in the camp.

America. In this commando, his job was to sort out piles of clothes and luggage taken from the most recent transport. That's how members of the team got food items that were hidden in the pockets of those who died, as well as other treasures that they could use for barter."

"Have you been to Canada?" I asked.

"No. But, unsurprisingly, Rudolf Vrba lives there now. In Vancouver."

"You said you're still in touch?"

"As I said, we met in Israel and, since then, we have kept in contact by letter and by phone."

"He's one of a kind," I said.

"Have you seen the movie Arbinka?"

"Yes. By Kishon. With Chaim Topol."

"That's right. Kishon, a Hungarian Jew, took the character of Arbinka from a Hungarian Jew named Ervin. He always reminded me of Vrba too. A man of many exploits and great resourcefulness."

"So, Arbinka is a real person?"

"His character is based on a real figure, Ervinka. I encountered him in Israel and before that in Hungary. The point I'm trying to make is that there are people with courage and resourcefulness who thrive in chaotic situations," Kraus said sadly.

"And especially when they are surrounded by people who are going like sheep to the slaughter," I broke in, regretting what I had said before I even finished the sentence.

"I wouldn't be so quick to judge."

"Yes, you're right..." I said thoughtfully, and hurried to change the subject. "And Vrba just met up again with Alfréd Wetzler, someone from the town he grew up in. In a little while ..." I said, flipping through the remaining pages, "I'm going to get to the target page, 204. Then can we move on to soccer?"

"Finish the reading; that way you won't have a reading assignment for tonight, and tomorrow we can jump right into the story of the escape."

I went back to join Vrba as he became deputy registrar, responsible for the daily coordination between the number of arrivals, the number of new corpses, and the total number of prisoners at the end of each day. Later I would understand the critical importance of this job that he had. I wondered if Kraus also bore a number tattooed on his body. The long sleeves that covered his arms in the hot summer hid the mystery. The Krauses did not resemble any of the survivors I knew: the lonely barber, Misha, the Sharshavsky couple who ran the grocery store in Masrik Square, 'Sonia' who wandered screaming through the city streets, and 'Crazy Ibn' named after Ibn Gvirol Street where he walked around dressed in rags, muttering quietly to himself. I flew past page 204 and continued on.

In January 1944, the Germans began to lay new railway tracks parallel to the road that connected Birkenau 1 to Birkenau 2. Vrba noticed that the railway tracks extended towards the gas chambers and crematoria. It was clear to him that the era of selections had finished and that, from here on in, there would be only a direct line to death. Vrba concluded that Auschwitz was on the verge of a dramatic increase in its capacity to produce death. He and his friends estimated that the Nazis were preparing to take in about a million victims, and hence the target was Hungarian Jewry – the only remaining large European Jewish community except for Britain. As a privileged inmate who enjoyed access to the German press, Vrba had already learned of the unrest in Hungary, and now news arrived in the middle of March 1944 that German forces were marching to Hungary "to restore order." In time, the information leaked to the lowest ranks in the camp as well, and gossip spoke of "the Hungarian salami that they would soon have lots of."

I looked towards Kraus, as if afraid of what was about to happen to him. He sensed my gaze and came over to me.

"Are you finished?"

"Yes. Right now I'm at the part where the Germans are marching into Hungary."

"Now we're already getting close to my story. All hell broke loose in Budapest, especially in the provincial towns."

"Can you tell me more about the provincial towns?"

"Yes, Uri. What's not clear?"

"I would like to hear a little more about Mezőladány and… about your childhood… in that village."

"There's not much to tell. It's a small village, right at the eastern end of Hungary. We were about a hundred Jews in the village. We had a lively community life, but we relied on the larger community of Kisvárda."

"How did your family make a living?"

"My father, Shmuel HaLevi Kraus, may he rest in peace, was a Torah scholar who spent his nights studying the holy books but, during the day, he managed our little general store in the village."

"A big store? Like the *Mashbir l'Tzarchan*?"[17]

---

17. A large department store

"No. It was a small shop, but it was a nice family business which provided a living for two families."

"Did you work in the store?"

"I was the ninth child in the family, and the most spoiled one. The one who helped my father in the shop was Mrs. Balak, Big Bela's widowed mother. Of course Bela and I used to run around the store and hide among the shelves. That's how the disaster happened," said Kraus, holding his head, "but you're reminding me that I promised you at least one soccer story today." It was clear to me that he was avoiding something, but I wasn't against getting back to soccer.

"So when do you think the Maccabi Tel Aviv players gave up the blue-and-white uniforms, and who led the change?"

"I didn't know we were ever blue and white," I stammered.

"So the one who led the change is a player named Joseph Merimovich. Do you know him?"

"Yes, Yosa'leh, he coached us three years ago, and was a Maccabi player for many years."

"Right," Kraus nodded.

"And he also has a sports store in Hod Passage in Tel Aviv."

"I didn't know that. So it was Merimovich who suggested that, in solidarity with the yellow star badges, Maccabi should switch to playing in yellow uniforms."

"Wow. I thought we were born yellow."

"He came up with the idea as a player, and the whole team supported him and followed his lead," Kraus said, intending to go on, but I didn't let go.

"So what was the disaster that happened at the store? What happened to you and Bela?"

"I thought you wanted to hear the story of Vrba's escape," Kraus said, rushing on without leaving me room for any questions. "Vrba decided that the time had come to carry out the escape plan he had been working on for many months. Of course, he wanted to save his own life but, according to him," said Krauss, picking up the book and reading from it, "'Now it wasn't about reporting a crime that was already committed, but an attempt to prevent a crime, to warn the Hungarians, to get them to revolt, to urge them to form a Jewish army of a million men. An army that would fight instead of die.' That's it, Uri, this is where we're stopping for today," said Kraus just as the doorbell rang.

The three of us walked towards the door.

"Hello, cuties," Kraus began, "where's Gideon?"

"Gideon went up with Sima. She asked that we not eat cake before dinner," Dina said.

"Well, she's right," said Gusta. "Wait a minute and I'll cut you some slices to take home for after the meal."

"Uri, would you like to join us for dinner?" Rutha addressed me, to my surprise.

"Uri will eat with Grandma Tsipora," Gusta intervened, "I promised her that. You have the whole week, children."

"Okay. Too bad," said Rutha. "Tomorrow morning we're going to visit relatives, but we'll be around all afternoon and evening."

"Tomorrow. Great," I said.

"So, we'll see you tomorrow, Uri," concluded Rutha, leaving me with the sounds of my name ringing in her mouth.

"Tomorrow. Bye," I said, feeling my cheeks reddening again.

Chapter 3

"Uri, you need to get up," I heard my grandmother's voice, tearing me out of a sweet dream. I rolled over onto my left side, trying to bring Ruthy back into my dream, but Grandma's gentle hand on my cheek drew me into the Jerusalem morning.

"What time is it?" I asked blearily.

"Eight. I'm sorry to have to wake you up, but the maid already finished the kitchen and she has to collect the laundry and change the sheets. And besides, Gusta asked that you come at nine today because they are having friends over for bridge in the afternoon."

"Yes, I also made plans this afternoon with the neighborhood kids."

"Ah, your cousin Doron is supposed to come to visit. So he'll join you until six. You missed his birthday last week."

"Yes... but... not today, Grandma."

"Aunt Esther will pick him up at six, so you can continue with your plans after that," said Grandma, stroking my head as she used to do when I was little.

I quickly dressed and showered, leaving the cleaning woman, Aliza, to deal with all the mess I left on the floor of my room.

"I made a fried egg for you," Grandma greeted me in the kitchen.

"Thanks, Grandma."

"So, I understand that you and Mr. Kraus are getting along well together. Gusta told me that her husband has been positively beaming from the moment you entered their house yesterday."

"He's a very interesting man. We talk in English about World War II. He will also help me with the essay. I think I'll write about Vrba."

"Who is Vrba?"

"A great hero who escaped from Auschwitz."

"Well Uri'leh, I'm glad he's helping you. And how is Gusta? And the English?"

"Fine… but… they acted very strangely when they first saw me."

"Strangely? In what way?"

"It was as if they saw a ghost. They say I look like someone named Bela, who is the son of Big Bela, who grew up with Kraus in Mezőladány."

"Interesting. In any case, Gusta didn't charge me for the hours of your conversation with her husband, just for her lesson. And it's not like they don't need the money."

"Their apartment is small, but looks very well-kept and furnished in expensive taste," I pointed out.

"Uri'leh, you've developed a sense of taste… yes. Mr. Kraus had the furniture and the kitchen shipped by boat from Switzerland. Have you seen the Baroque sofa in the living room?"

"It's beautiful. I didn't know it was Baroque."

"And the kitchen is also modern and well-equipped. But don't let that mislead you. They are living on very limited means."

"So why doesn't she take more money for the conversations with Mr. Kraus?"

"He probably enjoys it a lot. It gives him satisfaction to talk to a boy like you. And she wants you to come back and continue the conversations with him. Are you enjoying it?"

"Yes. It's interesting. But I feel like he's avoiding some of my questions."

"Don't forget that he is carrying difficult memories, Uri'leh. You need to understand. Take it slowly."

"What memories?"

"In Hungary he not only had to face the Nazis, but also Jewish leaders. He had problems from all sides. And after that, in Israel, he didn't have an easy time of it either. Gusta told me that both the government ministries and the security forces took actions against him."

"Really? Why? Was he a traitor?"

"Oy, Uri. That's a harsh word... and I really don't know all the details... but I know there are some big secrets there. I think it's best not to drag him in those directions. Okay, Uri?"

"Okay. Today we are supposed to talk about Rudolph Vrba's escape from Auschwitz. Do you know anything about it?"

"No. I didn't know there were any escapes from Auschwitz."

"Yes. The historians erased it."

"Now you sound like your father... that explains why Gusta asked this morning if we are revisionists. I didn't tell her that your mother votes Mapai," Grandma sighed. "Gusta was quite frightened."

"Why?"

"As I said before, the Kraus family did not have an easy time with the Israeli authorities. Sometimes when we're sitting in the café and a police car randomly drives by, I can still see fear in Gusta's eyes."

"Well… the anxieties of Holocaust survivors."

"Not just that," said Grandma. "Not just that. Mr. Kraus must be keeping secrets that someone doesn't want to be revealed, and Gusta is afraid."

"So she holes up in the house?"

"Oh, not at all. Gusta is a woman who loves society and culture. Concerts, exhibitions, museums and lectures. She goes out with her group of friends, and sometimes with Miklós."

I couldn't tell if I heard jealousy or admiration in Grandma's voice.

"Tell me, Grandma, were they in the camps?"

"I don't think so, but I know that Kraus's parents and some of his brothers and sisters perished in the Holocaust."

"I'll check it out …" I said as I went to my room to get ready to leave.

"Not a good idea …" I heard Grandma's voice following me.

At a quarter past nine I crossed the road, my attention drawn to the top of the palm tree, hunting for a sign of movement on the upper floors. I knocked lightly on the Krauses' door.

Mr. Kraus opened the door for me wearing the same brown suit from yesterday afternoon, a white napkin folded into a triangle and tucked in the front pocket.

"Hello, Uri, I just came in," he said, taking off his yarmulke.

"I see there is no chessboard today," I pointed out.

"This morning at the café I replayed the game with Henrik... Zvi... my brother. Fischer lost."

"Oh no. Let's hope it's not another turnaround."

"Let's hope. He's still leading by two points."

"Mr. Kraus, did your brother make Aliyah to Israel with you?" I tried my luck.

"No. He's older than me. He's the one who studied at the Academy in Vienna until he had to leave because of racial laws. He was the first of us to come to Israel, and he came here before the war broke out."

"He made Aliyah alone?"

"Yes," said Kraus, looking at me in bewilderment. "He is single."

"And other siblings?"

"My sister, Rivka, came after him in 1935."

"And that's it? Only the two of them in Israel?"

"My brother Naftali made Aliyah after the war... he... and the others... didn't listen to me." He lowered his gaze and began searching his pockets irritably, exclaiming, "Where the hell did I put it?"

"What?" I asked.

"I asked my brother to bring me my photo with Vrba from 1958, during his stay in Israel. He also brought a picture of me with Gyula Mándi from Ramat Gan Stadium."

"Which game?"

"Against the English team," he said, adding, "the junior one, I think."

"We won four-zero," I exclaimed. "Were you at the game?"

"Yes, I was Mándi's guest."

"So he's the Hungarian coach you were talking about?"

"No, there are two others, much more famous internationally... but I'm afraid I forgot the photos in the café."

"Do you want me to run and get them?" I offered.

"No, I'm there every morning anyway. I'll pick them up tomorrow... even though it's likely that my brother Zvi took them... let's continue with Vrba for now. Where were we?"

"You promised to tell me today about the disaster at the store."

"There was no disaster in the store. There was an event that affected the rest of our lives."

"What event?"

"You're a stubborn one. Well. It was like this: Big Bela and I hid, as we usually did, under one of the shelves in my father's store, in a place where we could see but not be seen. The blacksmith, Henrich Kovács, entered the shop, dragging his son István by the ear. My father wasn't in the shop, so Agnes, Bela's mother, showed Henrich to the nail box. After she had rung up the purchase, she left to the back of the store, and that was when we saw István's father take a hammer off the shelf and put it in the big sack slung over his shoulder. Bela and I came out of our hiding place and chased after István and his father."

"And you stopped them?"

"Henrich Kovács was a big, strong man. When I shouted at him, 'Thief! Thief!' he grabbed Bela and me in his two strong hands and said that if we say a word he will destroy both of us and our parents. To reinforce his message, he landed a ringing slap on my cheek that knocked me to the ground."

"And you kept it a secret?"

"That's the end of the story," Kraus answered me evasively.

"Then why was it a disaster? I don't understand," I insisted.

"Because Jews should be smart, not right. Like Vrba."

"I don't understand..."

"Then listen," sighed Kraus, picking up the book next to him. "Ready?"

"Ready," I said in disappointment, opening my notebook and inserting a cassette into the tape player.

Kraus took off his jacket, hung it over the back of the chair, and adjusted his tie.

"Vrba's first attempt to escape from Auschwitz was in January 1944. He was supposed to join a prisoner named Unglik, who bribed a Slovak SS man that he knew. Fortunately, Vrba was delayed and arrived late for the meeting."

"Why fortunately?"

"Because the Slovak shot Unglik in the head, took the bribe money and hurried away to report to the camp authorities about the escape attempt that he had foiled. Vrba learned from the story that he could not rely on casual acquaintances from his past. Luckily, he had one true friend, from the city where he grew up, named Alfréd Wetzler. Wetzler was older than Vrba, and had a strong position in the camp. One day Alfréd Wetzler told Vrba that an escape of four prisoners from the camp was being organized, and that they would need the help of Wetzler and Vrba. The good news was that the man who was the brains behind the escape was planning to be at their disposal later." Kraus paused for a moment and raised his eyes, glad to see me enthralled, and then went on.

"The four analyzed the Nazi response mechanism to escapes, and realized that all the security and search circles were tightened for the first three days after each escape, but returned to normal on the fourth day after no escapees were found in the area."

"So there were escapes before?" I asked.

"There were escape attempts that managed to cross the three-day circles, but they were captured in the following days in areas far from the camp. So the four planned to hide in a pile of long, heavy wooden logs that had been collected for the purpose of gearing up the extermination plant in preparation to receive the Hungarian Jews. Vrba and Wetzler agreed with Sandor, the leader of the fugitives, that during the three days of hiding, the two of them would update those hiding about what was happening in the camp. And so it was. A week after the four escaped via the hideout, Vrba saw them being led by the SS men who had captured them towards the accursed Block 11. In the following days, Vrba managed to get closer to Block 11, where Sandor promised him that the secret of the pile of planks had not been discovered, and that it could be used by them in their escape."

"I wouldn't trust Sandor. It must have been a trap by the Nazis," I said.

"You're right to be suspicious, Uri. That's also what my brother Zvi said when he heard the story. He doesn't understand how it was that the Nazis did not immediately murder the four escapees."

"Your brother is right."

"Yes, Zvi is more suspicious than I am... that's why his apartment looks like a fortress."

"A fortress? Is that why he has your pictures?" I guessed.

"Very good, Uri," Kraus smiled and continued, "and also the important documents…" he stopped as though he had said too much.

"I don't understand. Who are you afraid of?"

"My apartment was once broken into, and important historical documents were stolen from me."

"Where? Here on Ben Maimon Boulevard?"

"No. During the short period when I lived in Hadar Yosef in Tel Aviv. The lawyer Shmuel Tamir warned me then not to walk at the edge of the sidewalk."

"Shmuel Tamir the member of Knesset?"

"Yes. We angered a lot of important people then, and he was afraid for my life."

"What? That's a bit much. Here in Israel?"

"Yes, yes. But I'll get to that later, Uri, let's continue with Vrba."

He picked up the book again.

"Before the escape, Vrba and Wetzler hid all the equipment they needed. Through his work in Commando Canada, Vrba had obtained two expensive Dutch suits, thick winter coats and heavy shoes. In addition, they collected Russian tobacco, dipped it in kerosene and let it dry."

"For what purpose?"

"Be patient and you'll hear. They made an agreement with two Polish prisoners who worked in the area of the lumber pile that they would cover the opening after they entered the hiding place."

"It seems to me a big gamble to share the secret of the escape with the Poles."

"I thought so too but, when I met Vrba, he told me that with the help of Wetzler's acquaintances, they were in contact with the underground that operated in Auschwitz, and that was a sufficient threat for the Poles." Here Kraus stopped and studied my expression as I tried to digest the fact that an underground existed in Auschwitz. "The escape was scheduled for April 3rd, but the first attempt was thwarted when Wetzler stopped on the way because of a suspicious SS man standing at the gate. In the second attempt, the Poles failed to reach the meeting point. This went on for four days. On the fifth day Vrba was detained by Otto Graf who used to torment him in Commando Canada but, to his surprise, he just turned to him kindly and offered him a Greek cigarette."

Here he stopped again and looked at me. "Remember the story of the Greek cigarette. That's when the last transports of Greek Jewry had just arrived in Auschwitz. The 'splendid work' of the evil mastermind Dieter Wisliceny. Remember the name," repeated Kraus, "Wisliceny."

"Okay. I wrote it in the notebook. I hope I spelled it right," I said.

"Graf said goodbye to Vrba, who hurried to join Wetzler. They crawled into the space between the boards and the Poles covered them up, placing thick beams over their heads. Vrba quickly spread the tobacco dipped in kerosene between the wooden beams to mislead the dogs would be sent to sniff them out."

"Now I understand," I smiled with satisfaction.

"The hours crawled by as the two wondered how it could be that their escape had not been discovered yet," Kraus continued. "Then a fierce siren shattered their thoughts, followed by a threatening silence. The calm before the storm... and that came minutes later. Hundreds of pairs of stiff boots marching in rhythm, thousands of voices shouting, and thousands more answering them.

The search began, typically German in its thoroughness. The voices came closer and closer to the lumber pile, climbing on it and searching around it and, with them, dogs that sniffed, barked and scratched the boards. Vrba and Wetzler pulled out their knives, ready for battle, but slowly the voices weakened and the danger receded.

"The second day was the key one. The camp authorities knew that within 24 hours the responsibility for the search would be taken from them and their negligence would be exposed to the higher ranks, and they spurred their men on mercilessly. Even the night didn't bring any comfort or relief. On the third day, in the afternoon, two Germans from the search forces became suspicious of the lumber pile and began to move the upper beams. They moved four beams, coming within 15 centimeters of Vrba's and Wetzler's drawn knives. Then a big commotion was heard from the direction of the camp gate. 'Here, they caught them,' said one of them, and they hurried away.

"On the night of April 9, loud noises were heard from the bomber planes that attacked the area near the camp."

"Why didn't they attack Auschwitz?" I asked.

"Excellent question, Uri. Write it down," Kraus said and went on. "The last 24 hours passed in relative silence and, at half past six in the evening of April 10, the footsteps of the last soldiers evacuating the external guard circle were heard. At nine, Vrba and Wetzler began their efforts to move the remaining wooden beams covering them. They blessed the two Germans who had, to their great fortune, moved some of the beams while searching, and came out into the cold night air. They returned the boards to their place, to allow other prisoners to use the escape route in the future, and set off on their journey.

"Crawling on the ground, they inched away from the watchtowers into the small grove of birch trees, where they got to their feet and took off running until they reached another exposed area. Dawn was breaking, and the next bit of forest could be seen far off in the distance. Five hundred meters away from them, they saw a group of women prisoners accompanied by SS men. They dropped to the ground and rolled for two hours from ditch to ditch until they reached the forest. When they arrived in the forest, they calmed down a bit and caught their breath, but only for a short time for, after a few minutes, they heard young voices and Vrba noticed that the area around them was filling up with a group of Hitler Youth. Fortunately, the onset of drizzling rain stopped the gang. Vrba and Wetzler continued on their way until they reached a wide area of dense bushes, crawled into its center and lay safely on a bed of grass."

Kraus closed the book and looked at me with a smile. "That's it, my young friend. This, in short, is the story of the escape."

"I'm sure it's not over," I protested. "Others ran away and were caught. You said you'd tell me the whole story."

Kraus looked at his watch. "It's already a quarter to eleven. Let's go to the kitchen, we'll make ourselves some soda pop."

I followed him, watching him with interest as he rolled up his sleeves and washed two glasses and small plates. I circled him from right to left, but I could not see any sign of a tattoo on his arms.

"We will also cut ourselves a slice of walnut cake," he told me with an appreciative look. "We will continue to follow them farther along their path, Uri ... but what's most important for me is to tell you what happened to Hungarian Jewry after that escape. Okay?"

"Of course," I said, realizing that his wish to convey a broader message was stronger than my curiosity.

Kraus went to the phone, dialed and waited a few minutes while the receiver emitted the waiting tone. When he finally gave up, he led us back to the living room. He picked up the book and leafed through it: "There are still a hundred pages to the end of the book, but the last 70 include appendices that we'll skip over." I nodded in agreement and he continued.

"Well, at this point in time, the distance from their hiding place to the Slovakian border was 130 kilometers, which is roughly the same as from the entrance to Jerusalem to Haifa's beautiful beach. They had no maps and relied on Vrba's memory from an atlas that had ended up in Commando Canada. Several times they took wrong turns and found themselves going in a circle and approaching Auschwitz again.

"On the third day, they were exposed by children playing in the park with their mother and their father, a Nazi officer. The father approached the bush, following the children's cries, and stared coldly at the escapees and the knives in their hands. Eventually the Nazi decided that his family's safety came first and rapidly fled the place, and our friends hurried away from the spot.

"They kept walking for hours until they found themselves standing on the outskirts of the Polish city of Bielsko-Biala. When dawn came they managed to find their way out of the maze of the city and reached the fields of a village called Fibrovica. They knew that they couldn't move around in daylight, so they took a chance and knocked on the door of a relatively isolated house."

"That was dangerous," I whispered.

"Yes," he agreed and went on. "The door was opened by a Polish peasant woman who assumed they were Russian soldiers on the run, and apologized for her halting Russian. She fed them breakfast and they spent the day at her house, helping her with household chores. In the evening they fell asleep and at three in the morning were woken in a panic by the peasant woman shaking them, urging them to get up and continue on their way. She gave them drinks and paid them four marks in exchange for the work they did. Our friends thanked her," Kraus said, looking at me. "They're our friends, aren't they?"

"Right," I answered with a tight smile, caught up in the story.

"They left her house for the second half of the journey. This was the difficult part that included climbing the snowy Tatra mountains. Their progress became slow and, after two more days... are you counting the days?" he checked my alertness.

"Yes! It's been ten days since they ran away," I said proudly.

"Very good. During one of the breaks they took between climbing and shuffling through deep snow, they lay down to catch their breath, but the click of a rifle bolt made them both leap up. The whistle of the bullet that followed sent them running. They saw that 70 meters behind them, on the neighboring hill, a German patrol accompanied by tracking dogs was advancing. Their goal was to make it past the top of the hill, where they had rested, so that the hill would cut them off from the German patrol. Wetzler bypassed the summit first. Vrba fell on his way, hearing the bullets whistling around him. The fall saved his life. The German commander shouted, 'Stop shooting, we hit him.' Then, while the Germans were sliding to the bottom of the hill, Vrba jumped up and rushed to the summit, joining Wetzler as they ran towards the trees. The patrol started firing again, but the terrain conditions protected the runaways, and the wide river at the bottom of the valley helped them cover up their tracks and delay the dogs."

Krauss stopped and looked at his watch. "Excuse me a moment," he said and walked towards the telephone. He dialed again and this time it was answered. After a brief conversation, he returned.

"They chose the most deserted paths, sure that the Polish border would soon be behind them. The next day, while they were still climbing, they walked into the fields of an elderly Polish peasant woman. They stood there for a while just staring at each other. She showed no fear. In light of their positive experience with the previous farmer, our friends decided to gamble again. They knew that their filthy appearance betrayed them, and they decided to reveal their identities to her. 'We escaped from Auschwitz. We want to reach the Slovakian border. Can you show us the way?'

'I will send someone to help you,' she said."

"That was a mistake," I said.

"We'll see. Vrba was ill at ease too. He followed her and saw that she was crossing a bridge. He called to Wetzler and they both chose a high point overlooking the bridge, which would allow them sufficient warning time if she returned with hostile forces. At twilight, when visibility was reduced, they spotted her crossing the bridge with an elderly man. They waited until the two got closer and then noticed that man was holding a pistol. Their hands immediately went to the knives in their pockets, ready to pounce on the farmer. 'I brought you food,' said the peasant woman, 'clearly you're hungry.' They followed the farmer while devouring the food and stuffing it down their throats, when, to their astonishment, the farmer burst into raucous laughter. He pocketed his pistol and said, 'You really are from a concentration camp. Only really hungry people can eat like that. I was afraid you were Gestapo agents. Sometimes they try to deceive us. Come to my house and tomorrow morning we will go on a journey to the border.' At this point, Vrba was already struggling to walk since his injured legs, which had been paining him all the way, had become so swollen that they prevented him from walking without frequent stops. They entered the farmer's house, where Vrba tried with all his might to remove the boots from his swollen feet. From his pocket he took out the razor that he had kept in case he needed to commit suicide, and carefully sliced through the fine Dutch leather. 'You won't be able to keep walking in boots. Take my felt shoes. That's all I have to offer you,' said the kind-hearted farmer.

"That night they got to sleep in beds and, the next day, they stayed in the house while the farmer went about his work. After he returned, the group sat down to eat supper, and then the farmer told them about the guarding and the frequent German patrols. However, he reassured them and said that he knew the patrol schedule very well.

"They set off. The old man surprised them with his rapid pace, while Vrba trailed behind in the felt shoes. 'The

German patrol passes by here every ten minutes,' said the farmer calmly. 'We'll have to wait until the next patrol passes by.' They continued on their journey for two days until they finally reached an open area.

"'You see the forest over there?' said the farmer. 'That's Slovakia. The German patrol passes there every three hours. Wait until the next patrol passes before you continue on.' Vrba and Wetzler looked longingly into the forest, fighting the urge to run towards it immediately. Then they turned to the Polish farmer and thanked him warmly. They waited for the German patrol to pass and then dashed towards Slovakia," Kraus concluded with excitement.

I was also excited and asked for a glass of water, as if I, Uri, was the one who had just finished an arduous journey, full of tension and obstacles.

Kraus returned with a glass of water and a glass of soda pop as well, leaving me the choice.

"Well, Uri, what do you think?"

"I think they are two brave and talented guys who had a lot of luck. What happened to them after that?"

"They did escape the worst of all, but Slovakia was no safe place. The country was under the rule of the anti-Semitic pastor Jozef Tiso, and his Hlinka Guard was just as dangerous as the German Gestapo. The safest thing for them was to continue hiding in the forests or join the partisans who were fighting the Nazis."

"And they joined the partisans?" I asked with sparkling eyes.

"They planned to join the partisans but, before that – and this is actually the reason for this whole story – it was important for Vrba to spread the 'truth about Auschwitz.'

For this purpose, they wanted to meet the Zionist leadership in Slovakia and tell them that the 'new settlement areas' meant the gas chambers. Their goal was to provide Hungarian Jewry with accurate information."

"And at that stage, in Budapest, you still didn't know about the gas chambers?"

"We knew that Polish Jewry had been exterminated. We did not know about the sophisticated extermination machine and, most important of all – we lived in the complacent belief that it wouldn't happen in Hungary. If you remember the dates of the escape, at the stage when Vrba was crossing the border to Slovakia, the Germans had already occupied Hungary, but in April they had not yet begun deporting Jews from there. The various Jewish leaders in Budapest differed in their views regarding what awaited us and the best ways of coping with it."

"Did we finish the book?"

"No. We have a few pages left."

"Can we finish them today?"

Krauss glanced at his watch. "Yes. We have almost an hour before Gusta gets back. I'll pick up the pace."

"Thank you," I said.

"Oh, Uri," he smiled, "for children like you, here in the Land of Israel, all this suffering was..." he wiped a tear from his eye and left the sentence unfinished as though catching himself from getting carried away. "After two hours of walking they met a Slovakian farmer and asked him for help and directions to reach the city of Čadca. He helped them change out of their mud-spattered Dutch suits, they dressed in peasant clothes, and joined him in shepherding ten pigs to the Čadca market. The date was April 24, and Vrba realized that they had to hurry before the transports of Hungarian Jews began. The farmer promised to help them meet up with the Jewish leadership and, indeed, after they finished selling the pigs, and after he had generously given them a portion of the proceeds, the farmer led them to the clinic of Doctor Polak. Two Hlinka soldiers were stationed at the entrance to the clinic. Screwing up their courage, they walked by the guards as two local patients and, a few minutes later, they were sitting in a small room with Dr. Polak, telling him their story."

"They were very lucky," I said.

"Yes. He put them up in his house for one night and, the next day, took them to meet with the leaders of the Jewish community in Žilina.

"Now I'm going back to our conversation from yesterday evening. The official Jewish leadership was the Judenrat, appointed by the Germans but, in Slovakia, within this leadership, an underground group called the 'Working Group' had been organized. This small group, which took actions that risked the lives of its members, met with Vrba and Wetzler in Žilina. Dr. Oskar Neumann, Oskar Krasnansky, and Irwin Steiner were there at the meeting, along with another man named Hexner, when the fugitives told their story. They sensed in their listeners a lack of trust."

"What? They didn't believe them?"

"No, Uri. The Auschwitz camp was an inhuman place. It's hard to believe that human beings could develop such a mechanized extermination system. It was hard for them to take in that the story was true."

"So the whole escape was in vain?"

"Not quite. After a meal, the interrogation began. The members of the Working Group pulled out a large book containing the names of all the Jews who were sent from Slovakia to 'resettlement.' Vrba easily disproved this farce of the deportation to a new settlement. From memory, he reeled off the names of 30 Slovakian Jews who had travelled with him in a train to Auschwitz, and whose names appeared in the community's record book. Disbelief gave way to shock.

"The leaders placed Wetzler and Vrba into two separate rooms and began taking down detailed statements from each one, in order to prepare a report that would stand up to external criticism. For long hours, the fugitives dictated detailed statistics on the transports that had arrived at Auschwitz and on the exterminations. The descriptions included the countries the victims came from, the dates, and the numbers tattooed on their arms.

"I will read you a sample from the report:

'The numbers 109,000 to 119,000: At the beginning of March, 45,000 Jews arrived from Thessaloniki. 10,000 of them entered the camp, including a small percentage of women, about 30,000 were sent directly to the crematoria. Out of the ten thousand, almost all of them died after some time from infectious diseases and the conditions of the camp.'

"In the same exact way, they dictated a long record that included everything that had happened from the day they arrived in Auschwitz until the day they escaped."

"It's really unbelievable," I said. "How did they remember the details? How can it be?"

"It really is amazing. There are several versions. One says that they took the data with them, written in small print and rolled up into small containers. Another version claims that one of the containers fell in their possession while they were running away from the German patrol that they encountered in the hills. Remember?"

"Yes."

"In any case, one thing is clear. Rudolph Vrba has a phenomenal memory. In a meeting with me in 1958, he also recalled all the tattoo numbers by the date the people had arrived in Auschwitz."

"Really amazing."

"Yes. The Israeli historians who were loyal to the government, those who made sure that the Vrba-Wetzler story was kept secret and undocumented, also claimed that it was a legend and that the data came from another source."

"Why would they do that?"

"Because..." Kraus stopped. "We'll get to that," he said finally, and I thought I saw fear on his face. "Let's continue. Now I'm quoting Vrba's closing remarks after giving the detailed testimony: 'One million Hungarian Jews are about to die. Auschwitz is waiting for them. If you reveal this to them, they will revolt. They will never go to the furnaces willingly.'

"'Don't worry,' the Working Group leaders reassured him. 'We have daily contact with the leaders of Hungarian Jewry. Tomorrow morning the report will be in their hands. Now come on, you're tired. You and Mr. Wetzler should stay here. You'll get proper clothes, money and identity documents.'

"After a day of resting, Wetzler and Vrba met with Dr. Oskar Neumann and Oskar Krasnansky and asked them if they had sent the report. The two replied that the report was already in their hands and that, at this very moment,

Dr. Kastner was checking it. He was the most important person on the Hungarian committee.

"Remember the date, Uri. On April 27 at the latest, Dr. Kastner received the report. You can write it down."

"I wrote it," I said, noticing that Kraus was upset.

"Day after day, Vrba inquired about the progress of handling the report, and was answered that the translations into different languages had been completed. He wanted to know if an uprising had begun among Hungarian Jews, and was answered that the issue was being handled by the Jewish leadership in Budapest."

"Is that true? Did you get the report?"

"It's partially true. The report reached Budapest, but it did not reach me."

"Why not?" I asked suspiciously.

"I'm asking the same question myself. I only received a copy of the report more than a month later, when it was already too late."

"But why?" I insisted.

"That's a story in itself. I want to finish the book and we'll get to it at our next meeting, okay?"

"Okay," I shrugged.

"And then one morning, when the maid brought breakfast to his room, Vrba noticed that her eyes were streaming with tears. When he asked the source of her sorrow, she answered, 'They're deporting the Hungarians. Thousands. They're passing through Žilina in cattle cars.'" His throat went hoarse at the end of the sentence and he looked away.

"Are you alright, Mr. Kraus? Should I get you a glass of water?" I asked.

With his back to me, he waved his right hand. "Everything is fine, Uri. Just memories."

"Memories of what?" I persisted tactlessly.

"The trains the maid spoke of also carried the Jews from the towns in the book, including Mezőladány, my hometown."

"Members of your family?"

"My father, brothers, sisters, relatives, neighbors. Yes, Uri," he sighed. "The whole backdrop of my childhood."

"I'm sorry," I whispered. "Little Bela too?"

"No. Without little Bela."

"So he was saved?"

"Yes... so... you could say that." He sounded impatient.

"And you knew about those trains at the time?"

"I feared greatly for their safety... but... but..." he stammered and stopped. "But in the meantime, we will continue with Vrba." He got up and went out to the balcony, where he lit a cigarette. When he came back, he acted as if nothing had happened as he picked up the book, flipped through the pages and continued:

"Vrba stormed down the stairs, but there was no sign of Neumann or Krasnansky. Hexner, the junior clerk, told him they were doing their best and sending milk and sandwiches for the children. He reiterated that 'Kastner is an influential person and he will fix the situation.'"

"So he was a liar?" I asked in disappointment.

"Who? Hexner? No, he wasn't a liar, Uri'leh. Just naive. He believed his leaders, and perished with his family in Auschwitz." He took two deep breaths and went on: "When Vrba calmed down, Hexner informed him that the Germans had issued an arrest warrant against him and Wetzler." Kraus looked up from the book and looked at me. "Vrba claims that he found out later that Kastner showed the report to Eichmann and asked for clarification about the disaster. Eichmann, who understood the report's potential to slow down the quiet process of extermination, ordered an immediate search for Wetzler and Vrba."

"Do you think that's true?"

"Vrba is convinced of it. For me, it fits with other events that were happening in Budapest at that time, but it's third-hand testimony."

"Why would Kastner do such a thing?"

"If he did it, he did not mean anything evil. His intentions were good. He had a fantasy of saving all of Hungarian Jewry. We'll get to that. He believed in the plan along with Rabbi Weissmandel, one of the leaders of the Slovakian Working Group."

"And what happened to them... to the leaders of the Working Group?"

"With the exception of dear Gizzy Fleishman, who perished in Auschwitz, all the others were saved."

"Vrba?"

"Vrba and Wetzler stayed in Slovakia. Vrba still managed to meet that Weissmandel in June, and later joined the Slovakian partisans with his friend Wetzler."

The sound of the key in the door startled Kraus, who went over and greeted Gusta with an embrace as if they hadn't seen each other in months. I could tell from the tone of their conversation that Gusta was reassuring him.

"Hello, Uri," Gusta turned to me.

"Hello, Mrs. Gusta. Is everything alright?"

"Yes. Miklós just worries too much. He sent Henrik to look for me..." She rummaged through the bag that hung from her shoulder. "But, as a result, we have pictures that Miklós brought from Henrik especially for you." She handed Mr. Kraus the pictures and continued, "First we need to complete our English lesson! Will you have lunch with us later?"

"No, thank you, I have to eat with Grandma today."

"And we've already spoken enough English for today, Gusta," interjected Mr. Kraus.

"I think Uri needs some rest. Shall we continue tomorrow?"

"Miklós. Tomorrow at noon we are going to Tel Aviv."

"Oh, yes, you're right. Then we'll start early tomorrow. Here, look," he showed me the pictures. "This is with Vrba, this is with Gustav Sebes, and this is with Benfica's coach... Bela Gutman."

"Wow," I came over and looked at them closely.

Kraus smiled. "We'll save the rest for tomorrow."

"And Hannah Szenes too," I added.

"If we have time to get to it."

"Okay. Thank you Mr. Kraus. Thank you Mrs. Gusta," I said with a certain amount of disappointment as I collected my things, comforting myself by thinking about meeting with Ruthy that afternoon.

Chapter 4

"Don't make noise before four o'clock," we heard Grandma Tsipora's voice from behind the door we had slammed after us while my cousin Doron and I were already skipping down the stairs. To my disappointment, there were still no children in the street so, at Doron's request, we began playing the game 'Corners' with the new ball that Grandma Tsipora had given him for his birthday.

I was mesmerized as the approaching figure of Rutha, in shorts and a tight t-shirt, caught my eye. The ball that struck my face and bounced back from the edge of the nearest step pulled me back to reality and brought a burst of loud laughter from Rutha and the girls around her.

"That's great, I see you brought a ball," she said, coming up to me. I looked away, using my sleeve to wipe away the tears caused by the blow to my nose.

"It's my ball," interjected Doron.

"Are you okay?" Rutha asked, ignoring him.

"Yes. Thank you, Rutha."

"Call me Ruthy," she stated, combing her golden hair with the fingers of her right hand. "Let's play dodgeball."

We spent hours playing the game, with me taking pity on Ruthy every time the ball landed in my hands though, when it came to her turn, she bombarded me mercilessly, accompanying each shot with peals of laughter. While Ruthy and I were playing a game within a game, Doron made friends with Gideon, her younger brother. We wandered between the street and the park, all the way to the area of Jason's Tomb, alternating between games of stickball, mumblety-peg and jacks. Around six in the evening Aunt Esther arrived and shouted to us from the sidewalk to come home for dinner.

"Let's meet in the dark by the grave," said Gideon. "Like last year," he added, raising my hopes.

"Forget the séance nonsense," Ruthy said. "We'll meet at eight. Bring a bottle. We'll play Spin the Bottle."

When we entered Grandma's apartment, the table was already set for four people. Aunt Esther began her typical family interrogation:

"How is Hayuta? I haven't seen her in a long time."

"Fine."

"Your sister hasn't been to Jerusalem for a long time either. Right, Tsipora?" Esther glanced at my grandmother.

"They were here on Saturday," I answered, lowering my eyes at the implied criticism.

"Hayuta seems to be very busy," said Grandma.

"Is she? What, she started working?" Esther continued.

"She helps my father," I said as I stood up and turned my back, taking out a bottle of cola from the refrigerator.

When she realized that I was not cooperating, she moved on to the next topic:

"I heard you're spending hours with Kraus."

"Yes."

"It really interests me."

"What?" I asked.

"What exactly did he do during the war in Hungary? I understand that his activity is still unknown. There are all kinds of rumors."

"I know he did less than he wanted to… but tomorrow or the day after tomorrow I'll know more."

"You know that the Holocaust struck Hungarian Jews only when the war was almost over," she said.

"Yes."

"They didn't flee east en masse," Aunt Esther declared, "even though the Russian army was really close. The leaders must have already known about fate of the Jews in other European countries. I really don't understand what happened there."

"Kraus knew about the Holocaust of the Jews in Poland," I jumped to his defense, "but no one knew about the extermination machine of Auschwitz or the expansions that were made there to absorb Hungarian Jewry until Vrba fled from there."

"Who is Vrba?" Esther asked. "We haven't heard of him."

"That's exactly what I said to Uri," Grandma Tsipora chimed in.

I was going to answer, but Doron suddenly burst out, frustrated at being left out of the conversation, "Uri and Rutha are in love!"

"Is that so, Uri'leh?" Grandma asked with a loving smile.

"That's nonsense, you idiot," I answered. "Where did you get that from?"

"Her brother also told me!" Doron stood his ground.

I was torn between the urge to change the subject and the desire to hear more information from Doron.

"I'm going to take a bath," I said and got up from the table. "Are you coming to the room, Doron?"

"Take a bath at night," Grandma said, but Doron and I had already left the dining area.

Once in the room, I tried to interrogate Doron, but I couldn't get any information out of him. Before eight I was the first to go down to the quiet street, an empty juice bottle in my hand. I knew I was early, but I made a circuit around the street and went down the steps leading to the park next to the tomb. There was a young couple sitting on the bench in the park. I recognized the guy – the son of the neighbor on Grandma's floor. He was busy trying to shove his hand under the girl's shirt but, when she noticed me, she seized the opportunity to repel his advances and push him away. I passed by them as if they were invisible but, out of the corner of my eye, I caught his angry look. I passed the grave and continued in a wide circle along Alfasi Street to avoid encountering the couple again on the way back.

At the end of my big detour, I met the children who were walking along Ben Maimon Boulevard towards the park, where Ruthy was already sitting in the center of a half-circle which we made into a full circle with our arrival. I sat down in front of her, placing the bottle in the center of the circle. The game progressed lazily, with me breathing a sigh of relief every time the bottle missed me and waiting in tense anticipation whenever it came near Ruthy. Eventually, at the end of a round, it pointed at me.

Gideon jumped in. "Truth or dare?"

"Dare," I said, avoiding the question that he must have prepared for me.

"I dare you to kiss Rutha," he said with triumphant joy. I went up to Ruthy and kissed her gently on the cheek.

"No. On the lips!" Gideon demanded. We brushed each other's lips, and I was happy that the blush that rose to my face was hidden by the darkness of the night. I returned to my place, my heart pounding with excitement, and avoided looking at anyone else in the circle. After a few more rounds, the bottle pointed at Ruthy and this time Haim, one of the neighborhood urchins, jumped up.

"You must show us your bra," he said, rolling with laughter.

"That's not going by the rules," I protested, defending her dignity.

But she remained tranquil. "It's okay, Uri," she said calmly and lifted up her thin shirt, revealing a bright white bra hugging an impressively large chest.

"Are you happy now? Babies," she said. "Come on Uri, let's get out of here."

"Rutha, stop!" Dina jumped up. "You promised Sima that you wouldn't leave the neighborhood."

"I'm not leaving it. Tell Sima that I'm with Uri," she said and pulled me by the hand towards the stairs.

We went up the steps of the park, turned right and walked as far as the section where the street turned into a boulevard and, there, in front of the kiosk, when she was sure that the other children couldn't see us, she pulled me to the right onto Alfasi Street.

"Where are we going?" I asked, allowing myself to be dragged along without resistance.

"We're going to say hello to Golda."

"Which Golda?"

"Meir."

"Golda Meir?"

"Yes. Just joking. All the gang is meeting up there now near the Prime Minister's building. Come on. It'll be cool."

"Why are they meeting up? Why there?"

Ruthy informed me that a demonstration of displaced Arab Christian residents from Bir'im and Iqrit was being organized for the following day, and that she wanted to support them. She explained to me that her kibbutz, Kibbutz Bar'am, sits on part of the displaced Arabs' lands, and that she and her friends were fighting this injustice.

We passed the broad Ben Zvi Boulevard and entered the dark, wooded area leading to the government buildings. Our conversation turned into an argument, with my right-wing opinions taking endless blows from her.

"Would you like to go to the movies tomorrow?" she suddenly veered off in an unexpected direction.

"Tomorrow?"

"Yes. Are you busy?"

"No. It's just that you changed the subject very suddenly. What movie?"

"The movie 'The Godfather' came to Israel; a friend of mine saw it in Paris a week ago."

"I heard about the movie. It's for adults only, isn't it?"

"Yes. And…? Is there a problem with that?"

"Will they let us in?"

"I look adult, don't I?"

"Yes… but…"

"Uri… there are laws that were made to be broken."

"Marlon Brando's in it," I said to avoid her last statement.

She nodded. "So it's decided?"

"It's decided."

"Good," Ruthy smiled. "We're getting closer. Come on... pick up the pace a little..." she goaded me. "You're out of shape."

After about a quarter of an hour of brisk walking we reached the illuminated area, and there we found three groups of protesters shouting and insulting each other while dozens of policemen were trying to restore order.

"Those on the left are the displaced residents. Look, they're getting ready to spend the night here," Ruthy commentated on the scene for me.

"What? Are you planning to sleep here?"

"No, silly. Not me. And those facing them are the people from my kibbutz and, next to them, all kinds of hot-headed right-wingers. Want to join them?" she teased.

"Why don't we get closer? Why did you stop?"

"I prefer that they don't see me. And besides, my friends are those," she said and pointed to a small group carrying banners of 'Matzpen.'[18]

"What's wrong with you, Ruthy? Matzpen? You've gone too far."

"What are you getting so excited about? They're all just cream puffs," she said as a good-looking guy walked up to us. To my surprise, she fell into his arms. "Meet Udi Adiv,"[19] she said to me, then pointed at me and told him, "And this is Uri, a problematic upbringing, but not a lost cause."

---

18. Matzpen [Compass] was a revolutionary socialist and anti-Zionist organization, founded in 1962 and active until the 1980s.

19. Udi Adiv was eventually sent to jail after being arrested for espionage on behalf of Syria.

"Hello, Uri," said Udi, extending his strong hand.

"Udi, what's happening here?" she asked.

"The displaced villagers don't want Matzpen activists to join them. Serves them right."

"You need to understand, Uri. Udi left Matzpen for the Red Front.[20] We are not extreme enough for his taste," Ruthy giggled.

"You're very much to my taste," said Udi, giving her another hug.

Ruthy smiled with pleasure, but suddenly her face froze. "Wow. I'm in trouble."

"Rutha Shorin! What are you doing here?" A bass voice resounded from a man with a mustache who led five more kibbutz members in his wake.

"Nothing, Yoel. Uri lives here in the area and he is now walking me to Aunt Sima's."

"Your father assured me you were done with these adventures. I understand that the traitors of Matzpen are no longer enough for you." Ruthy turned her back on him, which only incensed him further: "Wake up Rutha!! This is a battle for our home."

"First of all, it's their home," Ruthy turned to him, unable to restrain herself.

"You're not going to get away with this one easily. We'll bring it up at the next meeting. Your father has exactly one week to straighten your head out. That's it friends, let's go towards the gate," he said, leading the band in his wake.

---

20. A Marxist-Leninist faction of Matzpen that broke off to form an independent group in 1970.

"Someone here got into trouble ..." Udi chuckled. "Come on, you'd better scram."

We left the area of the government quarter, walking quietly between the trees. I suddenly realized that Rutha had taken advantage of me as a cover story. My feelings ranged from anger to insult. We walked on in silence until we got back to the busy Ben Zvi Road.

"I really wanted to be with you," Ruthy broke through the fog of embarrassment, reading my mind.

"It doesn't look that way. It looks like the main goal was to go to the preparations for a demonstration."

"That too. I could have asked you for a cover story and gone without you... but I wanted to go with you."

"Ruthy. It's not just that you weren't honest with me... also your friends aren't that..."

"Uri... let's just leave it behind us. You and I are together now," she said gently, taking my hand in hers. "Let's enjoy the rest of the evening. Okay?"

"Okay," I answered, embarrassed. I felt like I'd dissolved into a puddle.

"Come hug me, I need it now," she whispered and wrapped my right arm about her waist, leading us back towards the neighborhood. We walked up Alfasi arm in arm and onto Ramban Street.

"So tell me, what's your story with this Kraus?"

"He's a special man."

"That *dos*?"[21]

"He's not such a dos. At home he doesn't wear a yarmulke at all."

---

21. Dos [religious in Yiddish] is a pejorative term used by secular Israelis to refer to religious Jews, primarily ultra-Orthodox.

"Sima says there's a rumor that he saved tens of thousands of Jews. Do you think it's true?"

"Yes, he swam against the stream. Both in Hungary and in Israel. I don't know the whole story yet, but I think it's not easy for him here."

"Yes. I understood that he is not a favorite of the government," she said.

We turned onto Ussishkin Street and found ourselves facing the park where we had started.

"Let's sit for a while," she said, leading us down the park steps.

We sat down on the bench in the empty park, still in an embrace.

"He's kind of a lone horseman. Different from his surroundings," I said thoughtfully.

"Like the Mexican fan palm in their Jerusalem yard."

"Mexican...? I didn't recognize it... yes... in Budapest Kraus took a stand against the Zionist and Haredi organizations and, in Israel, against the ruling party. The security agencies probably also took action against him. It all sounds pretty extreme to me."

"No. It doesn't surprise me at all. My friends are getting arrested by the Shin Bet[22] right and left. I know that during the days of Isser Harel,[23] things were even more extreme. Then they also followed the members of Hashomer Hatzair."[24]

"But Kraus is really not a leftist," I said and immediately regretted it.

---

22. Israel Security Agency, Israel's internal security service.

23. Director of the Mossad from 1952-1963.

24. Hashomer Hatzair [the Young Guard] is a Labor Zionist secular Jewish youth movement.

"A rebel is a rebel. In those days, the Shin Bet not only took action against Maki[25] but also against Herut, without distinguishing between right and left." She paused for a moment, catching my gaze. "In any case, he sounds like an interesting character. I'd love to hear how you get on with him. In the end you'll also be a rebel," she said with a smile and reached out to caress my cheek. Her beautiful eyes misted over as she brought her lips to mine. My heart was pounding. I imitated her moves and placed my palm on her cheek. Her lips brushed mine, then moved up and gently brushed my closed eyelashes. She placed a palm on my chest, lightly teasing my nipple with her fingers and, while I was trying to figure out what to do next, she pulled my head close and pressed her mouth to my mouth, which responded by opening. Before I realized what was happening we were sucking each other in, exploring new places with our tongues. When I plucked up courage and placed my hand on her chest, she broke off the kiss slightly to say:

"I would happily keep going, but I have to report to Sima."

"You think she already knows?"

"I guess so. Thanks, Uri." She stood up.

"I'll walk you," I stood up with difficulty, trying to hide my excitement. We parted at the entrance to the stairwell with a long embrace.

I continued to stand there, following her with my gaze, before I crossed the road and skipped up the stairs of the facing building, beside myself with elation and emotion. I opened the front door quietly, praying that Grandma had

---

25. The Israel Communist Party

already gone to sleep. The light in the living room was on but the apartment was quiet. I went into my room and tossed and turned for hours in bed. I finally fell asleep at three in the morning with Arik Einstein's[26] voice caressing me and, on my lips, playing like a prayer, "I have a girl and her name is Ruthy."

26.[27] Arik Einstein (1939-2013) was a well-known Israeli singer.

Chapter 5

"What's wrong with you this morning?" Grandma asked me, clearing her plate from the table to the sink.

"Everything's fine. Why?"

"You came home so quietly last night and got up by yourself this morning..."

"Yes, I set an alarm clock. I agreed to meet Kraus at half past eight."

"And you hardly ate anything," she added.

"I'm not hungry."

"Did you eat out in the evening?"

"Yes, thanks Grandma, I'm in a bit of a hurry and I need to get a few more things ready. I'll see you in the afternoon. Don't worry, I promise to come back hungry."

I hid away in my room until twenty past eight, lying on the bed and reliving the events of the previous evening. My feelings for Ruthy overflowed, filling me with delicious pleasure tempered by concerns and questions. Ruthy was different from any of the other girls I had known until then. I didn't know if it was due to her kibbutznik roots, her brazen rebelliousness, or the fact that she was older and more mature than me. There was something liberating but, at the same time threatening in her free behavior.

I hoped with all my heart that she was also lying in her room at that moment and thinking about me.

A glance at the clock made me jump to my feet. I hurried downstairs, crossed the road and entered the well-kept garden of the building across the street. I bypassed the tall date palm, my eyes trained on the second floor in a disappointed hope of seeing Ruthy's waving hand. I returned to the stairwell, lingering a few seconds to see if I could hear her voice before knocking on the Kraus family's door.

"Good morning, Uri. Come in," Mr. Kraus opened the door for me with a wide smile.

"You won't believe who I was talking to about you ten minutes ago."

"With who?" I asked in surprise. "With Ruthy?"

"No. With Vrba!"

"With Vrba??"

"Yes. The time in Vancouver is ten hours behind us so, for him, it is only half past ten at night."

"But Vrba doesn't know me."

"True, but I told him about a nice, grown-up and curious boy from Tel Aviv who listened attentively to his life story and the tale of his escape from Auschwitz."

"Thanks," I grinned in embarrassment.

"Then he asked your name."

"And...?"

"I told him, 'Uri,' and he asked, 'Uri Even?' It turns out his cousin's son is also named Uri and about your age, also with curly black hair, but I understood from Gusta that your grandmother's family name is something else. I told him you find it hard to believe the story, and you are asking how it is possible that it was never publicized in Israel."

"I didn't say that at all," I answered defensively, even though that's what I thought.

"You said something similar. Anyway, he sends you greetings and promises to visit you on his next visit to Israel and explain everything to you, but also suggested that you might meet the other Uri. You live in Tel Aviv, right?"

"Right."

"So he lives not far from you. What do you say?"

"Sure, I'd be happy to meet him. So I understand that today we are speaking in Hebrew?" I changed the subject.

"Yes. We finished Vrba's book. You'll continue your English lessons with Gusta."

I nodded and told him about the writing assignment that I wanted to complete by Passover to be accepted as part of the delegation.

"Good, I can help you. You've earned it, honestly. Come sit down," he led me towards the table on which the chess board was laid out. "Are you still following the game?"

"No," I answered indifferently, "I was busy yesterday."

"Yes, I heard..." Kraus surprised me. "I understand that Dina's guest dragged you into an adventure."

"Who? Rutha?"

"Yes. Sima came by this morning. Gusta is in her apartment now."

"What did she tell you?" I was dumbfounded.

"I don't know the details, but I understood that this Rutha is one mischievous young woman."

"It was my idea anyway," I found myself defending her.

"Your idea? What does a revisionist like you have to do with the Matzpen movement?"

"We didn't go to the Matzpen movement," I protested. "I wanted to see the people from Bir'im and Iqrit from up close."

"I understand that there were people there who were even more extreme than Matzpen."

"Not that I know of... yes... maybe one named Udi."

"Well, so be it." He noticed my discomfort and rapidly changed the subject: "We have until half past ten."

I was deep in thought and did not respond. "Perhaps we'll have enough time to talk about the German invasion of Hungary," Kraus said.

"I don't understand this whole story. It doesn't make sense," I said in frustration.

"What story don't you understand?" he asked, gently touching my palm.

"Yesterday you told me how Vrba, the hero, ran away from Auschwitz to save the Hungarian Jews, and today you want to tell me about the Holocaust of the Hungarian Jews."

"Yes. You're right. And what doesn't make sense?"

"If they wrote such a detailed report, how come Hungarian Jews didn't stage an uprising? What did the heads of the leadership do with it? And how come the whole world didn't cry out? And how come I haven't heard about this report until today? And not just me, my grandmother and my aunt haven't heard of it either."

"Uri, these are difficult and legitimate questions. The entire way these events played out was puzzling and sounds illogical. But was there anything logical in that whole period of darkness? Does it make sense that all this happened at all?

"In any case, getting to the point, it's hard to believe, but the report arrived in its entirety to the hands of the Jewish leadership in Budapest. And yes, again hard to believe, but the leadership did not publicize the report to the world. Hard to believe, but neither did they share it with the masses of Hungarian Jews, and this is a great sin. A sin that has been kept secret to this day."

"To this day?"

"Yes, Uri. You are one of the very few who is open to hearing these secrets."

"But why? Why?"

"You're shaken, Uri. I understand that last night's events are also troubling you. Would you rather skip our conversation today?"

"No. And it has nothing to do with Ruthy. None at all. Sorry for bursting out. Please go on."

"It's okay, Uri, it really is inconceivable... now you're feeling a tiny fraction of the abysmal frustration I felt then," he said and pondered for a long time before continuing. "The terrible disaster that was looming finally reached us, and was hidden until today for several reasons. The first was because there was no cooperation between the various Jewish organizations and, as a result, no information flowed between them, and there was no concentrated effort either." Kraus stopped and watched as I wrote in my notebook. "The second reason is that some of the leaders thought there was no point in spreading the information because it would just create a big panic, without giving the masses any solution. The third reason was that some of the leaders believed that they would bring about salvation in some miraculous way and, when their mistake became clear to them, they were already trapped by their actions. The fourth reason is the concealment of people's shared guilt in what happened, and that explains why the details I want to share with you this morning have been kept secret until now."

"I'm writing it down."

"Should we start?"

"Definitely," I said, turning on the tape recorder.

"So the first point you had trouble believing was the lack of cooperation in the face of the approaching Holocaust. Mapai representatives, who controlled the Zionist Federation institutions, tried to push me away because I was a representative of the Mizrahi movement from the administration of the Eretz Israel[27] office. This split affected the day-to-day work so, towards the end of 1943, it was decided that all the Jewish movements would band together in an effort to save the remaining refugees in Europe, as well as the Hungarian Jewish community. To achieve that unification, it was agreed to establish a central committee for rescue affairs in Budapest."

"Excellent. You led it?"

"No, not at all. The idea of banding the ranks together, as well as the budgets for the rescue committee, came from the Land of Israel and, therefore, the Mapai representatives were appointed as the heads of the committee – Kastner and Brand."

"And you?"

"Not only was I not appointed head of the commit-

---

27. Trans.: Land of Israel

tee, I was not even invited to become a member." Krauss watched me digesting the situation before he went on. "And not just me. The Orthodox, or the Haredim as you call them, were not invited either."

"So it wasn't a combined effort..."

"That's right, that's why the Orthodox established a separate Haredi rescue committee and started to transfer funds from Haredi donors and from the Joint.[28] Later, following pressure from the Diaspora, the two committees were united, but I was left out.

"Hashomer Hatzair, who were my partners in the Eretz Israel office, nominated a new representative named Baumer. Uri, are you with me?"

"Yes." I pulled my attention back to what he was saying.

"In February 1944, about half a year after his appointment and a month before the German invasion, Baumer left Budapest and made Aliyah to Israel. And he was not the only leader to leave, other leaders did too."

"Why?"

"Because they felt that their personal danger had increased."

"And you and Gusta didn't think of making Aliyah?"

"I won't deny it, I was very worried and, indeed, I sent a request to Israel to make Aliyah via the same leaders who left... but the answer I received from Haim Barles, the head of the Istanbul office, was negative..." Kraus stopped and flipped through his thick binders, pulling out a piece of paper with a handwritten note on it and reading it to me: 'Kraus is the key to the Aliyah from Europe.'"

He re-filed the paper and looked up. "He, Barles, meant

---

28. The Joint Distribution Committee, a global Jewish humanitarian organization founded in 1914.

well and I was forced to respect his decision. It's possible..." he said and took a deep breath. "It's possible that if I had been married to Gusta at the time, I would have refused Barles' instructions and made Aliya."

"Are you sorry you stayed?"

Kraus sank into his chair, closing and opening his eyes repeatedly before sitting up straight and answering, "It's true that if I had left then, I would have been spared the countless hardships that found me and have stayed with me to this day... but, on the other hand, I wouldn't have met and married Gusta, and the privilege of saving the lives of a hundred thousand Jews would have also been taken away from me, including Gusta's life."

"When did you meet Gusta?"

"I met her for the first time at the end of February 1944. There was a festive reception for the Hungarian Ministry of Finance. Her name was Gusta Stahl, and she came to the event with the management of the Polish-Hungarian Chamber of Commerce... and she was as beautiful then as she is today..." A dreamy look came over his face.

"Did you talk?"

"Gusta stole my heart the moment I saw her. She was with an older man, and I relaxed when she introduced him to me as her father. He, Nessa Stahl, was a Zionist activist in Poland and they had come together to Budapest and were living there as refugees. As you know, Gusta knows many languages, so she worked in the Chamber of Commerce office as an interpreter and secretary. At that event we found a quiet corner and talked for a long time, ignoring the commotion around us."

"What commotion?"

"Cocktails, toasts, courtesy speeches and a host of representatives from neutral and hostile countries."

"Nazis too??"

"Nazis too. Before the invasion, there were such events." Kraus stopped and glanced at me before continuing: "And so, while we were still standing and talking, a tall German approached us. I knew he was assistant to Edmund Wiesenmeier, German ambassador to Hungary. We had met a few weeks before at a meeting in the office of the Hungarian Interior Ministry, shortly after he arrived. He approached us wreathed in smiles. 'Hello, Mr. Kraus,' he addressed me. 'How come you don't introduce me to the beauty of the evening?' He turned to Gusta and introduced himself, 'Dieter Koch,' then kissed her hand. Gusta thanked him and tried to indicate that we were in the middle of an important conversation, but he did not take the hint and instead returned with three glasses of champagne. We were finally rescued by the head of the Chamber of Commerce who approached us at the request of Gusta's father and pulled her away, with apologies, on the pretext that her help was needed for translation. That's all," Kraus concluded, "that's how we met – and we've never been apart since then."

"And this Dieter?" I asked.

"Oh... we didn't part from him for many months either... but again I got carried away," Kraus recovered his composure. "Where were we?" he scratched his head. "Ah, yes, the attempts to bring together the Jewish organizations in Budapest."

I nodded. "So you couldn't form a collaboration?"

"No, although I never stopped trying for a moment.

In the days before the German invasion of Hungary, the Polish consulate in Istanbul published details that had been provided by the Polish underground. According to the consulate, between the summer of 1942 and the fall of 1943, 850,000 Jews were killed in Poland."

Kraus went to the bookshelf, pulled out a binder and opened it in front of me. "Look. The Jewish representatives in Istanbul ignored the information," he continued, flipping through the pages, "as well as Allied representatives in Istanbul. They also buried the notification."

I reviewed the questions Kraus raised in the letters he sent to Istanbul, which remained unanswered. "So how did you hear about it?"

"Rumors spread, as they will do. They passed from mouth to mouth but lacked solid facts like those contained in the later Vrba report."

"And you continued to fight among yourselves in Budapest?" I asked sharply.

"That day I went to a meeting with Segdi Masek from the Hungarian Foreign Ministry. I entered his elegant office and found him in despair, holding his head in his hands and supporting his arms on the heavy wooden desk. He told me that the German ambassador had demanded that Miklós Horthy, the regent of Hungary, together with the Hungarian Chief of Staff and senior Cabinet ministers, report to Hitler."

"Why was this Masek in despair?"

"He understood that it was a German trap but, beyond that, he had a serious personal problem. You see, Segdi Masek was married to a converted Jew. He wasn't sure that the protection he'd provided her up till then would be effective if the Germans invaded Hungary."

"And he thought that was what was about to happen?"

"Certainly. So did Kallay, the Prime Minister. But contrary to their entreaties, Horthy and the entourage went to Germany... I understood from this that the German invasion was getting closer."

"How is this related to Jewish cooperation?"

"Given the news from Istanbul, and after my meeting with Segdi Masek, I renewed my efforts to establish a representative all-Zionist rescue committee, but again I met with refusal in Budapest."

"Maybe, unlike you, they didn't know the invasion was getting closer?"

"Them?" His voice rose in anger. "I told them everything I knew, and those on the rescue committee knew everything I knew and much more." He paused again and flipped through the pages of another binder. "Look here. Peretz Reves, the head of Young Maccabi[29] and a member of the rescue committee, writes that he heard about the anticipated occupation three days before it actually happened. That is, on the same day that Segdi Masek informed me. Together with Yoel Brand, a fellow member of Kastner's committee, he attended a social gathering which included strippers and a lot of alcohol. Dr. Schmidt, who was also present at the gathering, warned Brand that he should get his wife and children out of the Majestic Hotel because... and I quote: 'Within a few days, with the German invasion, the hotel is supposed to serve as the Gestapo headquarters in Budapest.' Here, look at the document." He handed me Peretz Reves' testimony.

---

29. Young Maccabi is the youth movement of the Maccabi World Union, a Zionist organization focusing on athletics, officially founded in 1921.

"So they knew?"

"Of course they knew. And then the invasion did come," Kraus announced dramatically, adjusting his glasses on his nose as he stood up and began circling the table with small steps while speaking slowly: "It was a Sunday morning. The Nazis delayed the departure of the Hungarian entourage that met with Hitler until the moment when the German army began its invasion of Hungary. The Hungarian army, cut off from its leaders who had been detained in Germany, and lacking information, met the Germans without resistance."

"It really was a trick."

"Yes. A well-known Nazi trick. I remember the balmy early spring weather. It was a fine morning that started pleasantly and took a turn a few hours later. Columns of German vehicles followed by soldiers captured the capital, Budapest, without firing a shot. By the late afternoon you could already see German officers sitting tranquilly in the cafes of Pest."

"Where were you that day?"

"When the soldiers entered the city, I was in the community building on Sip Street, in the provincial towns department. I tried to reach my father as well as Big Bela in his office in Kisvárda on the only phone there was in the village, but without success."

"And Gusta?"

"Fortunately, the Chamber of Commerce had installed a phone in her apartment. Quite rare in those years. She called me and whispered that Dieter Koch was standing outside her door and ringing the bell. I told her to close the curtains of the front window and not to open the door. We agreed that when she saw Dieter leaving the building, she would place a blanket on the side windowsill and when I arrived I would knock four times on her door before she would open it. I asked her and her father to pack light suitcases for staying away from their apartment."

"Why?"

"Because I was afraid that Dieter would come back there, and if he didn't find her, he would harass her father.

"Before I left the community building I called Carl Lutz from the Swiss consulate, who had generously invited Gusta and me to stay in the consulate building. Gusta's and her father's apartment was in the Jewish Quarter, not far away from the community building. I passed by a triangle of the three largest synagogues. Residents of the Jewish quarter were streaming towards the synagogues, each according to the faction to which he belonged, hoping to find counsel and protection in the house of God. When I arrived at Gusta's house the blanket was in its place on the windowsill, and I ran up the stairs and knocked on her door. The door opened and Gusta fell into my arms, pale and trembling.

"We said goodbye to her father, who moved to shelter with friends near the Great Synagogue on Dohany Street, while Gusta and I, after coordinating by telephone with Carl Lutz, rushed towards the Swiss legation. The kilometer and a half to Liberty Square where the legation was located we covered in 10 minutes. Carl Lutz was waiting for us at the entrance to the building and arranged a bedroom for us. I got an office in the Department for the Representation of Foreign Interests headed by Lutz, and from then until the liberation of the city, Liberty Square became our home."

"And the Jewish leadership didn't get organized?"

"The Jewish leadership called an emergency meeting that day at Brand's house."

"Were you there?"

"No. Representatives of Mizrahi like myself were not invited to the meeting, nor were representatives of the general Zionists."

"Did they reach any decisions?"

"No, but by the next day the Germans had already set up the Judenrat. Eichmann was the chief engineer. He had three demonic deputies, commanders in the SS Judenkommandos. The first two were Hermann Krumey and Dieter Wisliceny."

"I remember we talked about the evil Wisliceny, who is Krumey?"

"A member of the Gestapo who started by rounding up the Croatian Jews in camps, personally commanded the transports from Poland to the extermination camps and came from there to serve in Hungary."

"So who was the third?"

"The third was Kurt Becher. A special kind of bastard."

"Why special?"

"Because not only was he never punished for his actions, he grew his family fortune from the extermination of the Jews. In Hungary he dealt with the economic side, trading lives in exchange for property."

"So he wasn't an accomplice to the killing?"

"Of course he was. Kurt Becher was formerly an officer in the Death's Head Units which ran the extermination camps. Before gassing was perfected they took part in slaughtering the first million in mass shootings and burying the survivors in pits."

"So this is the group that chose the Jews of the Judenrat?"

"That's right. These were the experts. They had shared expertise in destroying the Jewry of Poland, Slovakia, Thessaloniki, Croatia... and more." Kraus stopped and took a breath.

"The day after the occupation, the Germans rounded up 500 heads of the Jewish community, chose eight members from the various streams of Judaism to be on the Judenrat of Budapest, and appointed Samu Stern, a tycoon and Jewish-Hungarian community leader, as the head. At the end of the meeting, the community committee convened. Kastner and I were also at that meeting. Kastner said that he would like to contact the Germans and see what could be done. Everyone present except me agreed with him. Two days later he returned and reported that there were indeed chances of obtaining positive results from the Germans."

"Did you believe him?"

"I believed him that he believed in the possibility, but I didn't believe in the Nazis for a single moment. That's why we agreed that he would continue his talks with the Germans while I focused on my ties with the Hungarian government."

"The Hungarian government continued to function?"

"Yes, absolutely. Despite the German invasion, the Hungarian government remained sovereign, and the regent Horthy was left at the head of the system.

"At this point, Uri, I believed that, given the circumstances, cooperation among the Jewish institutions was indeed beginning. I sat with Kastner, and we agreed that in his future meetings with the Germans he would be obliged to insist on four very important points. One – maintaining a Jewish way of life; the second – no ghettoization, meaning Jews being rounded up into one place; the third was to promote the emigration of the 600 who were certified, bearing transit passes; and the fourth, no deportation of Jews from Hungary. He agreed with me."

"That sounds good. But I understand he didn't succeed?"

"He certainly tried, but the Nazis tricked him, and he sank very quickly into attempts to buy the lives of the Jews with two million dollars in the framework of the fantastical Europe plan. I think we mentioned it sometime yesterday or the day before."

Kraus fell silent when he heard the sound of Gusta's footsteps and then the rustling of her keys. He got up from the chair, motioning to me to stay where I was, and hurried towards the door as it opened. I heard them whispering in their foreign language.

Kraus returned to his chair. "Gusta will be back shortly," he said, but my ears were focused on the drumming of her heels on the stairs as she went back out and climbed up to the second floor. I tried to think what she might have told him now, and what news had caused her to go out again and up to the second floor. My curiosity overcame my embarrassment.

"What's new with Rutha?" I asked, feeling my cheeks getting hot.

"Things are hopping up there... um... It's better if you hear directly from Gusta. OK, Uri?"

"Do I have a choice?"

"There's always a choice, Uri. There's always a choice."

He looked at me kindly, recognizing the question mark on my face. "Even when nothing can be changed, you can decide how to relate to something." I wasn't sure if he meant my actions the night before or his actions 30 years ago.

"Well, let's continue..." he said. "It's important for you to know that Gusta loves you very much."

"Thank you," I answered shyly.

"So, Kastner and Brand met with Wisliceny, Eichmann's deputy, on the fifth of April. They explained to him in detail the Europe plan for redeeming Jewish lives with money, as they saw it. Wisliceny greatly enjoyed the fact that instead of his having to make the Jewish leadership swallow the bait and convince them that he honestly intended to save Jewish lives in exchange for money, the leaders themselves came to him with the plan."

"And what about your four demands?"

"Kastner kept his promise, and in another meeting with Wisliceny, they specified the four demands, including the issuance of those 600 certificates that I had dealt with, which had yet to be assigned individual names. Wisliceny considered the four demands in detail and asked: 'Why only 600? Why shouldn't a hundred thousand be deported?'"

"But you didn't want deportation," I burst out.

"True, but the fools were so excited by the Germans' very willingness to make the deal, that they swallowed the bait without paying attention to the details. Four days later, on the second of May, they sobered up. Kastner then met with Krumey, Eichmann's deputy, following the lack of compliance with the four demands I had specified."

"The 2nd of May? That's already after he read Vrba's

report," I said. "He must have understood from the report that they had no intention of meeting those demands?"

"That's right... and it's nice that you remember the dates, Uri. At the same time a report from the railway company of Slovakia was leaked, stating that it had been asked to prepare for the transport of 300,000 Jews through its territory."

"Yes... those must have been the Jews who later passed by Vrba's residence in Slovakia and caused his maid to cry?"

"You surprise me with the connections you make. That's exactly right."

I grinned shyly and he went on, "At the meeting, Kastner was told that 600 certificate holders would be able to leave, not by ship from Constanta but rather secretly, in sealed train cars under the guise of deportation, and that the Jewish representatives were not allowed to speak about this with Hungarian representatives."

"Why?"

"The excuse, according to the Germans, was that the Hungarians were demanding the deportation of all Jews from their country, and not just a small minority that would make Aliyah to Palestine. The emigration of a small number, they said, would just enrage the Hungarians."

"Really?"

"Absolutely not. Kastner came back to me and confessed that, despite all his efforts, the Germans refused to hear of any option other than deportation. To Spain."

"To Spain of all places?"

"Yes, basically deportation westward. Spain was neutral and safe. I emphasized to Kastner that such cooperation would be understood by the Hungarians to mean that the deportation was being done with the Jews' consent."

"Why?" I asked.

"I already explained to you," Kraus lost patience. "Deportation is something done by force to a destination decided on by the deporter. The position I took in my meetings with the Hungarian authorities from the beginning of the war was that it was forbidden to deport Hungarian citizens. One day you cooperate with the Germans on deportation to Spain, and the next day you have no claim against the Hungarians when you ask for their assistance in preventing deportations to Poland."

"And Kastner didn't understand this?"

"He completely ignored me! And so, at the beginning of May 1944, my relationship with Israel Kastner came to an end," concluded Kraus in a furious tone, leaving the table. I heard the sound of running water from the kitchen and after a few minutes he returned carrying two green apples. He sat down at the table and began to peel the first apple. When he raised his eyes I asked:

"So that's it? That was the end of the collaboration?"

Kraus looked at me sadly and said: "It was a lack of collaboration until the time of the mass deportations of May-June 1944. Unfortunately, it was not the end of the 'lack of collaboration.'"

"I don't understand. Even after hundreds of thousands of Hungarian Jews were sent to the camps, you continued to argue among yourselves?"

"We didn't continue to argue. We just stopped communicating with each other. We got disconnected."

"And the leaders in the Land of Israel didn't intervene?"

Kraus lowered his eyes and said in a whisper, "The leadership in the Land of Israel was fed information by Kastner and Brand, and it had its own interests."

I watched the spiraling snake of apple peel that got longer and longer as the peeling motion continued. The room fell silent. Kraus pushed the plate with the first sliced apple towards me and set off on the task of peeling the second one.

"But they sent the paratroopers, they sent Hannah Szenes," I broke the silence.

"They sent her to warn the Jews. To organize them. Unfortunately, Uri, I will have to disappoint you again. Both about the story of the capture of the paratroopers, and also about the lack of cooperation in the attempts to rescue them.

"It goes a little beyond the four topics I said I would explain to you, but the story of the paratroopers is also a clear example of the lack of cooperation."

"I want to hear about it," I declared firmly.

Kraus took off his glasses, breathed on them and polished the lenses with the crumpled handkerchief tucked in his pocket. He chewed a slice of apple and went on.

"So, in those days, at the height of the great deportation of the rural Jews to Auschwitz, three paratroopers from the Land of Israel landed near the Hungarian-Croatian border. Hannah Szenes crossed the border into Hungary on June 9th and was captured immediately. The other two, Yoel Palgi and Peretz Goldstein, managed to cross the border and arrived in Budapest on June 20th. Their arrival was coordinated in advance with the rescue committee which, as usual, did not inform me."

"Until now, I've only heard of the name Hannah Szenes. How is that?"

"Excellent question, Uri. I don't have a complete answer, but I suppose that later in the story we will see several possible reasons for this. The day after their arrival, they contacted Kastner, who informed Clages, head of the intelligence department of the Gestapo in Budapest."

"What? Why did he do that?"

"According to him, he did it to protect them."

"Protect them? How?"

"He made up a story that they came from the Land of Israel to check the truth of the Germans' willingness to make a deal that had replaced the Europe Plan, a deal of trucks in exchange for Jewish blood. Since, according to this cover story, the paratroopers came to Budapest for the purpose of promoting a cause acceptable to the Nazis, they should come out of hiding."

"Sounds completely illogical to me," I insisted. Kraus smiled bitterly at me.

"You're right, Uri, but Kastner wanted to keep his promise to the Germans to maintain 'Industrial calm,' and this was in stark contrast to the purpose of the paratroopers' original mission."

"So he tricked them."

"Yes, Uri. That's why on June 24th, Kastner tried to convince the two paratroopers that their staying in Budapest was endangering the city's 200,000 Jews, as well as the safety of the heads of the rescue committee and, most important of all – was endangering the departure to Spain for those who were waiting for the train that would take them westward."

"The Kastner Train?"

"That's right, Uri and, for these reasons, he asked them to turn themselves in to the Gestapo."

"What?" My jaw dropped.

"Yes. Yoel Palgi agreed to turn himself in, but only on

the condition that Peretz Goldstein would not be turned in, but instead, would be smuggled to Romania."

"He was brave," I said.

"Yes. He also argued that if both were in the hands of the Gestapo, it would be easy to break the cover story that Kastner had constructed for them."

"Not exactly... After all, Hannah Szenes was already in the hands of the Germans, and anyway she had not coordinated the new cover story with them."

"You're right, Uri, you're right, but there was not a single Jew there as smart as you, and anyway, Palgi was convinced, and the next day he reported together with Hansi Brand."

"Where did they report to?"

"At the Gestapo headquarters, to the deputy head of the Gestapo in Budapest. Palgi underwent an extradition process and, at the end, he asked for a pass from the Gestapo so that he would not be arrested."

"So Kastner kept his word. He succeeded."

"A short-lived success; a short while later, Palgi was nonetheless arrested by the Hungarians."

"The Hungarians? That was already in your territory, Mr. Kraus."

"Yes," he chuckled bitterly. "But I wasn't told, and I didn't even know of their presence in Hungary."

"What do you mean, you didn't know?"

"Just like with every other matter, they didn't inform me in advance that paratroopers were expected to arrive from the Land of Israel, even though they knew; they didn't inform me when the paratroopers arrived, and not even when they were captured."

"Unbelievable. So what happened to Goldstein?"

"That day, Kastner brought Goldstein to the camp for the high-status people who were supposed to emigrate to Spain by train. His parents were there among those high-status people from Cluj."

"Wow. Did he know they were there?"

"That I don't know, Uri."

"But Kastner kept his promises."

"Kastner was a true Zionist. His original intentions were good. It's just that he made a mistake along the way and fell into a demonic trap."

"And Goldstein? Did he get on the train…?"

"On June 30th, the day the train left for freedom, the Hungarian counter-espionage detained Kastner as well as several members of the rescue committee, and delayed the train's departure. During their interrogation they were asked about the whereabouts of Peretz Goldstein. Kastner and Hansi Brand went to the high-status people's camp and convinced Peretz Goldstein to turn himself in. Goldstein, who knew that refusal would delay his parents' departure, agreed, and found himself in the Gestapo prison together with Palgi and Szenes."

"So different from the stories we grew up on at school," I sighed.

"You're right."

"But I still don't understand how you didn't know," I insisted.

Kraus looked at his watch and continued, "I first heard the story of the paratroopers at the end of August 1944, three months after their arrival and two after the arrest of Palgi and Goldstein."

"And then you couldn't help anymore?"

"No. Palgi and Goldstein were transported on a deportation train to the camps. Both of them planned to escape from the train, but only Palgi succeeded. He returned to Budapest and joined up with the rescue efforts. Then I helped him too."

"And what happened to Peretz Goldstein?"

"He arrived in a concentration camp in Germany and perished in March 1945, two months before Germany surrendered." Kraus got up, pulled out a cigarette, took the apple peels to the kitchen and went out to smoke on the balcony.

The Haaretz[30] newspaper lay folded at the far end of the table and I took advantage of his exit from the room to pull it towards me. I read the article describing the demonstration of the displaced residents, as well as the mobilization of Uri Avneri from "Olam Hazeh,"[31] and the Rakach[32] movement, to support them. I was happy to see that unlike yesterday's "Maariv,"[33] this morning's "Haaretz" supported Ruthy's position. Kraus came in from the balcony and circled the table to see what article I was reading.

"What do you think, Uri? Should they be returned to the provincial towns?"

"It's not a simple case. There are hundreds of thousands of refugees in the countries around us," I said.

"But these displaced persons are not refugees, Uri. They are residents of the State of Israel."

---

30. An Israeli newspaper (trans. "The Land") founded in 1918.

31. A non-Zionist political party in Israel (trans. "This World").

32. The original name for a non-Zionist political party in Israel supported by Arab voters (trans.: Hebrew acronym for "New Communist List")

33. Another Israeli newspaper (trans. "Bringing on Evening") founded in 1948.

"True, and they are not Muslim either," I quoted Ruthy's words. "I'm reading that they were given an explicit promise that they would be able to return to the provincial towns two weeks after they were evacuated from them," I added.

"Yes. It was an evacuation for security purposes, like the residents of South Tel Aviv were moved to the center of the city in preparation for the battle for Jaffa."

"Then Rutha is right," I said.

"There is some justice in her position," Kraus said.

"I'd love to know what's going on with her," I tried again.

"We'll have to wait for Gusta. Shall we continue?"

I nodded.

"Good. So have I provided sufficient evidence for the first point?" Kraus asked.

"Yes." I looked down at the notebook and read what I had written. "Lack of clear cooperation, and also withholding of information between the Jewish organizations," I stopped. "But what I argued is that it can't be that the threat of the coming extermination was never publicized among the hundreds of thousands targeted for extermination."

"Of course it can," Kraus declared. "I'll give you the most concrete example of not informing the victims of what was about to happen to them... In the beginning of May, Kastner traveled to his hometown of Cluj. In Cluj, the roundup of 18,000 Jews into a ghetto had already begun. Kastner, in coordination with the depraved Nazi Hermann Krumey, met there with the tyrant Wisliceny and with the local Judenrat. Together, they prepared the list of the local high-status people that would be included in the 600 to leave Hungary by train to freedom."

"That was a few days after he read Vrba's report," I said, flipping through the notebook.

"Right. The Vrba-Wetzler report was certainly in his possession, but neither he nor the community heads shared it with the masses of Cluj Jews."

"Why?"

"Later they would claim that everyone knew anyway, and that there was no chance of rescue."

"If they knew, some of them would have tried to resist, wouldn't they?"

"Most likely. But most of them didn't know. What's worse, they were told of a journey to a new settlement Kenier Mezo – "Fields of Bread" in English. They were read postcards allegedly written by the first Jews who settled in that 'wonderful' place."

"They took away their chance to fight," I said. "At least that's what Vrba and Wetzler had hoped for."

"Yes, Cluj was the most Zionist city in Hungary, and there were youth movements there that could have been organized... but there was a better option than fighting."

"What was that?"

"Cluj was close to the Romanian border, only 15 kilometers away. The youth movements had done many border smugglings before. In May 1944, Romania already saw the Soviet troops approaching from the east."

"What does that mean?"

"That means that the chances of survival for those who crossed the border into Romania in May 1944 were infinitely better than entering the ghetto in Cluj. Given the short distance, and the thinning out of the border guards in the area, many could have escaped across the border and been saved."

"So why? Why weren't they told? It's so frustrating."

"The Germans demanded silence from the leaders. As I said, Cluj was known for its Zionist activity, and Eichmann feared a repeat of the Warsaw Ghetto uprising scenario. That is why he demanded complete silence in exchange for continued cooperation."

"And you? Why didn't you tell people?"

"At the beginning of May 1944, I still didn't know about the Vrba-Wetzler report, Uri. How many times do I have to explain?!" He was losing his patience.

"My mistake," I caught myself. "Sorry. I didn't think..."

The room fell silent. Kraus got up and went to the kitchen, returning with two glasses and a pitcher of water.

"Kastner brought copies to Budapest, and gave them to some of the leadership that was close to him. He did not give me a copy. I only found out about the report a month later but, by then, it was already too late for the Jews of the provincial towns and, for that, I have never forgiven him. He had the report in his hands. If he saw in front of his eyes the citizens of his city... being rounded up in the ghetto in preparation for being sent to extermination and he did not tell them, you can be sure he didn't tell other provincial towns, not Mezőladány, and certainly not me." His hand trembled as he poured water into the glass.

I looked at him wide-eyed. In a broken voice he continued: "On May 15, 1944... began the most intensive deportation in the history of deportations to Auschwitz... probably in all of human history. Eight weeks of extermination and murder at an unprecedented rate. Every day 8,000 deportees from the provincial towns were transported by trains."

"From your village too? From Mezőladány?" I asked hesitantly.

"Of course. From there too."

"And up till then you hadn't managed to reach your father on the phone? ...or Big Bela?"

"The phone in Mezőladány was disconnected during the month of March. I was able to get hold of Big Bela in Kisvárda. I gave him the address of the consulate in Budapest and tried to convince him to come to us with my whole family."

"And why did he refuse?"

"He quoted my father's constant excuse that, 'Mezőladány will be freed by the Russian army before Budapest.' God knows how hard I tried," Kraus said, as tears flowed from his eyes and he turned his gaze away from me, towards the balcony.

I got up quietly and filled his glass with water from the pitcher. Kraus dried his tears and thanked me with his glance.

"You did the best you could, Mr. Kraus," I tried to comfort him. "Big Bela must have had good plans."

"Bela had more hopes than plans, and talking to him made me even more worried."

"Why?"

"Because he told me that István Kovacs, remember him?"

"Yes. The son of the thieving blacksmith."

"This István was recruited to the local police under pressure from the Germans."

"Then he could protect your family."

"The opposite..." began Kraus and stopped.

"Why the opposite?"

"Because István Kovacs hated the Kraus family, and he hated the Balak family just as much."

"Because you called his father a thief?"

"I wish it had ended there. As a child, I was very afraid of Henrik Kovacs, but mischievous Bela didn't restrain himself and, one Friday night dinner, he told my father the story."

"And how did your father react?"

"My father listened to the story of the theft of the hammer and dismissed it with a wave of his hand. But when Bela told him that Kovacs knocked me to the ground with a hard slap, Father turned red. Although he changed the subject, and Bela and I thought the matter was forgotten, the following week Father went to the nearby village of Kisvárda on business. He knew the chief of police there and the day after his visit two policemen arrived in Mezoldani and arrested Henrik Kovacs. I never saw him again."

"And the son? István Kovacs?"

"We saw István every day. From a little brat, he grew into a violent thug. Every time he passed me he promised me that he would fulfill the 'promise' that Henrik made us before the slap."

"And he beat up you and Bela?"

"Father's connections in Kisvárda deterred him, but all that changed after the German invasion. I was no longer in the village, but Bela told me that he got punched by István, and a couple of my brothers did too."

"And your father?"

"My father was already more than 80 years old, and I

know he regretted until the end of his life that he had not kept his anger under control. As I told you, as a Jew you don't have the luxury to be right. You have to be smart. I also should have been smarter..."

"You tried to convince them to come to Budapest, Mr. Kraus," I tried to comfort him.

"I begged them, Uri. I gave Big Bela the address of the Swiss legation at Liberty Square. He talked to my father, but Father claimed that in Mezoldani they were closer to the Slovakian border, the Ukrainian border and the Romanian border."

"And what happened?"

"The day after our last conversation, the Jews of Mezoldani were rounded up into the ghetto in Kisvárda, and at the end of May they were sent to Auschwitz in two transports."

"And your friends in Miskolc?"

"From there too... in June... 15,000 Jews on five trains."

"And they were all killed?"

"105 survived."

"Why, Mr. Kraus? Why?"

"Why what, Uri?"

"All those horrors. Why did they refuse to work together?"

"Why Uri...? I ask myself this question every day. Like I already told you, it was not from evil intentions. It started from a German deception, continued with Jewish megalomania, and developed into a death trap."

"I don't really understand."

"I'll go back a little. You have to understand that the whole story started with the belief that Jewish lives can be bought with money."

"And that's not true?" I asked.

"It's true for small numbers of survivors. It's true when a certain Nazi saves a few lives because he's greedy for money. It's even true when it helps the Nazi authorities to obtain the Jewish leaders' cooperation ... but... The exchange is always for small numbers of Jews. The great task of the complete extermination of European Jewry always remained the Third Reich's supreme goal."

"Where did the Jewish leadership get the idea that it would be different in Hungary? That there would be no mass extermination?"

"If you remember, in 1942, two years before the Germans entered Hungary, the Nazis began transporting Slovakian Jewry to extermination camps. As part of that deportation, Rudolf Vrba was also sent to the extermination camps in Poland. After this wave of deportations, only the Jews who were essential to the Slovakian economy remained."

"I remember."

"The Germans had to stop at that point, because they had no candidates left for deportation. The heads of the Slovakian Judenrat, who had paid a $50,000 bribe to the tyrant Dieter Wisliceny, mistakenly thought that it was their bribe that halted the deportation."

"This was the same Wisliceny who coordinated the transport of Greek Jewry."

"Nice. You're following."

"And writing."

"So the heads of the leadership in Slovakia believed that if they managed to save 20,000 Jews for $50,000, they would ultimately be able to save all the remaining European Jews for $2 million."

"Mathematically, it's pretty close," I said.

"Yes, this criminal, Wisliceny, on his way to Budapest, stopped in Bratislava and collected from Rabbi Weissmandel –" he stopped, giving me a questioning look.

"Yes, I remember. The Haredi head of the Slovakian Judenrat."

"Good. So he collected a letter of recommendation from him addressed to the leaders of the Budapest Jews. Wisliceny's goal was to revive the Europe Plan that he had fabricated a long time before, together with the Slovakian Judenrat, that is – saving all the remaining survivors in exchange for millions of dollars."

"And why would the Jews in Hungary believe that he had the authority to achieve that goal?"

"Wisliceny was Eichmann's deputy and under his command in this task. Both of them were crafty and passed the letter of recommendation from the Slovak, Weissmandel, to the Orthodox representative on the Hungarian Judenrat. That representative, who was Rabbi Weissmandel's contact person, indeed fulfilled his duty and delivered the copies of the letter of recommendation to the 30 community leaders, including Kastner."

"Did you get it?"

"You know I didn't. And then, as I've already told you, Kastner and Brand met with Wisliceny and explained the 'Europe Plan' to him, as they saw it, and Wisliceny was delighted to hear them make the offer instead of him."

"Why did he want the plan?"

"He and Eichmann understood that this was the best way to occupy the heads of the community while the Nazis were organizing to start the extermination. I'll remind you that this was at the beginning of April, when the Germans were already in retreat on all fronts. They had a severe shortage of manpower and they needed the cooperation of the Jewish leadership."

"So they actually made the Jewish leadership believe that the plan to save the Jews in exchange for money was a Jewish plan."

"Right. When Wisliceny realized that the leaders of the committee had swallowed his bait, he surpassed himself by demanding payment for Kastner's meetings with him. He received the first payment on April 8th, a day after Vrba and Wetzler entered their hideout in Auschwitz. That was the compensation the Germans gave for the order requiring Hungarian Jews to wear a yellow star, issued at the beginning of that week," he said sarcastically.

I smiled and he went on, "He received the second payment on April 21st, when Vrba and Wetzler crossed the Polish-Slovakian border. Four days later, Eichmann summoned Brand to discuss a new deal: 10,000 trucks loaded with basic staples in exchange for one million Jews."

"But there were only 850,000 Jews in Hungary."

"That's right, Uri. They chose a round number, apparently including the remainder of the survivors from other countries and from concentration camps. Four more days passed before Kastner received the complete and detailed Vrba-Wetzler report. Do you remember the date?"

"I have it written down. Just a second... on April 27th, 1944."

"As a reward for the Jews' exemplary behavior at the beginning of the deportations," Kraus snickered, "Eichmann increased the number of people going to Spain from

600 to 750, and allowed Yoel Brand to travel to Istanbul, on his and Kastner's behalf, to promote their illusory plan."

"Which one? The trucks?"

"Yes, 10,000 trucks for one million Jews."

"But, in those days, many of that million had already been exterminated."

"Right. You're right, Uri. But the talks continued. Brand was replaced in the meetings with Eichmann by his wife, Hansi, who shared with Kastner, among other things, the efforts to save the high-status people from Cluj."

"Among other things?" I echoed, detecting sarcasm in his voice.

"Among other things..." he repeated, without elaborating.

A knock on the door interrupted our conversation. Kraus went to open it and Gideon burst into the room holding a Maariv newspaper. "They sent me to switch Maariv for Haaretz," he said jubilantly.

"Ho ho," smiled Kraus. "They already finished reading it?"

"Sima said she wouldn't read it today and Uncle Mordechai had already read it at work," said Gideon, standing next to me and secretly passing me a note.

"Bye, Uri," said Gideon, picking up the Haaretz newspaper and disappearing the way he came.

The sharp-eyed Kraus took advantage of the break for another cigarette, purposely standing on the balcony with his back to me, giving me time and space. I opened the note and read its contents:

"Hello Uri. Thank you for defending me. It helped but now I'm grounded. I'll be at the window above Kraus's balcony at midnight. If you come I will try to slip away (drawing of a heart) Ruthy." I sniffed the note and read it over and over, trying to envision the face behind the writing. When Kraus began to stub out his cigarette and move the chairs on the balcony in a particularly noisy manner, I folded up the note and shoved it into my pants pocket.

"Everything okay, Uri?" he asked as he sat down.

"Yes..." I answered dizzily, trying to absorb the information in the note and decipher the feelings coloring it, "...yeah, okay." I felt my cheeks redden again.

"I think Ruthy is a brave girl," Kraus surprised me. "Perhaps reckless, but definitely brave..." he added. "And you too... are brave, for defending her."

I looked away from him, leaning my head on my right hand. Kraus got up without a word, went to the kitchen and brought us both some soda pop. "Should we continue?" he asked.

"Sure," I nodded.

"On May 27th, two Jews named Mordovicz and Rosin used the hideout that had served Vrba and Wetzler seven weeks earlier, and escaped from Auschwitz. On June 6, they crossed the border to Slovakia and went through the same series of meetings as Vrba and Wetzler had done in Slovakia."

"And they confirmed the Vrba-Wetzler report?"

"More than that. They didn't just confirm the past data... they also confirmed the predictions, and reported on those Jewish-Hungarians from the provincial towns who had arrived in Auschwitz in the period after the Vrba-Wetzler escape."

"So what did they do with this report?"

"This report had already reached me but, before I

discuss my activities, I owe you an explanation of the third reason we talked about – 'the motive.'"

I nodded in anticipation.

"On June 10th, 388 high-status people from Cluj arrived in Budapest. They were followed by other groups of high-status people from the provincial towns."

"This was in the midst of the massive deportations you mentioned?"

"Yes, and Eichmann increased the number of high-status people who moved from other provincial towns from 300 to 800 and then to 900, most of them according to lists prepared by the local leaders."

"So, at the time of the mass deportations, the heads of those communities were busy preparing lists of a few individual survivors?"

"Yes, Uri. That was Eichmann's diabolical plan. That's how he diverted the leaders' attention and obtained their cooperation."

"So how many survivors were there?"

"The total of the high-status people of Cluj, together with those from the provincial towns, and additional ones added at the last moment, was 1,685 people. This is the number that left on the Kastner train from Budapest on June 30, 1944."

"But hundreds of thousands were deported to Poland."

"That's right, and about 400,000 perished."

"You couldn't have arranged for...?" I stopped myself mid-sentence and changed direction. "The train arrived in Spain?"

"No, Uri. No. I couldn't...!" Kraus read my thoughts, "and the train never made it to Spain. Eichmann kept the 1,685 people so important to the Hungarian Jewish leadership as hostages inside the train, and parked it in Bergen-Belsen."

"And they were exterminated?"

"No. Some of them were released to Switzerland after a month, but most of them were held until they were released in December."

"Hostages for what?"

"For continued cooperation in Budapest. Don't forget that the Allied landings in Normandy were on June 6th. Eichmann saw the end coming, and he was not ready to give up on the extermination of 200,000 Budapest Jews."

"At least you got to judge him, and hang him."

"He was indeed tried and hung in the Land of Israel. But I didn't 'get to' do it. I was prevented from testifying at the Eichmann trial."

"Why?"

"This is the 'fourth reason.' It's why your grandmother and aunt never heard the story you heard today. I think you got a complete answer for 'why.' At first, silence was obtained in exchange for a big dream of saving hundreds of thousands and, later, after the leadership rounded up its most important people in one train, they became hostages to ensure the cooperation of Kastner and his friends. Is it clear to you now what the leadership's motive was?"

"Yes. And that also explains the big hush-up that's lasted until today."

Gusta's footsteps were heard in the stairwell. Kraus got up and hurried to the door.

"Hello, Uri," said Gusta in her heavy accent, sitting down next to me and placing her handbag on the chair.

"Hello, Mrs. Kraus."

"You must want to hear how Rutha is doing," said Gusta kindly.

"Yes."

"She's fine. She's currently grounded. Her aunt and uncle are very angry."

"Why?"

"I understand that her parents called from the kibbutz. People are really angry at the family. Before she and Gideon even went to Jerusalem, her parents promised the kibbutz that she wouldn't meet with her friends from Matzpen."

"But it was me, Gusta."

"Yes, dear Uri. That's what Ruthy says too."

"You see?"

"It's very noble of you to defend her. It's even quite moving. Miklós..." she said, turning to Kraus, "...he always defended me. He was always loyal."

I smiled contentedly and she continued, "But everyone knows, Uri, that it was she who dragged you there."

"That's not true," I protested, realizing that my chances of seeing Ruthy before our secret night-time rendezvous had shrunk considerably.

"No one is mad at you, and I'm sure that Ruthy will eventually be forgiven for everything as well. Just a little time and patience."

"Is she staying in Jerusalem?"

"I really don't know. I'm not sure if Sima knows. Maybe she'll stop by here later... Anyway, I guess they'll decide tomorrow whether to return the children to the kibbutz at the end of the week. Shall we start our English lesson?"

"Just a moment, we were in the middle of something," I

turned to Kraus. "What about the fourth point... how it is that this has not been publicized until now?"

"We'll see if there's time left after your English lesson," said Kraus and left the room.

The lesson with Gusta dragged on. Gusta, noticing my lack of focus, got up and sat down facing me. I surprised both her and myself with my mastery of English grammar, as well as the correct use of verbs and the various tenses. Kraus, wandering between the kitchen and the bedroom, joined us towards the end of the lesson, watching Gusta with great pleasure.

I glanced at Kraus expectantly. Reading my look, he said: "We have to finish now, Uri. Gusta and I need to pack some things for the trip to Tel Aviv, and to eat lunch."

I sat for a few more moments before getting up to leave, feeling disappointed by Kraus's revelations. The heroic plots of my childhood had been painted in dark shades that troubled me.

Kraus, as if reading my thoughts, came back into the room. "Tomorrow I will tell you the more encouraging parts. The rescue operation I put into place, thanks to which most of the Jews of Budapest survived. Then you will also hear about Bela Gutman from soccer and our meetings in Budapest."

"I thought Bela was just a nickname. What kind of name is Bela for a soccer player anyway? And a guy?"

Gusta, entering the room, answered instead of him: "It's true that Little Bela was an affectionate nickname but, in Hungary, Bela is a man's name."

"Did you know Little Bela too, or did you just see pictures?"

"No... I mean yes. I met Little Bela in Budapest. He came to us in the middle of June 1944."

"What? He managed to escape from Kisvárda? From the ghetto? How?"

"It's a long story Uri, and we need to pack for the trip to Tel Aviv. Tomorrow, okay?"

"Fine," I nodded. They left the room and I continued to sit there, lost in thought. A warm breeze wafted in from the balcony. My mind was flooded with information and my heart full of emotions. I looked around the room, listening to its sounds, aware of the contradictions.

The side of the bookcase in front of me and the furniture next to it seemed to be playing the melody of history, while the balcony and the entrance hall, giving way to the kitchen, sang the song of life. I got up and walked slowly towards the door of the apartment, trying to find a balance point for my emotions, somewhere between the two extremes.

Chapter 6

"Uri, turn down the music, it's not four yet," my grandmother called as I got ready to go down the street.

"It's not me, Grandma. The downstairs neighbor is pretending to be Mike Brant."

Grandma smiled. "It's probably Yaron, Cooperman's son."

"Doesn't sound like a very promising singer to me. Well, I'm going downstairs, Grandma."

"Dinner's at seven. Don't be late. I want to go with Esther to see 'The Godfather' later."

"To the movies?"

"Yes. Would you like to come?"

"It's only for adults, isn't it?"

"Right. Would you like us to choose a different movie?"

"No. Enjoy, I'll be on time for dinner."

I closed the door behind me and went downstairs, hearing Mrs. Cooperman scolding Yaron as I skipped down the last steps on my way to the street. I didn't like Yaron. He was my age, quite a braggart, and worse, a good-looking guy who had stolen Nurit Zilber's heart the previous year.

The neighborhood was quiet. The weather was particularly hot and, in the burning afternoon hours, most of the neighbors had gone to rest. I crossed the road and looked towards Ruthy's floor, hoping for a sign. I entered the yard, walked counter-clockwise around the building and completed half a circle, my steps accompanied by the rustle of dry leaves and the crackle of the twigs as I stepped on them. I stood in front of Kraus's smoking balcony. The apartment was locked and sealed up. The shutter on the floor above, in Ruthy's room, was open, but no sound could be heard from it. I waited a few minutes, trying make noise with my pacing back and forth.

At four I gave up and returned to the street, towards Grandma's building. The noise from the Cooperman home had been replaced by the aroma of stewing meat with tomato sauce. I continued to the left towards the park, where the neighborhood children had already gathered. I was disappointed to find that Gideon and Dina weren't there, but I joined a three-on-three soccer game, in which the team opposing me included the same Yaron Cooperman, the 'singer' who took every opportunity to hit me hard.

Thoughts of Ruthy continued to trouble me. I quit the game, promising the group that I would come that night for the séance they were planning near Jason's Tomb, and returned to my observation post in front of Grandma's house. While I was watching two floors up across the street, a light blue Ford Cortina pulled up in front of the building, discharging a girl with a big backpack.

"Uri?" she turned to me.

"Nurit? Wow, I didn't recognize you."

"You've completely changed too. I recognized your eyes. You've really grown! How long have you come for?"

"I've been here since Saturday so I guess I'll stay until Sunday. We'll see."

"Good. I'll also be here until Sunday. Wow. I can't believe how you've grown."

"A year, Nurit. A year has passed." I surprised myself with my ease.

"Well, I have to go up to put my things away and say hello to Grandma. Are you staying in the neighborhood?"

"Yes, I'm here until seven."

"Good, see you around."

Nurit came down an hour later wearing real Levi's jeans and a tight-fitting tricot t-shirt that showed how much she had matured, too. She stood beside me, leaning on the fence like I was. The children who had finished the soccer game moved from the park to the street. Yaron, upon seeing Nurit, broke away from the group and approached us.

"Nurit... what a doll," he said shamelessly and came up to kiss her.

"Hello, Yaron," Nurit answered, turning her cheek to him.

"How are you? When did we last see each other? At Passover, no?" Yaron asked.

"Yes. At Passover."

Yaron started chatting with her while I was focused on Ruthy's balcony. Towards seven o'clock, I apologized and said that I had to get something from the Kraus family and go up to dinner.

"Maybe we'll go to the movies tonight?" Nurit suggested. "I want to see 'Peepers.' I love Arik Einstein."

"Sounds great," Yaron responded enthusiastically.

"Have fun," I said. "I already promised the group to join the séance after dinner."

"Wow. A séance? Really?" Nurit said. "What time?"

"We arranged to meet at half past eight near Jason's Tomb."

"Good. Then maybe we'll postpone the movie and join in," Nurit said, and I nodded as I crossed the road. When I returned from another fruitless walk around Ruthy's building, the dinner table at Grandma's was set, and Grandma was dressed in her festive clothes.

"Are you going out already, Grandma?"

"No. Esther is picking me up at a quarter past eight. I like to be ready."

I took a quick shower before dinner and joined Grandma, who was sitting in the chair facing the TV in the living room. The 'Mabat' evening news broadcast caught my attention when the headlines mentioned the displaced persons from Bir'im and Iqrit and the conflicts they were having in the north. Haim Yavin reported that the displaced people had driven out Matzpen members from the abandoned church in the ruins of the village.

"Did you hear, Uri'leh?" asked Grandma, who had probably been informed by Gusta.

"I heard. It doesn't surprise me. They expelled the Matzpenists from the demonstration as well."

"Uri, I want you to promise me that you won't go there tonight."

"I promise, Grandma... shhh... I want to hear." Yavin continued to report that "the detainees will be brought to court tomorrow morning."

"I promised Hayuta... your mother," she corrected herself, "to keep you from going wild. She's going to call today. Do you hear, Uri?"

"I hear, I hear," I blurted out impatiently, noticing Grandma's fear of violating my mother's instructions.

The rest of the news broadcast dealt with the severe crisis between the Soviet Union and the president of Egypt, with the military commentator declaring that Egypt posed no security risk to Israel in the foreseeable future. I finished eating and walked to my room while, in the background, Yavin reported that Yitzhak Rabin was expected to finish his post as ambassador in Washington in three months and return to Israel. The news broadcast switched to coverage of the big strike in the Elite[34] factory and Grandma turned off the TV and kissed me goodbye.

I sat in my room pondering the events that awaited me that night. I hadn't managed to figure out Ruthy's plan for getting out of the apartment. I was trying to think of where we would go if she did manage to get out. Would she perhaps agree to make out? Maybe without shirts? I asked myself, excited and anxious at the same time. Maybe I'll sneak her into grandmother's apartment? Or maybe I'll climb the palm tree and she'll open the balcony door for me? I decided that I would wear sneakers anyway, and long pants so I wouldn't get scratched.

I went down to the street to make another circuit of Ruthy's building, noticing that the Krauses's apartment was still dark. They hadn't returned from Tel Aviv yet. I continued down the street and joined the group sitting in a circle near Jason's Tomb. I was disappointed to see that Dina and Gideon were missing this time too. Nurit welcomed me with a big smile and motioned for me to sit next to her. She exuded a pleasant freshly-showered fragrance of shampoo, and her hair was pulled back to reveal her pretty forehead.

---

34. Elite is a nationwide food manufacturing company in Israel.

The séance was led by Rakefet. She laid down a huge cardboard circle bearing inscriptions in English. Unlike the séances I attended in the past, Rakefet didn't use a cup, but held a string with a flint pendulum at the end of it. She managed to scare the little kids who were sitting with us while Yaron helped her and tried to make us laugh. We spent hours raising up Jason's spirit and, after that, the figures of Judean heroes from thousands of years ago which, according to legend, were buried throughout the area around us. After a while, Nurit suggested that we play Truth or Dare, and I took that opportunity to leave the group. I made another circuit of the building, noticing that the light was on in the Krauses' apartment, heralding their return from Tel Aviv. I went up to Grandma's apartment and, as I was finally alone, passed the time daydreaming. I assumed she would be back as soon as the second showing was over, so I went back down to the street at a quarter to twelve. The lights were already out in the Krauses' apartment. I passed by the park, happy to see that the group had finished their nighttime capers.

Five minutes before midnight I circled Ruthy and the Krauses' building again, this time careful to step only in places where the ground was exposed to avoid making noise. All the apartments in the building were completely dark. Not a sound could be heard from the Krauses' apartment. I stood under Ruthy's window, looking at my watch nervously. Suddenly I heard a rustling sound that got louder and louder and, to my right, I noticed two figures groping their way into the yard in the darkness. I froze for a moment and then pressed myself to the back side of the porch, hoping the darkness would hide me. I could hear the two whispering: "I don't see their phone line. Are you sure the apartment is on this side of the building?" one asked.

"Totally sure."

"Excellent, it looks like everyone is asleep."

Ruthy's balcony window opened. The slight noise made the two strangers bend down close to the ground. My heart pounded violently. The two strangers were bigger and stronger than me. I didn't know if they were thieves or security personnel. My thoughts were racing. From the exchange between them, it was clear to me that they were there for a specific purpose. I wanted to warn Ruthy, but I was afraid of being exposed. "Uri," her whisper could be heard from above, "Uri." Cowering and frozen in terror, I couldn't answer her.

"Uri," Ruthy whispered more loudly. "Uri."

The two strangers crouched down. I wasn't sure if they had seen me.

"Uri, are you here?" Ruthy asked, almost out loud. Suddenly the light came on behind her and her figure could be seen. The two strangers straightened up and fled the yard. "Who are you?" shouted Ruthy.

"Who are you talking to?" Sima's voice could be heard. "Rutha?"

I stood up, signaled to her with my hand and moved deeper into the yard, opposite to the direction of the two strangers' flight.

"Who are you talking to?" Sima asked again.

"There were two scary people here."

"And how did you know they were there?"

"I heard a noise and, when I turned on the light, I saw them and they ran away."

"But you called 'Uri' before that."

"I thought maybe it was him, but no."

"Bless your heart. You bring nothing but trouble. I don't know what attracts suspicious people under your window, but I do know you're waking up the whole building. The whole neighborhood!" said Sima angrily. Her last words were interrupted by the closing of the shutter.

I moved away, deeper into the yard, going around the back of the building. The passage to the street from this side of the building was dark, as was the street itself. The darkness protected me as I pressed close to the fence, but it also prevented me from making sure that the street was free of threats. I stood still at the side of the yard, listening to the noises in the street against the background of my pounding heart, trying to decide what my next step should be.

The lights on the second floor went out and the building returned to the silence of the night. I remained bent over in hiding, fearful of what awaited me on the street. My watch showed that it was already one o'clock in the morning. I finally decided that I should take the risk to sprint the short distance to my grandmother's house. I pulled my keyring out of my pocket and selected the key to Grandma's apartment, holding it in my hand like a gun. I counted to three and broke into a sprint. Out of the corner of my eye, I caught a white Escort with two passengers sitting in the front seat. I picked up my pace and dashed into the stairwell of Grandma's building, realizing that I had just thereby revealed my identity and my place of residence.

Chapter 7

I tripped on the last step and crashed on the landing near my grandmother's apartment. I jumped to my feet and picked up the keyring I had dropped. My hands were shaking and I couldn't get the key into the keyhole. I heard footsteps coming up the stairs and started shouting: "Grandma! Grandma!"

"What's wrong? What happened?"

I jumped at the touch of a hand on my shoulder. "Leave me alone!"

"Uri'leh, wake up, it's me. What happened? A bad dream?"

"I don't know, Grandma," I answered, my heart racing, trying to separate the dream from the factual events of the night before. "I'm not sure."

"Come on, Uri'leh, get out of bed and come have a drink of water." I followed her out and headed to the bathroom. I washed my face, which looked frightened in the mirror, and my pulse slowed a little. I drank the glass of water and sat down next to my grandmother in the kitchen.

"You arrived very late last night," she said. "Is something wrong, Uri'leh?"

"Yes," I said, and told her about the two strangers in the yard of Kraus's building, and then in the car.

"But they didn't really run after you, did they?"

"No, only in a dream, but now they know where I live."

"So what? You haven't committed any crime."

"No. But I'm not sure they were actually police."

"Uri'leh, if they were criminals, they wouldn't have stayed an hour at the scene of the crime," Grandma stated quite logically.

"So they were probably detectives who were following Ruthy."

"And maybe following Kraus, we don't know. I'm not sure Gusta shared all her secrets with me but even the little I know leaves room for the possibility that they are under surveillance by the security services."

"I have to go warn them."

"Who?"

"Sima and Ruthy."

"Come relax first, eat breakfast and we'll think about everything calmly and logically."

I went back to my room, got dressed quickly and brushed my teeth. "I'll be back in a minute," I called out to Grandma as I opened the door and ran down the stairs. It was eight in the morning and the street was bathed in the tranquility of summer vacation. There was no sign of a Ford Escort, and all the window shutters were raised in Kraus's building. Feeling calmer, I went back to the stairwell and slowly climbed up to the apartment.

I lovingly accepted Grandma's scoldings, both for my nocturnal adventures and for the carelessness I had shown this morning, understanding that, beyond her gentle concern, she was already preparing for the report call with my mother. She tried without success to dissuade me from leaving the house but, at ten o'clock, I showed up at the door of the Krauses' apartment.

The smile on Kraus's face melted all remnants of the anxiety I was carrying.

"How was Tel Aviv, Mr. Kraus?"

"We had a lot of fun. Family, friends and culture... what could be bad?"

"Did you get back late?"

"Very. We had trouble waking up this morning. Gusta missed her appointment at the hairdressers' and I cancelled the meeting with my brother, Henrik."

We sat down in our regular seats. I debated whether to bring up the events of last night and eventually decided to wait until Gusta got back.

He got up, pulled back the drapes and opened the balcony doors wide. "It's dark here in the morning," he explained apologetically.

"So you promised yesterday to tell me about your rescue enterprise. You said there were some successes too," I began hopefully.

"Yes, Uri," said Kraus, pausing to gather his thoughts before continuing: "I tried, over the course of a number of years, to build the foundations for saving Jewish lives. In the first years I saved Jewish refugees from all the countries bordering on Hungary. My activity involved three main elements until June 1944. I enlisted Christian assistants," he said, raising one finger, "I collected an increasing number of emigration certificates for leaving Hungary," he said, lifting a second finger, "and I performed mathematical tricks," he said while adding the third finger, a mischievous smile plastered on his face.

"What mathematical tricks?" I was intrigued.

"Oh ho. I knew this would interest you. Let's actually start with the recruitment of the Christian assistants. Hungarians and foreigners. I identified four types of assistants who were convenient to recruit. I'll make it simple for you: there were the good people and those who sought the good; there were bad people with useful common interests; there were bad people who recognized the change in the balance of power on the war fronts; and lastly, bad people that I deceived. I needed all my senses and experience to identify the recruitment candidates and their motivations, and it took some finesse to navigate among the interests that changed over the years as the course of the war shifted."

"So there were also really good ones?"

"Yes, Uri. Not the majority, but there were. For example, Interior Minister Krest Fisher. I connected with him in 1938 when we joined forces to rescue 240 Jews who had been deported from Burgenland. Fisher was a good man and a great liberal. He opposed the Hungarian-German alliance and the anti-Jewish policy, so he allowed the deportees to enter Hungary. The Eretz Israel office, under my direction, equipped them with Aliyah certificates on behalf of the British ambassador, and they were permitted to remain on Hungarian soil until their Aliyah."

"Nice."

"More than nice!" he scolded me. "By this act, we created a new status of 'Refugees immigrating to Israel.' An important principle was established there which said that the certificate to the Land of Israel certified that the holder was a British-Palestinian citizen who was, therefore, exempt from the punishments of the immigration police. I used this precedent many more times."

"Were there more?"

"Good people? Of course. I already mentioned the name of Segdi Masek."

"Yes. The one who was married to a Jewish convert."

"I met him for the first time in 1943, when he wanted to consult with me about how to respond to an appeal that came from the Jerusalem mufti al-Husseini."

"What did Husseini have to do with the war against the Jews in Europe?"

"Quite a lot. In this appeal, the mufti claimed that the Jewish immigrants to Palestine were joining the British army and were expected to fight against the Hungarian army. We again worked together when we appealed to Pestoi Ammon from the Ministry of Internal Security on behalf of Jews who held certificates but were taken to the eastern front to join labor brigades. Pestoi Ammon was an assistant of the second kind. He didn't like Jews, absolutely not. But he really wanted to cleanse Hungary of foreigners."

"So you took advantage of his xenophobia by getting him to help Jews leave Hungary."

"Right. Leave. Not deported. But I didn't finish with the good ones yet. Among them was Carl Lutz, Swiss vice consul. He had just returned from Jaffa where had finished his position as deputy consul and showed himself to be a friend to the Jews."

"You fled to him with Gusta on the day of the invasion."

"Yes. And, as I mentioned, there were also those who cooperated following shifting trends on the front lines. One of the most important men in this category was László Ferenczy. He was a commander in the Hungarian Gendarmerie and carried out the deportations from the villages with great enthusiasm."

"Not a good guy," I pointed out.

"Absolutely not a good guy. At the end of June 1944, when the Hungarians started to sense the end of the war, he was brought to Budapest. I feared his arrival but, later, upon consultation with officials at the Ministry of Foreign Affairs, I became convinced that there was a chance to influence him to change his position and, what's more, at that time I was exposed to a great threat against me and against Gusta and I had to gamble on his help.

"For his part, Ferenczy had his own reason to change direction. He knew that the Soviets were approaching and he feared for his own fate. I managed to arrange a personal meeting for him with the supreme leader, the regent Horthy, and he did meet with him and moved over to our side. I'll talk more about him."

"You knew all the important people, Mr. Kraus," I observed admiringly.

"Yes, Uri, and that brings me to the third point." Again he held up three fingers.

"The mathematical trick?"

"Yes."

Kraus got up and brought three binders from the shelf.

"What are those?" I asked.

"These are the documents that support the story I am about to tell you."

"The trick?"

"Yes. These are minutes of meetings and publications documenting the development of the trick. As I said before, in 1938 we came to the realization that the 'status' listed in the certificates changed from refugee to British citizen, remember?"

"I remember. The bearer of a certificate was protected from legal moves against Jews."

He nodded. "This was the first step. In 1943 we had 1,500 such certificates and, in October of 1943, we implemented a new practice with the consent of the British Government and with the understanding of Pestoi Ammon: each certificate represented a family of four to six people."

"Instead of a single person!" I was amazed. "And if the family was smaller?"

"So we included children from larger families or orphans, or whoever was without a family. As far as the Hungarian government was concerned, at this stage there was an understanding that the 1,500 certificates in our possession were for 7,800 individuals."

"Wow. That was a serious trick."

"And this was just the beginning. After the German invasion of Hungary, I applied heavy pressure on the government through the Red Cross representative in Budapest and via the Swiss axis. At the same time, US President Roosevelt made an urgent appeal to the government. As a result of these pressures, two weeks after the invasion, the Hungarian government approved emigration for some of the bearers of the approved certificates, but made their departure conditional on German consent. This consent was not granted, but a government decree was issued protecting Jews who had foreign citizenship. I received certificates with the help of Carl Lutz and we managed to release hundreds of people who were already at transit stations and detention camps."

"Wow, that's awesome!" I rejoiced.

"Then I began claiming that they were actually family certificates."

"The 1,500?"

"No, the 7,800."

"You went too far..." I said.

"I tried. At the same time, I continued my efforts to get British permits for 7,800 bearers of personal Aliyah licenses. I turned to my friend Lutz and, on April 26, he contacted the Hungarian Ministry of Foreign Affairs and requested a departure permit for 7,800 certificates. The office representative asked if these were family certificates, and he answered in the affirmative."

"He fooled him?"

"Yes, Lutz adopted my approach and made use of it. He seized an opportunity. When asked how many people were involved, he answered 40,000. We were sure that the mistake would be found out."

"And...?"

"After a few tense days, Lutz informed me that a reply had been received: 'We are willing to agree to your request, but you must contact the German authorities for their approval.' We debated whether to turn to the Germans and eventually decided to do it, so the legation sent the request to Berlin."

"Amazing!" I said.

Kraus opened a binder, pulled out a document and read: "Here is a summary written by Michai Shlamon, Chairman of the Eretz Israel Office committee, and I quote: 'Mr. Kraus, on behalf of the Swiss legation, insisted that 7,800 bearers of licenses to emigrate to Israel constitute about 40,000 people. The Hungarian authorities agreed to this, while the Germans claimed that the intention of the German Ministry of Foreign Affairs was for 7,800 people only. With this, a correspondence was started between the Hungarian government and the German government so that the Germans would also agree to the number of 40,000."

Kraus closed the binder and wiped sweat from his forehead with a handkerchief. "It was just a first step. I had to continue to implant the mistake with all the many parties involved."

"And the Germans were on to the trick?"

"Some of them were, but the prank had gone from 'nothing.'.. to 'disagreement.' My role from then on was to reinforce, promote and embed the high number in the heads of as many people as possible."

"So what happened?"

"The German ambassador, Wiesenmeier, and his deputy, Dieter Koch, were afraid of the Hungarian government's progress in the direction of the 40,000 and activated Berlin to thwart the move."

"Dieter again?" I asked.

"Of course. He called me at the Swiss legation and arranged to meet me in Liberty Square. Gusta was worried that he was setting me up. I promised her we would sit on a bench not far from the consulate door, so she could see me from the first floor window and call Lutz if necessary."

"That was dangerous."

"Yes, it was dangerous. Indeed it turned out that his intentions were not innocent. He began by saying that it was clear to him and to Wiesenmeier that the number 40,000 was a fiction. A forgery. From there, he went on to say that Gusta's documents were also forged, and that he was afraid he wouldn't be able to continue protecting her for much longer."

"I don't understand. He protected her?"

"Of course not, but that's how he put it."

"So what did he offer?"

"He offered that he would sponsor Gusta and protect her from all harm in the building of the German Embassy."

"And you agreed?"

"He said he would convince Wiesenmeier to let him handle the issue of the legality of the 40,000 certificates for individuals, and hinted that he would work with me."

"So what did you answer him?"

"I needed time, both to promote the concept in the hallways of the Hungarian government that 40,000 was the number, and because I wanted to consult with Gusta and Lutz on how to respond."

"So you didn't refuse?"

"No. I thanked him for his concern and promised to bring up the subject in my conversation with Gusta, and that's how we parted."

"And the Hungarians did accept your position?"

"Not officially. The Hungarians spoke out of both sides of their mouth. Historians today claim that the Hungarian government never approved the exodus of 40,000 Jews."

Kraus pulled out a document in English and presented it to me: "Kraus decided, on his own initiative, that the 7,800 certificates were intended for heads of families, and included about 40,000 Jews. Neither the Hungarians nor the others involved in the negotiations agreed to this statement." The name of the historian Randolph Braham was displayed at the top of the document.

"So what happened in the end?" I asked.

"Are you dragging me ahead again?"

"What? Is it that complicated?"

"It was very complicated... but I'll go with you. Following the publication of the Vrba report – and soon I'll tell you how I contributed to the report's publication – heavy international pressure began to be applied on the Hungarian government. The Hungarian Foreign Ministry looked for ways to ease the pressure, and suggested that the emigration of the 7,800 families could serve as a tool to satisfy the foreign countries. On June 26, the Hungarian Crown Council convened. On the table was the decision to completely stop the deportations from Hungary."

"Completely?"

"Completely. In practice, the Hungarians avoided a conflict with the Germans, and chose the emigration of the 7,800 families as a compromise decision. The decision became known as the 'Horthy Proposal.'"

"And Horthy's proposal referred to individuals?"

"Again. In the official documents the number did not appear, but most of the Hungarian administration began to adopt it. On July 17th, I met with representatives of the Hungary ministries and with Horst Grell, the representative of the German ambassador, to discuss the emigration."

"You? With the Nazis??"

"Yes, I know it's hard to believe. The Swiss introduced me as a clerk in the Swiss Embassy. In the German minutes of the meeting I appear with the title 'Representative of the Jewish Agency.'"

"So the Germans knew you??"

"Of course. Most of those present in the room knew

me well; they were trailing me, after all. That's why I was fearful every time I went out into the street."

"And Dieter wasn't at the meeting?"

"Dieter was in the building, but was not present at the meeting. He was waiting for me at the end."

"What did he want?"

He asked what Gusta had decided. I told him she was very touched by the generous offer, but she was afraid she wouldn't be able to do her job at the legation if she moved to the German embassy. We agreed that we would consult with Carl Lutz."

"And Dieter accepted that?"

"He said that time was of the essence and that we had to make a decision in next few days, and so we parted."

I was debating whether this was the right moment to bring up the incident that took place the previous night at midnight under the balcony of his house. Against the backdrop of his dangerous exposure to the Nazi oppressors, the dangers of surveillance in the Land of Israel suddenly seemed petty and insignificant. In the end I decided to hold back and wait for Gusta.

"Is everything alright?" asked Kraus, having noticed my uncertainty.

"Yes. So say, at the meeting itself… before the encounter with Dieter… the participants recognized the number 40,000?" I couldn't believe it.

"It was still up in the air at the meeting itself but, that day, I got some reinforcement. Following our meeting, another meeting was held in Istanbul between the Hungarian attaché in Turkey, Baron Thierry, Barlas, who informed the representative from Israel about the

Hungarian government's approval of the emigration of 40,000 Jews." From the binder, Kraus pulled out a document in which Barlas reported on the details of the meeting. A victorious grin spread over Kraus's face. "What do you think, Uri?"

"If the 40,000 were indeed saved, then that's very... really... wow." I searched for the right word.

"Yes and no," Kraus broke into my enthusiasm. "Unfortunately, Hungary changed its mind twice more, and we were subject to life-threatening danger and deportations, as I told you, but in the end many more than those 40,000 were saved."

The muffled sound of a door slamming could be heard on the floor above us.

"What happened, Uri? Are you curious about the news on your friend from upstairs?"

I couldn't hold back any longer: "Yes. Some things happened last night."

"Things? What happened?"

I told Kraus about the events in the yard of his building the previous night. He listened impassively and asked: "Who do you think they were?"

"I don't know. I was afraid they were criminals, but Grandma said they could also be from the security forces."

"And what brings security personnel to the courtyard of the building at midnight?"

"I have no idea. At first I thought they came here because of Ruthy's involvement with the Matzpen organization, and her appearance the other day in the area of the demonstration."

"And...?" asked Kraus.

"And... I remembered that you said that agents broke into your house and went through your documents, so I thought that ..." I waited to see what he would say.

"It's always a possibility," Kraus replied with feigned calm, but I saw that he was on edge. He glanced at his watch, got up and went to the phone, made a short call and came back to the table.

"Gusta will be back soon."

"Are you worried about her? I hope I didn't cause you any trouble."

"I always worry about Gusta," he said with a smile, "and no, you didn't cause anyone any trouble. You didn't bring them to our courtyard. But I hope you didn't get yourself in trouble."

"Do you I might be? And Grandma too?"

"I'm inclined to believe that if you haven't heard from them by now," he glanced at his watch again, "it means you don't interest them." We sat in silence, looking at each other for several seconds before continuing.

"Good. Shall we go back? But before we move on to the big rescue operation, I owe you an answer regarding the distribution of the Vrba-Wetzler report."

"Right. I forgot about it for a moment."

"As mentioned, at the beginning of June, a month and a half after the Vrba-Wetzler report was written, it finally reached me. I was very surprised by the level of accuracy and detail, and I was even more surprised to discover the number of leaders in Budapest who had already known of its contents for over a month."

"What did you do with the report when it finally got to you?"

"I started working with Gusta on the report which, by June, already included the reports of the other two fugitives who escaped from Auschwitz a month and a half after Vrba and Wetzler. Their report was dubbed the 'Auschwitz Report.' As I told you, they verified the concerns raised in the first report, and reported on the transports that arrived from Hungary during the month of May."

"So what did you and Gusta work on?"

"I was busy collecting and writing up the events that occurred in Hungary during the weeks that had passed since Mordowicz and Rosin's escape, while Gusta was busy translating and typing up the additional findings. We distributed the first booklets we prepared."

"To who?"

"At the first stage, to Hungarian officials, to the representatives of the neutral countries in Budapest, and to the Vatican representative. Two weeks later, we were busy preparing the booklets for direct delivery outside Hungary. At that time, an event occurred which was very significant for me, which was both happy and chilling," his voice cracked.

"What?"

"A week after the report reached me, a consulate official came into my office in the afternoon and reported to me that a wild and dirty stranger was at the entrance, saying that he had to meet with me. I went down to the entrance floor, and there I saw an emaciated, filthy boy standing next to one of the elders of the community. Only when I got closer to him did I recognize Little Bela."

"Alive… wow… how long was it since you had last seen him?"

"Exactly a year had passed., I went to visit Mezőladány in honor of his Bar Mitzvah[35] in June of 1943. In his terrible condition, I had difficulty recognizing that beautiful boy."

"How did he get to Budapest?"

"It's a long story."

"I'm interested."

"He escaped from the Kisvárda ghetto on April 30 and roamed the streets for a month and a half."

"So it was a happy event. Why was it chilling?"

"Bela's story about what happened in Mezőladány and Kisvárda was chilling." Kraus paused and took a breath before continuing. "I brought him up to my room and let him wash up. Gusta, who had never met him before, cared for him devotedly. She dressed his wounds and fed him. I tried to find out from him what had happened to my family members, but he fell asleep immediately after the meal. I picked him up in my arms, amazed at how little he weighed, and laid him on the couch in our room. He slept for 16 hours, until the next morning."

"What did he say in the morning?"

"He said that a few days after the German invasion, István Kovacs returned to the village. Under pressure from the Germans, István had joined the local police and had been given responsibility for the entire district. The first to suffer at his hands was Agnes Balak, Little Bela's grandmother."

"Big Bela's mother?"

Kraus nodded. "Her body was found on the balcony of our family home in Mezőladány. István told my father that he would keep him alive so that he could see all his

---

35. A ritual to celebrate a Jewish boy reaching the age of 13, the age when he becomes obligated in the commandments.

children die." Kraus stood up and began circling the table with small steps while speaking slowly. "Big Bela tried to convince his son to run away and save himself."

"Why didn't Big Bela run away?"

"He had to take care of his wife and daughters and, above all, he felt responsible for my father who had taken care of him all those years..."

He lit a cigarette and started smoking in the living room. "...all the Jews of the village were lined up to marched towards Kisvárda, a three-hour walk. Little Bela looked for opportunities to escape, but István stayed close by them, hitting him and his father with the butt of his rifle every time they fell behind or spoke. His opportunity arose after they had already been herded into the ghetto in Kisvárda. Taking advantage of a commotion that took place in the evening on the other side of the ghetto during the distribution of food, he climbed the fence and broke into a run, ignoring the lacerations on his arm from the barbed wire. He headed north towards the Slovakian border, but the area was crawling with German soldiers marching east towards the Russian front. Fortunately for him, at the beginning of May there were still remains of fruit in the fields and orchards, even if they were half rotten. He slept during the day and walked at night, avoiding German patrols and stray village dogs."

"Where did he want to get to?"

"He wanted to get to Miskolc and, later, to me, to Budapest. He hid for a few days in the Zemplén forests, subsisting on mushrooms and berries, only advancing westward at night. Ten days after his escape, he approached Miskolc."

"But they must also have been in the ghetto at the time," I said.

"Right, but Bela didn't know that. He approached Miskolc in the evening. He knew the place well, as his mother, Margit, was a native of the city. Late at night he crept towards the Jewish quarter around Kazinczy Street and was surprised to find the area surrounded by barbed wire fences. He turned north towards the home of his grandmother, who lived on an estate north of the Jewish quarter. The house was dark and the small estate seemed deserted. He was quietly climbing the steps in front of the house when he heard the cock of a gun behind him accompanied by a harsh command to raise his hands. Luckily for him, it was a fighter from the anti-Nazi communist underground that was operating in the area. The man, Sandor Kopacsi, took Bela to his home, treated his wounds and fed him. Bela wanted to join the underground to fight the Nazis, but Sandor refused and gave him only surveillance missions. In one of the underground's ambushes Sandor was wounded and taken by his friends into hiding in the Bükk forest. Bela had to part from them there and set out on a long and dangerous journey to Budapest."

"Do you know what happened to Sandor? You describe him as if you knew each other."

"I did know him. He recovered from his injury and continued his underground activities. After the war, he joined the Ministry of the Interior in Budapest and we met there. I learned that, in addition to Bela, he had saved other Jews. Years later I was at the ceremony where he was awarded the title of Righteous Among the Nations for rescuing Jews from the Miskolc Ghetto. Today he lives in Canada."

"Him too."

"Yes. Him too. In Toronto."

"And Little Bela?"

"Bela's journey from Bükk to Budapest took five days. On the way, near Hatvan, he was wounded in the hand by a rifle bullet after escaping from a checkpoint. He remembered the address of the Swiss legation that I had read to his father on the phone, but he was afraid to enter the city center with his disheveled appearance and blood-stained clothes. Luckily for him, the same elder of the Jewish community encountered him in Pozsony and brought him to the door of the consulate."

"So he stayed with you?"

"No. After he recovered, we moved him to the apartment where the management of the Jewish homes was located."

"And you?"

"We, as I mentioned, were busy preparing the Auschwitz summary report in order to distribute it throughout the world, but one thing led to another – and Dieter Koch's pressure on the Swiss Embassy increased. Lutz suggested that Gusta and I formalize our love in an official wedding, which would make it easier for him to fight off the German demands to expel Gusta."

"And you got married?"

"Yes. Our wedding was held four days after Bela's arrival in Budapest."

"Who was there?"

"Very few people. Little Bela, Lutz and his wife, Nessa, Gusta's father, and a distant relative of hers. From the wedding canopy we ran back to the office to finish preparing the copies which I had to deliver to Florent Manolio, George Mantello's representative."

"A modest wedding," I said. "But it's amazing that you even managed to get married at all."

"Yes, but the next day we received a 'big wedding present.'"

"From who? From this Mantello?"

"No. Bela called from the housing management office and told me that, when he looked out the window, he saw István Kovacs in uniform walking around the buildings."

"Oh oh. He didn't get to you?"

"Not that week. Wait. Anyway, I was very worried that Manolio was part of a trap that the Gestapo had set for me, and that István was involved in the plot."

"So you postponed the meeting?"

"No, but only after Manolio presented me with the business card of Haim Posner, my colleague from Switzerland, with his signature that I recognized, did I decide to trust him. I sent the copies of the reports through him to Posner in Geneva, to the United States ambassador in Ankara, and to the chief rabbi of Stockholm. When Manolio returned with my reports to Geneva, on June 22nd, he wasted no time and, at two in the morning, he met with George Mantello and his brother and gave them the reports and my letter. In the morning Mantello convened the members of the Rabbinical Council and the Switzerland-Hungary committee. Besides them, he recruited a group of students who spoke various languages to translate the reports and my letter. Mantello made thousands of copies and distributed them in universities, to political figures, to members of Parliament, to the Pope's representative, to Jewish organizations in Switzerland, to McClelland – the representative of the committee for war refugees in Bern – to the Joint representative Saly Mayer, to clergymen in Switzerland and the United States, to all the legations in the city and to the newspaper editors."

"Whoa, whoa, I can't write fast enough. Who was this amazing Mantello?"

"A Jew, originally Romanian, who served at that time as Honorary Consul of El Salvador in three countries in Eastern Europe, and then as first secretary at the Consulate of El Salvador in Geneva. He is still alive. I met him during his visits to Israel. He was persecuted after the war by the anti-Semites in Switzerland and moved to Italy."

"I thought the Swiss and the Swedes were our great saviors."

"The Swiss Carl Lutz was the great savior, but it was his personal initiative, like that of Raoul Wallenberg. Lutz suffered for this after the war, upon his return to Switzerland. Wallenberg paid with his life."

"I heard about Wallenberg."

"Yes, Uri, you must have heard. The world loves dead heroes..." Kraus observed sadly and went on, "but right now we are in June 1944 in Geneva, and the uproar that Mantello stirred up via my letters grew and grew. Following the publication in the media, wide-ranging diplomatic activity began. The report reached Washington and, as a result, the American War Office received a demand on June 29th to bomb the train tracks and stop the transports of Jews."

"That's what I suggested yesterday."

"That's right, Uri but, unfortunately, it didn't happen even after the publications. What did happen is, on June 25th, a letter was sent from the Pope to the Regent Horthy in Budapest, in which the Vatican protested and, more importantly, a day later a letter sent by Franklin

Roosevelt, the President of the United States, arrived to the same Horthy with a sharp warning that 'those who are found guilty of war crimes will bear heavy punishments.' The archbishop of New York joined the defenders and, a day later, the Swedish king issued a warning to the Hungarian government."

"Great!" I burst out enthusiastically.

"Now you understand why I insisted we go over Rudolf Vrba's story. He was the one who lit the spark of truth." Kraus paused and rubbed his nose before continuing: "This great man, via his report, was responsible for saving hundreds of thousands of Jews."

"And you too."

"I saw myself as Vrba's and Wetzler's ambassador, like Mantello was my ambassador, and so on... Anyway, in the first stage, all this big noise brought about the 'Horthy Proposal' that we talked about and, a few days later, the complete cessation of the deportations from Hungary."

"The deportations were stopped? Completely?"

"Yes, it's just a shame that the report didn't reach me a month earlier. We could have saved hundreds of thousands more... and maybe my family too."

"It's not your fault. You did everything you could. And what happened with István?"

"István was attached to the gendarmerie and, in the beginning of July, he was put under the command of László Ferenczy, who I told you about before."

"Now I understand why it was important for you to develop connections with Ferenczy," I said.

"Exactly. István also noticed the irony and, in one of the meetings he said to me, 'Connections with the police in Kisvárda did not save your father's life. Your connection with Ferenczy will not save your life either' – and he was almost right."

"Almost?" I asked.

"You see... obviously, I'm here," he said with a smile and stood up. "All right. We deserve some cake now."

Kraus came back from the kitchen with two slices of walnut cake and said: "But I still haven't told you about the big operation."

"Ahh... I thought the distribution of the report was..."

"That too. Distribution of the report brings us to the first week of July 1944, with 200,000 Jews in Budapest, and with an ongoing threat that the Germans would resume mass deportations. I had certificates for, apparently, 40,000 people, and I worked hard to fill them in with names and details. For the purpose, I expanded my support staff with those who were sitting in the Swiss consulate building, but the place was too crowded to accommodate all the required clerks and could scarcely handle the masses of Jews who heard about the rescue operation being put together and crowded around the entrance to the Foreigners Department building in Liberty Square."

"So what did you do?"

"I asked Consul Lutz's approval to purchase a building, and he agreed. In retrospect, there was no need for a purchase since many Jews offered to make their homes available for the cause in the hope that this would help them preserve their lives and property. I found a building that suited our needs very well. It was a building at no. 29 Vadas Street which belonged to Arthur Weiss, a Jew who was a big glass wholesaler. A beautiful three-story building, completely surrounded by large glass walls, hence its name, the 'Glass House.' I chose the building because of its location, adjacent to government offices and foreign embassies. I assumed its prominent location would make it harder for the Nazis to carry out hostile actions. We hung a large sign on the front of the building: 'Swiss Legation. Representation of Foreign Interests. Emigration Department.' The building had an ex-territorial status, which enabled freedom of action. As a result, many of the leaders of the pioneering Zionist movements also moved into the building."

"And you allowed them?"

"Of course. On the opening day of the Glass House, on July 24, 1944, László Ferenczy also visited. He came to confirm that the opening of the building conformed with the intentions of the Hungarian government. After the opening, I went on a tour with him to Pozonyi Road, where we marked the Palatinus houses where permit holders planned to stay until their emigration.

"After I got the buildings, I needed a police force to protect them. Ferenczy, who was recruited to help after that meeting I arranged for him with Horthy, and acting in accordance with the power of attorney he had received from him, transferred 1,400 Hungarian gendarmes to the streets of Budapest to ensure the safety of the city's Jews."

"It sounds like you were in total control of what was going on in Budapest. Now I have a completely different impression from what you told me yesterday."

"I definitely had extensive influence on the Hungarian government institutions, but the Nazis did not give up on their project and continued their incessant efforts to resume the deportations."

"How did the whole mechanism that you set up work?" I asked admiringly.

"I was personally responsible to the Swiss for managing the Glass House and all the annexed buildings. I put Arthur Weiss, the owner of the building, in charge of operations. Carl Lutz visited the building often, so we had to keep the place looking respectable despite the thousands who were staying there. Within the building, the clerks worked tirelessly to assemble books of group passports which were supposed to cover 40,000 immigrants to Israel."

"That's a lot of work."

"Yes. The clerks interviewed each of the applicants, helped them fill out forms, attach photos, prepare certificates, approve them and transmit them to the Swiss legation for an official stamp. When the whole process was completed, the records were sent to the Swiss Ministry of Foreign Affairs. In total, we prepared ten books of group passports, but there were some people, including Bela, for whom I had to arrange an individual permit."

"Why?"

"One morning, István Kovacs made a surprise visit to the Glass House and said that he came on Ferenczy's behalf to check that everything was being run properly. I pulled him into my office while I sent Weiss to make sure all those that were unprotected, and particularly Bela, disappeared from the hallways."

"Bela was in the Glass House then?"

"Yes. I moved him to the Glass House the day after it opened. 'I know that Little Bela is in Budapest,' Kovacs told me. 'I have some pictures that I would like to show him.' He pulled out an envelope containing some photos. 'Look at this, a picture of his father, he asked to send greetings before I shot him in the head.' In the picture, I saw my good friend lying on the ground, his arms spread out to the sides and a big hole between his eyes. 'I saved him a train ride,' he added wickedly.

"Shocked, I got up from my chair, but István stood and blocked my way. 'Sit down, I'm not done,' he said, pushing me back into my chair. 'I didn't want to forego the pleasure of watching my fellow villagers arrive in Auschwitz, so I joined the guards' car. Your whole family got off the train together. They tried to keep up a respectable appearance, but not for long. When the men were separated from the women and children, I did not neglect your father. He didn't send his regards to you as he was too busy with your brothers. Look here,' he pointed to a column of naked men, 'can you identify him? The one with the beard. Do you recognize him?' Although I tried with all my might, I could not hold back my tears. My decent, honest, beloved father covering his private parts with both hands, dragged helplessly like a sheep to the slaughter.

"At this point I got up and demanded that he leave the Glass House. He stood there and said with satisfaction, 'I promise to soon bring you pictures like that of Little Bela... or maybe you'll actually march together in the column.'

"I ran from there to Lutz and, together, we issued Bela a personal Schutzpass."[36] Here Kraus stopped and went out on the balcony to smoke a cigarette.

"I'm sorry," I said when he came back in from the balcony.

---

36. A 'protective certificate,' most of which were prepared by Carl Lutz, which identified the bearer as a Swiss subject awaiting repatriation and thus prevented his or her deportation.

"Yes, that's the way it was."

"How did the Schutzpass help?"

"The Schutzpass was a personal document which certified that the bearer was registered in a pre-emigration group passport."

"So you managed get the 40,000 to Israel?"

"The Germans conditioned the Aliyah of the 40,000 on the immediate deportation of the remaining Jews to camps in Poland."

A patter of heels was heard from the stairwell, followed by the rustling of keys. Kraus stood up, as did I, and we turned towards Gusta who was coming into the apartment bearing a new hairstyle and shopping bags in her hands.

"Hello, dears," she said, turning away from us towards the kitchen. Kraus hurried after her, and five minutes later returned with her to the living room.

"Come sit, Uri," said Gusta. "Miklós told me about the events of last night."

The transition from Budapest to Jerusalem was too sudden for me, and I knew that it demanded even more effort from Kraus. I followed him, but he was completely focused on his wife. After some deliberation, I asked Gusta: "Didn't you talk to Sima?"

"Not yet. I'm going up there now. Or I'll talk to her after our English lesson."

"I'm not sure I'd be focused enough for an English lesson right now. Can we make it tomorrow?"

"That's possible, but we'll have to start early. I have a dentist appointment."

"So are you going up to Sima's now?" I asked.

"Oh, Uri. Stick to the task at hand," laughed Kraus.

"Miklós, fix Uri something to drink, I'll be back shortly," Gusta said and left the apartment.

I went with Kraus to the kitchen. After I drank some soda pop I watched him labor for five minutes preparing the foam for a cup of coffee for Gusta. We returned to the living room table and Kraus lit another cigarette. I marveled at the huge difference between the feverishness with which he inhaled the cigarettes and the moderate, calm rhythm with which he nibbled the delightful walnut cake.

Kraus hurried to put out his cigarette when Gusta came back in.

"What's going on upstairs?" I burst out.

"Things still haven't calmed down. Rutha's parents will probably arrive tonight or tomorrow morning. Sima is afraid to send Rutha back to the kibbutz by herself."

"So she's really going back to the kibbutz?" I asked sadly.

"Yes, Uri. Probably tomorrow."

"Can I see her?"

"No. She is locked in her room and refuses to talk to Sima."

Without thinking, I got up from the table and went towards the stairwell, racing up the stairs to the sound of the Krauses' shouts behind me.

I rang the bell of Sima's apartment and added three extra knocks when I got no answer.

The door opened and Sima, clad in an apron, stood before me.

"Hello. I want to see Ruthy," I said simply.

"Rutha is locked in her room."

"I need to talk to her. Just five minutes."

"That was you last night, wasn't it?"

"Yes," I admitted, lowering my eyes, "but not just me."

"Yes. That's what I understood. You've already caused enough trouble in the last two days. I think it's better that you stay away from each other."

Gideon's head appeared behind Sima. "Gideon, go back to the kitchen," she said, turning to face me. I was surprised to see Gideon walk past her and go down the stairs. It was not clear whether Sima noticed, as she was concentrating on me. "I'm sorry, Uri, I hear you are a nice boy but, at the request of Rutha's parents, I can't let you in."

"Just for a minute," I tried.

"Uri, the security forces also prefer that you two not meet."

"Why? Because of her membership in Matzpen?"

"Worse than that," she said before closing the door.

I went down the stairs and outside. I met Gideon in the front yard of the building.

"Can you tell me what's going on?" I asked him.

"Gideon, come in to the house right away!" Sima's call sounded from the balcony, her face hidden by the tall palm tree.

"I have to go up now. We'll meet in the park at four in the afternoon."

"At four," I confirmed, still standing in place, leaning my back against the bare trunk of the palm tree.

Chapter 8

"I had a visitor today," Grandma greeted me when I entered the apartment.
"Who, Grandma?"
"He did not specify what organization he was from."
"I don't understand. Who is he?"
"He introduced himself as Hanoch. He said he was from the security forces."
"And you let him in?"
"I had to. He came together with a policeman."
"What did he say?"
"He knew your whole family history. He was very kind. He said he understood that you were well-meaning, and suggested that you avoid meeting with Rutha Shorin. According to him, she associates with extreme subversive organizations."
"Matzpen is extreme?"
"He said it was worse than that."
"Did he also visit Sima?" I asked.
"Why?"
"Because she recited the exact same speech to me."
"I don't know, Uri, but it seems like she's really a troublemaker, this Rutha…"
"It doesn't really matter; she's locked in her room any-

way until her parents take her back to the kibbutz tomorrow," I said and went to close myself in my room.

I went down to the street at five minutes to four only after I agreed to eat a sandwich and promised Grandma not to do anything foolish. Nurit, who had got there before me, was waiting, leaning on the fence.

"You disappeared on us last night."

"Yes, I didn't feel like dealing with Yaron and his nonsense."

"I also left a bit after you. What are the plans for today?"

"I don't know. I don't have any."

"Hello, my beautiful!" Yaron's voice could be heard announcing his arrival from the entrance to the building. "Uri! What's up?"

"Everything's cool," I said without turning towards him.

"Are you cool too?" He came up and stood in front of Nurit.

"Absolutely."

"I have two tickets to 'The Godfather' tonight. What do you say?"

"I prefer Arik's 'Peepers,'" she said, glancing at me.

"Could be..." I was interrupted by little Gideon pushing himself into the center of the circle.

"Kid, will you get out of here?" Yaron addressed him rudely.

"It's fine, Yaron, I'm taking him to the kiosk." I put my arm around Gideon's shoulder and led him down the street.

"What's that Yaron's problem?" Gideon complained.

"Just a stupid bully. Let's stay away. Tell me what's going on over there at Sima's."

"It's a big mess. My parents are coming tomorrow morning from the kibbutz. They're taking us back."

"And you agreed to go?"

"Of course not. Is it my fault Ruthy makes her own messes?"

"And Ruthy?"

"She's not talking. The parents wanted her to come back today but they were afraid she'd run away."

"Run away? Where would she run away to?"

"To Gan Shmuel. She has someone there."

"Who? That Udi Adiv?"

"I don't know any Udi. There's someone named Gonen."

"From Matzpen?"

"I don't think so. He's a high school student. Two years older than her."

"And he's her boyfriend?"

"Kind of a boyfriend. He was her first."

My heart sank. I felt like my world had gone dark. "First what?"

"Well, you know… the first one that …"

"I don't understand. Is he her boyfriend now? Why would she run away to him?"

"Mom says that Ruthy thinks boys are like socks."

"Like socks?"

"Use them and change them, but don't throw them away." Gideon saw that I had stopped and he fell silent.

"Didn't you want to go to the kiosk?" he asked.

"I forgot I didn't bring money," I said and started walking in the opposite direction.

"I have a few pounds," said Gideon.

"Then buy yourself something, I'm going back."

When I got near the park, the gang had already gathered. I was approaching them when Gideon caught up with me at a run, holding a Lux popsicle in his hand.

"I understand you're not coming to the movie," said Yaron, "you have a new friend, huh…"

"Or a new brother," Nurit added sarcastically.

"I might come. I have to help my grandmother now," I said, abandoning the gang.

Nurit ran after me: "Wait Uri, I didn't mean it."

"Everything's okay," I said, making an effort to smile at her.

"I talked to my grandmother. She told me that you're spending a lot time with the Kraus family. They say he whispers all his secrets to you."

"How does she know? There are some real gossips in this neighborhood."

"Neighborly chats, you know. She sits a lot with Tsipora… your grandmother."

"I have deep conversations with Kraus," I said gravely.

"And you find it interesting?"

"Sure, it's even exciting. It's just not clear why he's intent on talking to me."

"That's how it is, those who came from 'there' are divided into two groups. My grandmother is a Holocaust survivor, and she always tries to get her grandchildren to listen to her stories. Even though we usually get restless quickly, she doesn't give up. My grandfather, on the other hand, has never said a word to us about what happened in the war."

"So Kraus is probably like your grandmother."

"Probably. It's just that he doesn't have grandchildren, so he tells you. By the way, my grandmother made a great cremeschnitte,[37] would you like to come and try it?"

"Okay," I agreed.

Nurit's grandmother opened the door for us with a broad smile. "Oh, how you've grown, Uri. Finally we get to see you."

"Thank you, Mrs. Zilber."

"Come sit down, children," she said and went to the refrigerator before Nurit could even say anything, bringing out the magnificent cake. "How are you doing, Uri? Are you planning to spend the whole vacation holed up at the Krauses'?' Nurit barely sees you."

"Grandma..." Nurit groaned.

"It's very important to him," I said, adopting Nurit's approach.

"I can understand that. Survivors... without children... it's not easy for them. Especially for those who lost children there."

"But Mr. Kraus and Mrs. Gusta didn't lose any children... they only got married half a year before Hungary was liberated."

"Are you sure?" Nurit's grandmother said, and stopped. The three of us fell silent, focusing on the cake.

"Wow. This is the tastiest cremeschnitte I've ever eaten. Thank you, Mrs. Zilber."

Nurit's grandmother nodded with satisfaction. After a short silence she said, "You know, Nurit – Gittel, your aunt, told me that Kraus saved a lot of people. She even

---

37. Cream cake

knows someone here in Jerusalem who Kraus saved in Budapest."

"Who?" Nurit asked.

"I don't remember his name... you met his son... in the sukkah,[38] he's your age."

"Oh, Ze'ev... Ze'ev Maor, I think."

"Yes, exactly. Maor. His father was a little younger than you children when Mr. Kraus forged his documents and smuggled him to Greece."

"Yes," I returned to the conversation. "Kraus is very modest. Only after many hours of conversation did he tell me that he saved tens of thousands of people." I flaunted my knowledge.

"And that's true. I heard it from several other people who passed through the Glass House."

"So you've heard about the Glass House?" I was amazed.

"Of course. Although I'm from Slovakia, any survivor from Budapest will tell you about it."

"So how come Kraus didn't get the honor he deserved?"

"Because those who live in a glass houses shouldn't throw stones... and Kraus... oh oh, bless his soul... he threw a lot of stones and stirred up a lot of resistance against him."

"I brought some issues of 'Lahiton'[39] from home. Do you want to see, Uri?" asked Nurit, who had lost interest in the conversation and pulled me into her room. We sat on her bed. She put a music cassette in her tape player and start-

---

38. A temporary outdoor hut built during the 8-day Jewish festival of Sukkot.

39. 'Lahiton' (from the word 'lahit,' hit, and 'iton,' newspaper) was an Israeli weekly covering music and pop entertainment. It was published from 1969 to 1989.

ed telling me about her family's trip to the Sinai, while I remained withdrawn, digesting the depth of the insult I felt from Ruthy's 'betrayal.' The fact that it had happened before she even met me didn't change anything.

"What's going on, Uri?" asked Nurit, noticing that my mind was somewhere else.

"I really need to help my grandmother." I was watching the clock.

"So are we going to the movies tonight?"

"Okay," I answered, without listening to her question. I got up and left her room sunk in thought, feeling lonely and betrayed. As worthless as a single sock.

Chapter 9

"Good morning, Uri'leh. You're up early today," Grandma greeted me in the kitchen.

"It's already half past eight," I said innocently.

"A few days ago, it was impossible to drag you out of bed. Have something to eat... look what I made you..."

"I'm not hungry."

"I made you pancakes."

"Thanks, Grandma. I'll eat."

"Some vegetables? An omelet?"

"No. Thanks, Grandma."

"What's wrong, Uri'leh? Don't you feel well?"

"I'm fine."

"You came back early from the movie last night. Didn't you have a good time with Nurit?"

"It was fine."

"Fine... fine," my grandmother murmured. "It's impossible to get anything out of you. Okay, so I'm putting strawberry jam and cream cheese on your pancakes... and drink another cup of water, the weatherman is predicting a *hamsin*."[40]

We finished our breakfast in silence, with me hiding behind yesterday's sports section.

---

40. A hot wind from the desert.

At nine o'clock I crossed the street and knocked on the Krauses' door. He opened the door, dressed in a button-down shirt with short sleeves for a change. I looked at his thin fingers and well-kept nails as he led me to the living room. The chess board was on the table. "As I expected, it ended in a draw," he said proudly.

"So, what's the result?" I asked indifferently.

"Seven to five in favor of Bobby Fischer."

"Good morning, Uri," said Gusta, storming into the room. "There's no time for chess discussions this morning, remember?"

"Yes, Mrs. Gusta," I replied as we sat down side by side.

"Rutha's parents are arriving later this morning," she said casually. I picked up the pen, seemingly ignoring her words, and raised my eyes. She glanced at me with a questioning look and continued:

"Today we will go over relative clauses and the infinitive." I tried to concentrate, take a lot of notes, and ignore her looks. For her part, she was trying fervently to get me to converse in English, and required me to create sentences in my notebook and read them out loud. When we reached the last page, she looked at her watch and realized that we had finished the material earlier than expected.

"You know everything worked out in the end with the police," she said.

"Worked out for whom?"

"For Rutha. The police decided to close the case."

"The police?"

"The security forces... I'm not sure exactly who," she answered hesitantly.

"So it's quiet up there. Great."

"I see you're already done," Kraus said, popping up

behind us after having disappeared from the room while the lesson was going on. Gusta stood up and motioned for him to follow her. After extensive whispering, Kraus returned to the table, a plate with orange slices in one hand and a glass of water in the other.

"Do you remember where we were yesterday?" he asked, handing me the plate.

"Thank you, I'm not hungry," I said, reaching for the glass of water. "Yesterday we got to the end of the summer of 1944." I opened my notebook and read: "When the Glass House you set up was already in full operation and the group certificates of 40,000 people were ready in thick books."

"Yes," said Kraus. "A relatively calm period. The Soviet army continued to advance. The town of Cluj we talked about was liberated, and we all expected that Transylvania and the Carpathians would soon be liberated at the beginning of October. And then..." he said with a dramatic flourish, "October 15th came and everything turned around."

"What was the turnaround? The Germans started to win?"

"No. A turnaround in our living conditions," he explained. "It was a Sunday. In the morning we celebrated the happy news of the liberation of Athens by the Allies from the west, and the liberation of Riga by the Soviets in the east. We also got the news that Hungary was requesting armistice terms from the Allies, and we could see the beginning of the end of the war."

"And...??"

"In the afternoon, Horthy did indeed announce Hungary's move to the Allied side."

"So that was good, wasn't it?"

"Not for us, because the Germans were quick to react. They arrested Horthy and his son. The father was sent to detention in Germany, and they threatened to kill the son if Hungary violated its alliance with them. The Germans brought the anti-Semitic Arrow Cross Party to power and its leader, Ferenc Szálasi, was appointed prime minister."

"And what happened to you in Budapest?"

"The same Holocaust that destroyed the Jews of the Hungarian villages began in Budapest in full force. The Jews were herded together into buildings marked with yellow stars, and no one was allowed to leave. At night people were pulled from their beds, and men and women over the age of 16 were taken, allegedly to work on fortifications, and handed over to the Nazis. The new interior minister reached an agreement with Eichmann on the transfer of the first group of 50,000 Budapest Jews to Germany, followed by more groups, until the 'final solution' was complete. We feared that all the achievements we had made with the Hungarian authorities would be erased, and that the Schutzpass status would be canceled."

"The Glass House continued to operate? What happened to Bela?"

"In the first days, no one was seen on the streets. I didn't leave the Swiss legation building either. Over the next few days we found a way to get to the Glass House. On October 22nd, the authorities publicized announcements exempting foreign subjects from 'work service.' I then pressed Lutz to issue individual Schutzpasses for each one of the 40,000 registered in the collective certificate books. The righteous Lutz gave us approval to do so and, at the same time, turned to the Szálasi government and presented him with the agreement of the previous government, providing for a collective Swiss passport for 40,000 people."

"And Szálasi's government approved it?"

"Not right away. It took more pressure. We went through two more tense days. At the same time that Lutz appealed to the authorities, I appealed to the United States embassy in Istanbul and the Eretz Israel office in Geneva, and I asked them to press for American intervention. The next day a sharp protest letter arrived from the United States demanding that the deportations be stopped immediately, while personally threatening all government officials involved."

"And you knew about that?"

"The letter was delivered via the Swiss embassy in Budapest. Lutz showed me the letter before he handed it over to the Prime Minister."

"To Szálasi?"

"Indeed. Szálasi told Lutz that they had no intention of deporting the Jews, but just to employ them in various jobs, and invited Lutz and the Swedish envoy to visit the camps where those able to work were being held. Lutz and the Swedish Danielson immediately went with the prime minister to the camp, located in Buda, and there they witnessed the arrival of a transport of children, women and old men. At this shocking sight, Szálasi ordered them to be immediately released from the camp and returned to their homes. At the end of the visit, Prime Minister Szálasi summoned Lutz and Danielson to continue the conversation about the fate of the Jews."

"Why was he being so nice?"

"Szálasi also understood that the end was approaching, and it was very important for him to obtain the neutral countries' support for his government. In the conversation, Lutz and Danielson presented the agreement that had been reached with the previous government. It was agreed that until those Jews emigrated from Hungary, their personal safety would be guaranteed by Schutzpasses on behalf of the Swiss and Swedish representatives, and that they would be rounded up into special houses. The wording of the protection form had not changed, but this time the same date, '23 October 1944,' the date of the meeting with Szálasi, was stamped on all the certificates."

"Wow. This time, it was with the consent of the Arrow Cross Party."

"It was a huge achievement, but I didn't stop there. The next day I appealed to the Pope and to the representatives of Portugal and Spain, and I asked them to contact Szálasi with a request for the same arrangement that Switzerland and Sweden had obtained. The government approved the request, and placed the buildings at the disposal of the neutral consulates for receiving the candidates for emigration. A sign was hung on the front of the buildings reading: 'This house is under the auspices of the legation of country X. Entry to foreigners is prohibited.'"

"Like you said, Mr. Kraus... it really was a big rescue enterprise."

"That's still not everything. Remember Mantello from the publication of the Vrba-Wetzler report?"

"Yes. The El Salvador Consul in Geneva."

"The day after Szálasi's approval, I sent Mantello pictures and personal information of Jews from Budapest who were not included in the list of 40,000, and I asked him to approve Salvadoran citizenship and passports for them. Thus, from the beginning of November, holders of Salvadoran papers were also protected in Budapest. The rumor spread about the existence of individual Schutzpasses for everyone who was listed in the collective passport and, as a result, crowds gathered around the Glass House in hopes of obtaining a Schutzpass and entering a safe house."

"I don't understand. How could a Schutzpass be issued to someone whose name did not appear in the collective passport books?"

"An excellent question, and the answer is 'forging names in the collective passports.'"

"Who forged the names?"

"Lutz did not actively participate in the forgeries, but he didn't prevent them either. Our representatives went to the printing house where the original forms were printed and managed to print additional forms for a bribe. The problem was that we needed a stamp that was locked in Lutz's office. Lutz, who understood the problem, solved it by writing to us that 'approved forms were returned with errors,' and asked us to stamp them. We took advantage of the stamp being in our hands to stamp all of our forged forms. The representatives of the pioneer movements, who saw that we were forging documents, pressured us to turn our operation into a large factory that would cover tens of thousands more Budapest Jews, and that became a problem."

"Why a problem?"

"My fear was that the forgery operation would be discovered, and then all the existing Schutzpasses would be disqualified. It was a heavy moral question, Uri." Kraus stopped and looked at me, "What would you have done?"

"I don't understand."

"Would you risk 40,000 who have documents that are guaranteed and turn them into ... let's say... 70,000 with documents that are not guaranteed?"

"That decision would be beyond me. What did you decide?"

"We continued producing modest quantities of forgeries, but the pioneer movements tried to produce forgeries in larger quantities, and we fiercely clashed over this. They brought us to the brink of disaster..."

"How?"

"Representatives of the Zionist movements prepared fake seals of the Swiss legation. On one of the stamps, the letter 'I' was omitted from the word SUISSE, so that it was misspelled 'SUSSE.'

"Wow, what happened then?"

"The authorities had begun to suspect the possibility of forgeries even before that. Only 32,000 Jews arrived in the Budapest ghetto, which was designated for all Jews not protected by the police, and this was less than 30 percent of what the authorities expected. They started looking for the missing Jews, and discovered that bearers of forged Schutzpasses had taken refuge in the safe houses sponsored by Switzerland. The Hungarians demanded to be allowed to enter those houses. Lutz announced that the legation itself would immediately begin searching the safe houses. Not all officials in the Swiss legation were our supporters like Lutz, and the forgeries were discovered during these searches. Then the legation had no choice but to allow the Hungarian police to search the houses. They seized 10,000 forged Schutzpasses and their bearers were transferred to the large ghetto. Many were murdered on the way there."

"So most of the forgeries were not caught."

"That's right, Uri, most of them were not caught, and more forgeries were also made after the searches. The tension among Lutz and me and the Zionist movements reached a peak. Despite the heavy pressure we managed, as I said, to avoid turning over the list of names of the 7,800 certificates that stood behind the 40,000 original Schutzpasses. However, many of the holders of original Schutzpasses were murdered because they were suspected of holding forged certificates."

"So it was still worthwhile?" I asked.

"It was worthwhile for those who survived. It wasn't worthwhile for those who were murdered. We can't determine whether something was worthwhile or not in such cases. Carl Lutz had a sentence he would utter frequently."

"What sentence?"

"He would say: 'I go crazy when I have to make a decision on who to save. Where is God?'"

"Where is God?" mumbled Kraus again, and went out to the balcony to light a cigarette.

• • •

"It was great negligence on their part," I said, when Kraus returned from the balcony.

"Whose?"

"The pioneer movements... about the forgeries."

"Yes, it was great negligence but, to their credit, they

showed a lot of courage. Not just in the forgeries, but also in saving people's lives with acts of heroism."

"What heroism?"

"Members of the pioneer movements disguised themselves as fascist officers and followed the deportation marches, pulling friends out of them. They had military vehicles. Others, dressed in Hungarian army uniforms, roamed the ghetto houses and labor camps and rescued Jews from there."

"And where did they hide them?"

"Mostly they were brought to the shelter on Vadász Street."

"Sounds like a big mess in the Glass House."

"Yes, lots of people staying there, and a big operation."

"Operation?"

"At the Glass House we gathered all the activists of the Zionist movements and their families. The staff numbered 150 people. Every activist had assistants, so the total number was over 500. The attorney Rudy Mezei was in charge of keeping order in the building. Don't forget it was a Swiss legation building and it had to look like that, ready for any Swiss visit or Hungarian inspection."

"Of course..."

"But, along with all the strictness, we also found the designated spaces and the time to maintain a Jewish way of life. On Sabbath evenings we made Kiddush[41] and sang Sabbath songs and, on Hanukkah,[42] we lit candles."

"Hanukkah candles? How?"

---

41. A blessing sanctifying the Sabbath, made over a cup of wine.

42. A Jewish festival on which candles are lit over the course of eight days to celebrate the Jewish victory over the Greeks and the rededication of the Temple in the second century BCE.

"We put a strip of wood on a table, put walnut shells on it, and filled them with oil and a wick; Michai Shlamon lit them. His wife managed to improvise some potato fritters, and there was great rejoicing." Kraus paused, observing the impression this had made on me and, when he saw that I was busy writing, continued. "The Zionist movements took care of teaching Hebrew, and there were Torah classes in the attic where the Mizrachi movement was housed. In the basement where the Orthodox were staying, there was even a Torah scroll."

"What happened in the end with Bela?" I changed the subject.

Kraus looked at me reproachfully, but answered my question: "He got bored in one of the safe houses and, despite my pleas, he went out to the streets and came to visit the Glass House."

"How far was that?"

"About half an hour walk. What he didn't think about were the lookouts that István had stationed to watch the Glass House, and they called him."

"And you didn't warn him?"

"I was in my office at the Swiss consulate when, one afternoon, Bela left the Glass House and disappeared. Only late that night Bela's neighbors informed me that he did not return to the building."

"And the unit that disguised themselves in the Arrow Cross uniforms couldn't save him?"

"I didn't know where he was taken to. Carl Lutz convinced me to wait until the morning and took me to the gendarmerie offices in a consul vehicle. We were greeted by László Ferenczy. After a few nerve-wracking minutes he informed me that his investigation had revealed that

Bela had arrived at the gendarmerie building the previous night, and that this morning he was supposed to join the death marches towards the border. Ferenczy went down to the detention cellar with us, where we were informed that István and Bela had just left the building five minutes before our arrival. László Ferenczy asked us to stay in the headquarters building while he left with his driver."

"He didn't know about it before you arrived?"

"I'm not sure. It's possible. A quarter of an hour later the car returned. Bela was sitting in the front seat next to the driver, bruised and beaten. Ferenczy got out the back door, followed by István with a downcast face, muttering a curse as he passed by me."

"Lucky you had Ferenczy against István."

"It didn't last long. Maybe influenced by this event, István left the gendarmerie and took up a senior position in the Arrow Cross companies. Gusta, who didn't like my leaving the legation building even before this event, now pressured me to stop completely. Her great fear was, as I said, of Dieter possibly joining forces with István Kovacs."

"Did they know each other?"

"No, but the circumstances made it extremely likely that they would meet."

"There's something I don't understand. What stopped the Arrow Cross from going on a rampage and destroying the Glass House?"

"Good question. They did try, and sometimes they succeeded in taking small actions. For our part, we recruited 200 deserters from the Hungarian army who got housing, a salary and food from the Glass House storerooms."

"That must have cost a lot. How did you finance

something like that in the middle of such a crazy war? It sounds unreal."

"The money was donated by wealthy Jews who found refuge in the safe houses."

From the direction of the stairwell, Gusta's clicking heels alerted us of her arrival. Kraus stood up as she approached us, smiling when she appeared as if they had just gotten married a week earlier. "How are you? Did it hurt?"

"You know Doctor Flum, he never hurts me."

"I'm glad."

"It's nice how you worry about me, Miklós."

"I was just telling Uri how you worried about me when I would leave the consulate."

"Oh. Did you tell him about the times you disappeared all night?"

"No. There's no need, Gusta," he said, caressing her palm.

Gusta agreed. "Would you like something to drink? I see you haven't touched the oranges."

"I wasn't hungry."

"How about you, Miklós?" she asked with a pleasant smile.

I watched the pair of lovers whispering together. I'm sure Kraus was never Gusta's sock, I thought, feeling sorry for myself.

Chapter 10

Gusta said goodbye to us and went up to Sima's. Kraus and I remained at the table, listening to the clacking of Gusta's receding footsteps.

Kraus, who either noticed my mood or had been prompted by Gusta before she left, tried to cheer me up by moving on to a topic I liked: "I forgot to tell you about Guttmann and Sebes."

"The coaches?" I asked agreeably.

"The soccer players who became coaches. Gusztáv Sebes," Kraus began, showing me a picture of the two of them embracing each other. "He's about my age. He played and coached soccer throughout most of the war."

"People played soccer during the war?"

"Towards the end of the war, official soccer in Hungary was shut down and, in a strange way, this shutdown also helped save Jews. Even though he was Jewish, Sebes had protection throughout the entire period. I met him after the war, when he started working as a coach of the Hungarian national team. He won an Olympic gold medal with that team in 1952. In the 1954 World Cup, this was the great Hungarian 'miracle team' with Kocsis and Puskás, which Sebes led to the finals."

"It lost to West Germany there," I hurried to flaunt my knowledge. "But I didn't know he was Jewish. Did you save him too?"

"No. As I said, he didn't need my help. Bela Guttmann, on the other hand, suffered a lot during the war. He was sent to a labor camp where he stayed from June to November 1944, exactly at the time we are in our story. In December, when he was about to be sent to Auschwitz, he managed to escape from the labor camp, came to Budapest and hid there until the liberation of the city. During this time we became connected indirectly, and we became friends after the liberation. Here is a picture of us at the Újpest stadium."

"In 1947 he returned and coached the Újpest team, then coached the Milano team in Italy, and won a championship with that team, then Puskás's Honvéd Budapest team, and the team of São Paolo, Brazil. When he returned to Europe, he led Porto to the Portuguese championship, then moved on to Benfica Lisbon which, as I said, won two European Champions League cups. Now he is coaching the Greek Panathinaikos."

"So it's a story with a happy ending."

"Not exactly. His sister and father were murdered in Auschwitz and he also suffered a lot, but Bela Guttmann chose life and still manages to give it a happy meaning."

"I didn't know the story of Bela Guttmann. And what happened to Little Bela? You left me in suspense."

"He stayed in the safe house. But those houses were less safe than before. Despite the soldiers I recruited who patrolled there, István and the Arrow Cross gangs would break into houses from time to time, carry away protected Jews and lead them to the ghetto or kill them along the way. That's the way it was until liberation.

"The rest of Budapest's Jews, those who were left outside the safe houses, were rounded up into the ghettos.

Starting from November 8th, every day groups began to leave, after a stay at the collection points, on a forced march towards the Austrian border. There they were turned over to Dieter Wisliceny, who had now been placed in charge of the death marches. Every day about two thousand people set out on these marches in treacherous weather conditions, after most of their equipment had been stolen from them. In the rain and without food, many did not survive the journey; some died of hunger and cold, and some were shot because they fell behind as they were walking."

"Lutz and his wife, and other employees of the Swiss legation, stood for hours in the snow and pulled out those who held authentic Schutzpasses from the long lines – some of them having been printed at the legation that same morning."

"Only the Swiss? What about the other legations?"

"The other foreign embassies also did their best. With the consent of the Hungarian authorities, they sent representatives to follow the marchers and return people with foreign protection certificates. Thus the vehicles of the foreign legations traveled along the road from Budapest to Vienna. Those who could not be rescued from the convoy were provided food and medicine."

"Why didn't the Germans send them to Auschwitz?"

"At this point, the Russian army was very close and the Auschwitz camp had already reduced its operations and was on the verge of closure. Every day we received reports about the plight of the thousands of Jews who had been marching for two weeks, spread out all along the route."

"But still, they managed to save some of the marchers."

"Yes, thousands," Kraus got up and pulled a black binder from the bookshelf. "Here, look at this document," and he read from one of the documents in the binder. "I'm quoting Breslauer: '... out of 35,000 who set out, I estimate that about 15,000 Jews were returned from the death marches.'"

"Fifteen thousand! That's a lot. Sounds made up."

Kraus nodded and went out to the balcony again.

When he returned, I asked, "You didn't mention Kastner's name today. Where was he at that time?"

"Kastner traveled around several countries in Europe. During the death marches, he came to Budapest for a short visit. I will read to you from a letter Kastner wrote to Saly Mayer, the Joint representative in Geneva: 'According to unequivocal reports from the border, the German authorities accept the Jews and treat them humanely. They are bathed and given adequate food and sent on by train. As one of Eichmann's subordinate officers explains: "The Jews' faces lit up when they reached the German border."' End quote of quote. That's how Kastner described it."

"Why did he do that?"

"At that point in time, he was pressured by his attempts to save the second group of passengers of the famous train. In August 1944, 318 of the train passengers were released to Switzerland. The rest – 1,366 passengers – were held hostage in Bergen-Belsen."

"And Saly Mayer didn't understand that?"

"Kastner claimed that the Nazis must be provided with another 20,000 Jews to work on the fortifications. According to him..." Kraus turned another page and read: "And I quote: 'If the demand is met, the Swiss legation will be able to grant 40,000 sponsorship certificates, as will the Swedes,' end quote." Kraus, his face flushed, slammed the binder shut.

"He was using your 40,000."

"Yes. And not to good use. There was no connection between the sponsorship certificates and the Germans' desire to send another 20,000 of Budapest's Jews to the death camps," he said, and went out to the balcony for another cigarette.

A commotion could be heard from the stairwell. Gusta entered the house and asked her husband if I was still with him. Kraus said to me, "Rutha's parents have come to take her. They are leaving for the north soon."

I kept silent.

"Uri, don't you want to go up to say goodbye to her?" Gusta tried. "She won't be coming back here anytime soon."

"Me neither," I answered rudely.

"Why?" Gusta asked.

"Sorry. I didn't mean it."

"It's okay," she came up to me and put a hand on my shoulder. "But why not say goodbye nicely? I thought you two were friends."

"I was a good friend."

"Right," said Kraus. "You were a good and loyal friend, and it is important that you're left with good memories."

"Thank you, I know you care about me and I appreciate it, but..."

I stopped. Silence enveloped the three of us. The commotion in the stairwell also subsided.

"But what, Uri?" Kraus asked.

"I'm angry with Ruthy."

"And does she know that?"

"She knows exactly what she's doing."

"What she did to you, you mean?" Kraus asked.

"I'm not the only one."

"The only one that what?" Gusta joined in.

"Never mind," I mumbled.

"Would you like to join us for lunch?" Gusta asked.

"No thanks. I'll go back to Grandma's. Do we have a lot left?" I turned to Kraus.

"We're almost done. I mean, it's up to you, I don't know if you'd like to hear about what happened in Europe and Israel after the war?"

"I'm not sure I need it for the essay I'm going to write, but I'm obviously interested in hearing about it."

Kraus scratched his brow and straightened his glasses. "Well, we have reached December 1944," he sighed. "I knew it was too late to organize rescue attempts. The anti-Semites at the Swiss embassy had isolated dear Lutz and left him with only limited influence. On December 8th, the German legation left Budapest. The next day, most of the members of the Hungarian government also left the city and moved to Odenburg. Chaos reigned in Budapest. The Arrow Cross militias were given full freedom of action and went off on murder sprees."

"Weren't you afraid for your life? And for Gusta's life?"

"I was always afraid, throughout the whole period but, of course, I became more afraid when the gangs took over. Gusta continued to pressure me every morning not to leave the building of the Swiss legation, but that was impossible. István became omnipotent. One afternoon I left the Glass House with a little orphan girl who had been brought to us that morning. I took her hand and was leading her to Pozsonyi Street to deliver her to a distant aunt who lived there. I also hoped to visit Little Bela on the same outing.

"When we approached the Margit Bridge we heard bursts of gunfire from the bank of the Danube. The most terrible sight..." he shuddered. "Men, women and children stood facing the river and were shot and thrown into the water. The water of the Danube turned red. I covered the girl's eyes and hurried to hide alongside one of the buildings. The firing continued for many long minutes. I gathered the girl in my arms and quickened my steps. Once we got to Pozsonyi street, I delivered the girl to her aunt, and there I was told that Arrow Cross gangs were raiding the houses and pulling out victims with no regard for age or certificates. The limited number of guards we employed were no match for the waves of gangs. One of those guards, armed with a rifle, escorted me to the house where Bela was staying, and I was relieved to see him safe and sound."

"So what did you do?"

"The next morning, from among the masses of Hungarian defectors roaming the city, we managed to organize another company that would protect the legation building and the dozens of safe houses. At the same time, Otto Komoly, president of the Zionist Federation, who was then head of the Children's Department of the Red Cross, reported to me that the government, from where it was sitting, had sent an instruction to transfer all the children to the large ghetto. I called a meeting with the Pope's representative, the Swedes Danielson and Wallenberg, the righteous Carl Lutz, and representatives from the Spanish and Portuguese legations, and we submitted a letter of protest to the Hungarian government. Following our efforts, the Hungarian government changed its decision and the children were saved."

"So you did a lot for the children."

"Yes, for other people's children..."

"I don't understand... there were children... who weren't other people's?" I stammered.

Kraus fell silent and looked at me.

"The next day I learned that István Kovacs and his gang had invaded Bela's safe house and removed him from there."

"Just him?"

"Just him. He knew Bela was in that specific building and came to take him."

"How did he know?"

"I'm afraid that my visit there, the day before, revealed his whereabouts," he said grimly.

"They followed you?"

"Either they followed me, or they saw me there, or our enlisted guards turned him in following my visit."

"And you managed to find him?"

"No. We turned the city upside down. I used all my connections. The next day two guards checked the corpses that washed ashore... and nothing... he disappeared without a trace."

"What did you do then?"

"I put my pride aside, I got my anger under control, and I went with Lutz, escorted by two soldiers, to search for István."

"And you found him?"

"We found him. In Lutz's presence he said he had no idea what happened to Bela but, when I got back to the

Glass House, an anonymous letter was waiting for me there: "Greetings, Miklós. Regards from Bela. We wanted to arrange a joint farewell for you, but you did not show up. He will wait for you on the river bottom."

"I'm sorry, Mr. Kraus," I stood up and put my hand on his shoulder. I went to the kitchen and came back with a glass of water that I handed him. "We can stop here," I said.

"Thank you, Uri. No, no, let's get it over with. What I went through with Bela was something thousands of other families went through, as you know. And I was one of the lucky ones."

"Still..." I started to say, but Kraus cut me off, getting his emotions in check: "The gangs' rampages increased and more and more people, from the safe houses as well, sought shelter in the Glass House."

"But where did you put them all?" I picked up the conversation, happy to keep it away from Bela's sad end.

"Do you remember that when we talked about Sebes and Guttmann, the soccer players, I said that we found a blessing in the cessation of soccer?"

"Yes." I wondered what the connection could be.

"The Hungarian Soccer Federation ceased its activities in mid-December 1944 and, fortunately, the Federation building was located at 31 Vadas Street."

"Next to the Glass House!" I exclaimed.

"Right. Next to the Glass House. With Weiss's consent, we broke down the dividing wall between the two buildings and about a thousand people staying in the Glass House moved into the Federation building."

"And they couldn't be seen from outside the building."

"No. Unlike the Glass House, the facade of the Federation building was brick. There was a fear that the tenants would be heard even if they were not seen, so we demanded absolute silence. In the evening, small groups moved from there to bathe and use the restrooms. István, who had found some of the safe houses empty in his most recent forays, suspected that their residents had escaped to the Glass House. The whole building went into 'István alert,' whenever the scout on duty on the first floor reported that he was approaching. On one such occasion, at the end of a meeting with Otto Komoly, chairman of the Zionist Federation in Budapest, the scout reported that István was standing by the front of the Soccer Federation building with his ear pressed to the wall."

"What did you do?"

"Lutz's car, which was supposed to pick us up to take us to the Swiss consulate, arrived just at that moment. We ran downstairs and called his attention to István as we got into the car. He lunged at us like a snake striking, but we were already on our way. I don't know how, but Otto and I were amazed when we got out of the car – István came up behind us with one of his thugs who held a drawn gun. István smiled and said: "Two birds with one stone.""

"And…?"

"Fortunately, Lutz's driver blasted his horn which made Lutz come down. He rescued us from the Arrow Cross car that had just pulled up. István, who was forced to leave us, whispered to us in Hungarian, 'Never mind. We'll hunt you down one by one.'"

"That was really lucky."

"Yes, luck too. At the end of the meeting, I tried to persuade Otto Komoly to come live next to me in the Swiss legation building, but he had left his home only days earlier and moved in with the Red Cross representative at the Ritz Hotel, and insisted that the place was completely safe. Three days later, on January 1, 1945, he was kidnapped by the Arrow Cross Brigade, and his body was thrown into the waters of the Danube."

"István?"

"Apparently, although that was an especially busy day for him."

"Why? What else did he do?"

"It started the night before, New Year's Eve. An Arrow Cross squad attacked the Glass House, threw grenades into it, and dragged many of its residents out to the street.

"Arthur Weiss, the owner of the building who I had appointed to manage it, came out to them and protested the violation of its ex-territorial status. In the meantime, the police commanders learned about the incident and they came and saved the lives of the 1,500 Jews who had already been rounded up in the street. The gangs returned the next day."

"The day of Komoly's death."

"That's right. This time Arthur Weiss did not have such good luck. He was taken away in their car and was never seen again."

"Gusta was right. No one should have gone out on the streets in those days."

"I had no choice and had to take risks, even if I did it in a calculated way, but there were those who behaved differently. Remember I told you about Erwin Berkowitz?"

"Yes. Erwin, whose character was portrayed by Kishon in the movie *Arbinka*."

"Very good, Uri. So Erwin arrived at the Glass House on Christmas Eve dressed in an SS uniform, right in the middle of the killings, and took his mother, Mrs. Berkowitz, out to dinner in a restaurant. He brought her black patent shoes and a fur coat that suited her straight black hair, and convinced her that she looked like a Spanish model, certainly not like a Jewish refugee. I tried to dissuade them but, with great confidence, he took her in a taxi to the 'Peace Café.'"

"Really Arbinka," I said.

"What courage! What audacity!" Kraus smiled at me, and continued: "There's even a happy ending to that story. He and his mother immigrated to Israel and he set out on an impressive career."

"And what happened to the Glass House after Weiss was murdered?"

"I appointed someone to replace him and we continued our rearguard battle. The riots continued into January. On January 15th, after murdering thousands, the Arrow Cross men began to flee the city, the bridges over the Danube were destroyed and the city was divided in two."

"Which part were you in?"

"I remained in Pest. Carl Lutz remained isolated on the other bank, in Buda. Without Lutz, I was helped by two dear officials, and Raoul Wallenberg, and we repelled the last attempts to raid the safe houses. Three days later, the Red Army conquered Pest, and four weeks later the liberation of Budapest was completed. That's it. End of story."

"Was István caught?"

"No. He fled the city in a Mercedes whose convertible roof was torn. Refugees that he passed said that a Russian Yak plane dived at the vehicle and blew it up with a shower of shells."

"Did you see his body?"

"You're a smart boy. No, I didn't see his body."

"And that's it?" I felt a strange emptiness.

"That's it. The city was liberated and 140,000 Jews survived."

"That's a lot, relatively speaking," I pointed out.

A commotion could be heard in the stairwell. Kraus got up and went to Gusta, who had opened the door, beckoning me to come. "Uri, come say hello." I stood up by the table with my legs turned to stone. Kraus came up to me and grabbed my hands: "Dear Uri. There are goodbyes that are not said and they stay with us for the rest of our lives. Believe me." I let him lead me towards the door.

"Come tomorrow at nine and we'll sum everything up." I nodded my head and thanked him. I went out to the stairwell and walked carefully towards the exit from the yard. The sun blinded me. I looked to the right, but there was no traffic on the street. The sun beat down on my head. A Peugeot 404 emerged from the left, and then I saw her. Ruthy was sitting in the back seat and opened the window. "Uri!" she exclaimed, sticking her head out the window. I remained rooted in place. The car drove on, turned onto Rashba Street and disappeared from my sight.

Chapter 11

Jerusalem, January 2022

The ringing of the phone made me sit up with a jerk. I had pins and needles in my right arm, on which I rested my head as I slept. The hands of the antique clock on the dresser showed three o'clock. I tried to think: "Who could be calling me in the middle of the night?" I shook my right arm, trying to restore the blood flow, as I reached out my left hand towards the smartphone that continued to ring and vibrate on the table. An unidentified number appeared on the screen.

"Yes?" I answered groggily.

"Uri?" I heard a young voice on the other end.

"Yes."

"Did I wake you up?"

"Who am I speaking to?"

"Ruthy," answered the female voice.

"Ruthy?" Still half asleep, I tried to sort out my dreams and my memories from the present reality.

"Yes, Ruthy. Rona's friend."

"Yes, Ruthy. What's wrong?"

"Nothing's wrong. You blew me off this morning."

"This morning? What time is it?"

"Three in the afternoon."

"Wow, I don't believe it."

"So I did wake you up."

"Yes. I spent all night and this morning reading, and I must have fallen asleep at the table."

"Oh, I'm sorry. Well, then call me when you wake up."

"No, no," I shook myself awake. "Ruthy Shor, right?"

"Yes, from the building across the street. Rona wrote me to check on you."

"Yes, I see now that she tried to call. I messed up."

"She was a little worried. She's coming back this evening."

"Ah... the key... I forgot."

"No big deal. You just missed some good coffee. When are you leaving?"

"In the evening. I'll bring the key. Is four okay?"

"Great, you'll even be able to earn your coffee again."

I went to the bathroom, washed my face and returned to the table, surveying the mess spread over it. I realized that I had gone through most of the notebooks and tapes. From the tape player, I took out the cassette marked 'Fifth Meeting' and put it back in the box with the others, together with the notebooks. The rumbling in my stomach reminded me that I had missed two meals, and I decided to return to Rachel on the Boulevard. I shoved the mobile phone in my pocket and went down to the street. Ben Maimon Boulevard greeted me with a blast of cold, making it clear to me that the heat of August belonged to my nighttime dreams and to the heating in Rona's apartment. I decided that I could withstand the cold for the short walk to the kiosk, and I set out at a brisk clip. The increasingly heavy rain made it impossible to sit at the open kiosk. I passed it and turned right to the Ephraim Café on Arlozorov Street. The owner greeted me with a smile, surveying my light clothing in amazement. The heating and the red shakshuka[43] thawed me out and enabled me to calmly plan the rest of my day. Rona wrote that she and Danny would be back around six, and asked me to consider staying another night in the apartment.

I considered the options as I ran back in the rain.

I loaded my backpack with the old cassette player, the recordings of the sixth meeting with Kraus, and the notebooks. I packed the rest of the materials destined for storage into the box and marked it with the letter 'K.' But, before I climbed up to put the box back in the storage space, I pulled out Ben Hecht's book 'The Denial' which Kraus had given me with a warm inscription 50 years earlier.

At five to four I crossed Ben Maimon Boulevard, my eyes fruitlessly seeking the tall, narrow palm tree. I lingered for a few moments, surveying the yard, realizing that the tall tree was still in its place but now hidden from view by the weeds that had climbed its trunk and covered its crown.

I knocked expectantly on Ruthy's door. The door opened and her tall figure filled the entrance.

"Hi, come in," Ruthy held out her hand.

"Hi, I'm Uri," I said and stole a glance towards the floor, discovering that she was not wearing high heels. When I saw that she had caught my glance, I added with embarrassment, "Barefoot in the Jerusalem frost."

"Yes. Strength of habit. A barefoot kibbutznik."

I followed her towards the living room, floored by her

---

43. A dish made of eggs cooked in tomato sauce with vegetables.

exotic looks. Bronze skin, straight black hair and a slim figure. No resemblance to Rutha Shorin, I observed to myself.

"Time has stood still," I said, pointing to the walls, "50 years and nothing has changed... the rooms, the floor, even the shelves on the walls."

"The books are all mine," she emphasized with a smile. "Have a seat, I'll bring the coffee."

She turned and walked away towards the kitchen, stepping gracefully on the frayed edges of her worn-out sweatpants.

"In which kibbutz did you learn to go barefoot?" I asked when she came back, even though I knew the answer.

"In Kibbutz Yotvata. There's no problem of cold there."

"So what brought you to Jerusalem?"

"My studies. I'm doing a master's degree in history."

"It's warmer in Tel Aviv."

"Yes, but I liked the department here... besides, I had enough leftists in the kibbutz."

"Ahh. A right-wing kibbutznik. How did this happen?"

"It happens. Trying not to go with the flow."

"Upbringing from home?"

"Father is actually an incurable leftist. He was one of the first children of the kibbutz, and was nursed on Ben Gurion from the day he was born. Mother was a closet right-winger."

"Why?"

"Why right-wing or why in the closet...? She made Aliyah from Morocco as a baby at the end the fifties and experienced the burning hot sides of the melting pot. Although she was my father's commander in the army, at home she's a private to this day."

"And when did you come out of the closet?"

"I've never been in it. Why, what are you?"

"Me? At your age I was like you," I said, again betraying the generational differences between us. "Today I am, let's say, much closer to the center."

"So you're happy about the new Lapid government?"

"Better than what was before, I guess. And you?"

"I'm right-wing, but definitely not a Bibi supporter. But let's not get into politics. Tell me what happened to you last night, that's more interesting. Rona told me you fell asleep over some historical recordings."

I took out the materials I had collected from the storage space and told her about my meetings with Kraus 50 years ago. I found myself sailing through the story, integrating facts as I spoke that I had not processed during the intensive listening of the previous night.

"Sorry, I got swept up in the story," I said.

"No, it really interests me." She got up to get a notebook and a pencil. "I heard that Kraus did great things, but the story that you are describing is much bigger than I knew."

"It turns out that's true. As a child, I did not appreciate the greatness of what he did."

"And why?"

"I was looking more for the warrior, the strong, proud Jew. Tonight I saw things with a new dimension. I'm also almost certain that, as an adult, I ran into one of the heroes that Kraus spoke about without even realizing it."

"How?"

"I suddenly realized that I have known Mickey, the son of one of them, Erwin Berkowitz, for 30 years, but we met 20 years after that week with Kraus, and at an age when all our momentum was directed forward, so we didn't put things in their proper place then. Now I'm starting to understand what I missed."

"How old were you then?"

"When I met Kraus? 14."

"It would be sad if your perspective didn't broaden over the years."

"Yes... but now I feel that I have a certain responsibility towards him."

"Towards the story?"

"Towards Kraus. It's a kind of deposit."

"Listen Uri... it's a historical treasure, and I'm even more amazed that it's completely connected to the period I'm researching."

"Really? On what subject?"

"The totalitarianism of the Labor movement before and after the establishment of the state."

"Yes. There's some overlap."

"I can understand why you didn't sleep last night. So, in the end, you just fell asleep while listening and reading?"

"Not in the process. I finished most of it, except for what I took with me," I pointed to the notebook lying on the table. Ruthy picked it up and paged through it.

"Absolutely illegible handwriting," she laughed. "Can you decipher it?"

"I can, but you're not the first to tell me that..." I chuckled.

"What's this?" She pointed to the last page in the notebook. "Open questions for a Passover visit. Is that from last night?"

"No, no. It's probably some kind of summary I wrote back then during summer vacation. I guess I was planning to come back again during Passover." I tried to take the notebook, but Ruthy pulled it towards her again.

"Let's read together."

"But you can't read the handwriting," I winked at her, as I picked up the notebook and started reading: "A. To check: Ask Grandma to get Ze'ev Maor's phone number from Mrs. Zilber."

"Who is that?" Ruthy asked.

"Mrs. Zilber is my grandmother's neighbor. I spent time with her granddaughter that summer, and they told me about an instance where Kraus saved the life of the father of that Ze'ev Maor."

"Got it."

"B. Open questions," I continued: "1. Why did Kastner act the way he did? 2. Why is Vrba's story not available in Hebrew? 3. Why didn't Vrba stay in Israel? 4. How is it that Kraus didn't manage to save more of his relatives? 5. Why don't Kraus and Gusta have children? 6. Why does Kraus open up to me and devote so much time to me?"

"Wow..." Ruthy whistled. "Heavy questions for a 14-year-old boy."

"7. Why were Kastner's murderers released? 8. Why did they capture Eichmann if they were afraid that problematic subjects would come to light? 9. Why were there detectives in the yard?"

"In which yard?" Ruthy asked.

"Just a second, Ruthy... let me finish reading."

"Yes, sir," she said, folding her long legs under her.

"So the next question... the last one... 10. Why didn't I talk to Ruthy? Should I call her?"

Ruthy's eyes widened.

"Should I explain?" I asked. She nodded.

I found myself telling her about my brief summer romance with Rutha Shorin.

"I wonder why she hasn't contacted you since then?"

"Isn't that the guy's role?"

"Nonsense. Sounds to me like she was the stronger of the two of you," she said, without noticing the blow she had dealt me with her words. "I think she's my relative."

"Who?"

"Rutha Shorin."

"Really?"

"Yes. You said her aunt lives on the second floor in this building."

"So?"

"So, my landlady, Dina, grew up here in the building. She's my father's second cousin, that's why I got this apartment under good terms."

"Amazing. Dina, Sima's daughter?"

"Yes."

"So you were also a Shorin once? I had a feeling it wasn't just a coincidence."

"Could be. I was born Shor. I remember a relative, a lecturer in literature, by the name of Shorin."

"Interesting."

"Do you want to explain the rest of the questions to me now?"

"Happy to. Questions seven and eight are not clear to me at the moment. They may be referring to a meeting that I have not yet gotten to in the recordings. I already told you about the detectives and Rutha... that leaves us with six long questions." I glanced at my watch.

"Tell me more about Vrba and Kraus. I'm familiar with the story of Kastner and Eichmann."

I told her the story of Vrba's escape and Kraus's publication of the Auschwitz reports. Ruthy listened attentively, scribbling notes in her notebook.

"It's amazing how a history student in the year 2022 hasn't encountered a single one of these names anywhere. Great people are hidden and unknown."

"Like the disappearing glory of the palm tree in your yard. The weeds bloom, grow wild and overshadow the crown of the tree."

"You're becoming poetic," she complimented me on the image. "Listen, it would really help me if I could use these materials for my thesis. What do you say?"

"I would be happy. I would be very happy."

"So, this is what I suggest," she said, checking the time on her cell phone. "It's already six o'clock, you must be hungry and want to see Rona. What do you say I prepare something for the three of us to eat, and we go over the material in a more serious way. How does that sound?"

"That means another night in Jerusalem," I said. "I'm sure Rona will be happy. She asked me to stay."

"Even better," she said, jumping off the couch, "Oops, I completely forgot about the coffee."

Ruthy's phone rang. "Hey, Rona," she said, switching the call to speakerphone.

"Hey, Rona'leh," I added.

"What's going on? Are you having a party without me?"

"We are waiting for you for dinner."

"I'll be late. We stopped on the way. Danny was hungry. I still have to drop him off at the station. I'll be there in an hour and a half, don't wait for me for dinner. Daddy, are you staying over tonight?"

"I might. It's possible that Ruthy will write a research paper based on the recordings."

"Wow. Cool. Now I'm definitely coming. I have to hear more. Well, bye, we'll see each other soon."

At dinner, Ruthy opened up and told me that she was currently in a long period of 'abstinence.' It turned out that she did not leave the kibbutz solely for ideological reasons, but also after being cheated on by a former boyfriend.

"We were together for five years. He was a child, and I always forgave him because of that. I don't understand how I didn't see what everyone else knew."

"What?"

"That the world was full of girlfriends for him, and I was only... I was only..."

"A single sock?" I suggested.

"What?" She was dumbfounded. "Yes..." she said after a pause. "...kind of."

"He stayed on the kibbutz?"

"Yes. One of the reasons why I avoided visiting there until recently."

"And these days?"

"Looks like I've gotten over it. I'm waiting for something more mature."

The phone vibrated in my pocket. "Sigal."

"Hey, Sigali. What's up?"

Sigal apologized for not getting back to me, and said that Hayuta had fallen in the bathtub and broken her hip. She sounded confused and distressed.

"I'm just leaving, Sigali, let Hayuta know," I said, as I

stood up and collected my things. I stopped at the door and turned to face Ruthy who was coming towards me.

"My mother took a fall and is injured. I have to go. I'll call you from Tel Aviv... Oh no, Rona..." I muttered.

"It's fine, I'll let her know," Ruthy said.

"She just sounded so excited about... us sitting together," I stopped and thought for a moment. "I would be happy if you choose this topic for your research."

"Are you leaving me the cassettes?"

"I'm only taking with me the cassettes I haven't heard yet. Ask Rona for everything else. It's in a box marked with a big K."

"You forgot something else," she said.

"What?"

"The key."

Chapter 12

Tel Aviv, February 2022

In the weeks after I returned from Jerusalem I was running between new business opportunities that emerged as the Coronavirus pandemic became less acute, taking care of my mother, and other family obligations. Thus I found myself on a Thursday morning, with my daughter Rona, wending our way slowly towards the congested La Guardia interchange. An incoming phone call interrupted our conversation.

"Hi, Mickey, how're you doing?" I asked.

"Great. What time did we say?"

"We didn't set an exact time. We agreed that I would arrive around noon and we'd talk before then."

"Then let's talk."

"First, say hello to Rona, who's in the car with me."

"Hi, Rona'leh, how are you? I haven't seen you in a long time!"

"Hi, Mickey. Yes, I miss you."

"We're on our way to meet my mother," I broke into the conversation.

"How is Hayuta? How is the rehabilitation going?" Mickey asked.

"Like always. Although she's trapped in the Tzahala

Estates,[44] she's still running the world ... but sitting this time."

"So we'll forget about today?"

"No, on the contrary. We'll finish our visit with her around twelve, and then we'll come to you... if that's okay with you?"

"It's great. So Rona, are you coming too?"

"I'd love to. If it's okay with you."

"It's more than okay! I'm getting lunch together. Are you still vegetarian?"

"You really don't have to do that..."

"Sure I do! So, see you soon, I'm glad you're coming," said Mickey and hung up.

"Mickey's a sweetheart," Rona said. "Do you mind if we switch off the music station?" she asked, leaning towards the radio.

"What station would you like?"

"Get with it, Daddy," she said, connecting us to Spotify, and singing along with Tuna.[45]

"You know that Ruthy is really interested?" she asked when the song ended.

"Ruthy Shor? She told me she was looking for a mature relationship..." I answered with a smile.

"Hello, Mr. 64. Hold your horses."

"I was joking. She is very impressive."

"The tapes and notebooks you left her have got her hooked. There are a lot of open questions there."

"I thought all the answers were there."

"We think they contain a lot of new materials and revelations, but also open up a lot of new questions."

---

44. A senior independent living complex in Tel Aviv.
45. An Israeli rapper, singer, songwriter and actor.

"We? You read them too? You listened to the tapes? When did you have time?"

"Daddy. She returned the material to me three weeks ago and, believe it or not... I went through the whole thing... including your questions."

"And what do you think?"

"I think you spent an amazing week there, a very powerful experience for a child... How old were you?"

"14 plus."

"In short, we're waiting for the tape and the last notebook. I'll take them with me to Jerusalem."

"Sorry, Rona'leh. I haven't gone over them yet."

"Dad! Are you serious?" she scolded me. "We need to move ahead. Ruthy is planning to include it as significant chapters in her thesis."

"Okay, okay, I've been busy. I promise to sit down with it over the weekend. Anyway, there's still a lot of investigative work to do. In Hungary too."

"A research trip to Budapest would suit me. My semester finishes in June."

"Hello!? What did you say before? Hold your horses."

"Why? Do you have plans for July?"

"We'll check, sweetie. I'll think about it."

"Is Grandma already moving around?" Rona changed the subject, identifying my mood with ease.

"Not really. I hope Hayuta will start going out to the public areas on Sunday."

"You know I've never seen her room before? She always waits for us in the lobby."

"Well... Hayuta always makes sure to present herself perfectly: make-up, refreshments, a committee of admirers in the lobby."

"It's strange that you don't call her 'Mom.'"

"Of course I call her..." I stammered, turning onto Sasha Argov Street.

• • •

Hayuta greeted us with a wide smile, carefully dressed and made up. Rona immediately embraced her in her wheelchair, bending down and carefully avoiding the bandaged leg.

"Grandma, did you go to the hairdresser?" asked Rona, concentrating on the magnificent hairdo – Hayuta's trademark.

"No. I hope to start going out on Sunday. The girls in my bridge group are already getting impatient."

"And the haircut?"

"Ilan the hairdresser came here, what do you think!?"

"Especially for you?!" Rona was amused.

"Well, with the publicity I give him... I arranged five more girls for him here."

Hayuta referred to any women younger than her by at least 15 years as 'girls.' At the age of 90, my mother was completely lucid and full of youthful vigor, a quality which had attracted young and constantly renewing social circles over the years.

"This room is really cool," said Rona.

"Yeah. It's okay... I'd make some changes here if someone asked me," replied my mother, turning her critical gaze on me.

"Tell me, Grandma," Rona got straight to the point. "Did you know the Kraus family who lived across the street from our building in Jerusalem?"

"Across from Tsipora?"

"Yes. My friend lives in their apartment today," Rona said and, to my surprise, she began telling my mother about the notebooks and cassette tapes that we had taken out of the storage space.

"I remember, I remember," said Hayuta, looking at me again. "It's a shame I didn't pressure you to return to Jerusalem at Passover to complete the project that you had started with that Kraus."

"You actually did put quite a bit of pressure on me," I said.

"Yes… but there was no one to talk to then. The swarthy Ricky had completely turned your head."

'Swarthy' was Hayuta's refined expression in the 2000s that replaced the 1970s expression 'schwartze.'[46]

"Anat Granit and the trip to Germany no longer interested you back then," Hayuta continued, demonstrating her sharp memory.

"What does that have to do with it?" I asked defensively.

"What do you mean? You were afraid that if you left the swarthy Ricky for Passover or, God forbid, for the summer, you would lose her forever. I tried, Rona," she said, looking away from me, "but it was like talking to a wall."

"Yes. My War of Independence," I muttered quietly.

"What did you say?" Hayuta asked, adjusting her hearing aid. "What did he say, Rona'leh?"

"His War of Independence," Rona said out loud.

"What independence? She destroyed all his grades at the beginning of high school, that Ricky. Traveling with

---

[46]. "Black" in Yiddish, in this case a pejorative term for Mizrachi/Sefardi Jews.

a respectable delegation to Germany? Anat Granit? No chance."

"Why did you bring up Anat Granit now? We haven't been in touch since sixth grade."

"That girl from the kibbutz didn't interest you anymore either."

"Who?"

"That communist from the north."

"It's because she pissed me off in Jerusalem."

"She chased after him, that communist," Hayuta turned to look at Rona, "wrote him love letters, with poems, you wouldn't believe it. But he didn't even want to read them."

"How do you know there were poems in the letters? What... did you read them?"

"Of course not..." stammered Hayuta, "you asked me to tear them up."

"Mom," I said, moving from exasperation to curiosity. "What was written there? Where are they?"

"I don't understand what he wants from me," said Hayuta, looking to Rona for help. "You asked me to throw them away 50 years ago."

"Let's go back to Kraus," Rona volunteered to save the situation. "What a sad story."

"Yes," Hayuta was happy to grab the lifeline. "I remember Tsipora telling me that they were a very nice couple. Without children or family. Very sad."

"He saved tens of thousands of Jews, but most of his family perished in the Holocaust," Rona said.

"That's what happens to people who put their work before their family," she said, narrowing her eyes at me. "I hope you will know how to take care of your family and, most importantly, your connection with your brother. In the end, that's all we have."

"Yes. My sister really takes good care of you," I said sarcastically, reading my mother like an open book.

"Really, Uri'leh. You know how hard things are for her."

I got up and opened the door to the balcony. Like Kraus 50 years ago, I thought to myself, finding refuge on the balcony, taking a deep breath of fresh air and relaxing as I faced the green yard. I reminded myself again that my childhood was behind me, and that the all-powerful Hayuta was already 90 years old. I looked back through the glass door at Rona'leh and Hayuta talking amiably, smiling, and I blessed the wonder of the skipped generation that united granddaughters and grandmothers.

• • •

A few minutes after twelve o'clock, I parked my car on Mickey's street. I tarried as I walked by the fence of his neighbor's house, enjoying the tall palm trees overshadowing their surroundings. Rona, who was ahead of me, had already leapt into Mickey's waiting arms as he stood at the entrance to his house. "I forgot how beautiful you are, Rona'leh. I think we haven't seen each other since the start of the Coronavirus," Mickey said, patting me on the back.

"I see your neighbor has two tall Mexican palms in their yard," I said, trying to show off Jerusalem knowledge.

"Oh, oh. Uri," Mickey responded with some sarcasm. "Those are Washingtonia palms."

But Ruthy Shorin said… I thought, as I took off my coat and sank into the armchair.

I let Rona and Mickey fill each other in on the past year as I checked the latest messages on my cell phone. Meanwhile, Mickey treated us to coffee brewed in the new machine he had just bought.

"Say, Mickey," I asked as he sat down. "What was your original last name?"

"Berkowitz. Why?"

"I knew it!" I rejoiced, looking proudly at Rona. "And your father was named Erwin Berkowitz, right?"

"Yes, but where is this coming from now?"

I told Mickey at length about my Jerusalem experience from last month and about the content of my meetings with Kraus, including the mention of the character of Arbinka. Mickey listened in silence while Rona occasionally broke in to add explanations and highlights. When we finished, Mickey said:

"What was the name of this man you met in Jerusalem? The one who built the Glass House?"

"Moshe Kraus, or Miklós Kraus."

"And the Swiss guy?"

"Carl Lutz."

"It's weird that, in all my conversations with my father, he never mentioned those names, not even when we were talking about the Glass House."

"That is weird. What did he say about the Glass House?"

"His mother, my grandmother, lived in the Glass House and he would visit her there. He told me that the place was protected by a foreign embassy and he also mentioned the name Raoul Wallenberg, but the names Lutz and Kraus never came up."

"And why didn't he live in the Glass House?"

"He didn't like how everyone was packed in so tightly,

or the smell that went with it. My father walked free on the streets of Budapest wearing an SS uniform. He carried out various rescue missions for the Jews of the city."

"Kraus told me about such heroes."

"He was unique because he held a legal certificate that he had obtained fraudulently from the Germans. All this is written in the book I transcribed from his oral account. Didn't I give it to you?"

"Not yet."

"It's a gray book with a picture of him on the front. It's called 'The Finger of His Left Hand.'"

"You read me several passages from the last version before editing, but you never gave me the printed book. Do you have a copy here?"

"Of course. I'll give it to you before you go. What are you doing with the story in the meantime?"

Rona broke into the conversation: "Ruthy, my friend from Jerusalem who is writing a master's thesis on the Zionist movements before and after the establishment of the state, intends to incorporate research on Kraus's whole story. She is mostly interested in his ongoing disputes with Kastner, who was a Mapai representative in Hungary."

"You know that a few months ago there was a Supreme Court decision regarding the discovery of Shin Bet documents surrounding Kastner's murder."

"I remember that there was a demand for document disclosure. I don't remember a Supreme Court decision."

Rona who, at this point, was already in the midst of a short Google 'research project' read: "The National Archive is not required to reveal additional Shin Bet documents on the murder of Israel Kastner – rules the President of the Supreme Court."

"When was this?"

"On September 13, 2021."

"Yes. We were in Morocco then, and that was even before I heard the tapes in Jerusalem. I guess I missed it when I was scrolling through Ynet."[47]

"It's a big story and a very strange one. You should investigate it. You or that student, the one in Jerusalem..."

"Ruthy Shor," Rona added, and continued: "I'm opening a WhatsApp group for you, me and Ruthy, called 'Budapest.'" To that group, she attached the Ynet article on the Supreme Court decision.

"Do you trust her? Ruthy? There's heavy material here."

"She's the top of the top," Rona quickly answered for me.

"Uri..." Mickey began, still thinking. "It's not just heavy material, your story is here too. This man, Kraus, entrusted a boy from Tel Aviv with a treasure. If you've already gone and opened the storage space, shouldn't you do something with it yourself?"

"I'm aware of the responsibility and the mission that goes along with it. It would be my great honor to bring national awareness to Moshe Kraus's memory, and to give him his rightful place. I just don't think I have those skills, or the time, and that's why I think I need Ruthy's help."

"Help, yes. But it seems to me that you are avoiding taking a leading role."

"Well, I need to finish reading and listening to my sixth session with Kraus first."

---

47. Israeli news website operated by the leading Israeli newspaper "Yedioth Ahronoth."

"You're just reinforcing what I'm saying."

"Yes, you're right, Mickey. But you know how it is, I returned to the fast pace of Tel Aviv and my million affairs. You move away from Jerusalem very quickly."

"Yes," Mickey mused aloud. "Jerusalem versus Tel Aviv, memory versus action."

"Holy versus secular," I added.

"That's precisely a good background for a book. Just saying," Rona elbowed me in the ribs.

"And I think you are the one who should write it, with a historian's help, of course. If you want, I'll also put you in touch with an excellent editor I know."

On the way back, next to me in the passenger's seat, Rona leafed through the book that Mickey had given us. I promised to give her the tapes and notebooks of meeting number six on Sunday.

After dinner I went into the study and looked for Rutha Shorin on Facebook, without success. Searches for lecturers in literature with similar names also brought up nothing. She's probably married and has a different last name, I told myself.

I turned off the computer, moved over to the armchair in the corner of the room, disconnected from Tel Aviv with a pair of high-quality headphones, and went back 50 years again.

Chapter 13

Jerusalem, August 1972

"Good morning, Uri. I'm glad you decided to come," Kraus said, looking at his watch.

"But we agreed that I would come at nine." I was confused.

"True... but we didn't exactly talk last night when you went out and I wasn't sure you'd come today... I was a little worried about you. Are you okay now?"

"Yes, Mr. Kraus, I'm fine. I'm glad she left. I'm going back to Tel Aviv on Saturday night... that is, tomorrow."

"Then we must hurry," said Kraus, passing me on the right and leaving a pleasant fragrance of eau de cologne. He sat down at the table and reached for the open binder. I understood that he had prepared the material in advance. I wondered what caused the special excitement that emanated from him that morning.

"As you know, after the war, Europe was flooded with waves of refugees moving both west and east, some returning to the ruins of their homes, others fleeing from their roots. Thus, in the first months after the liberation of Hungary, I found myself busy helping survivors, including those who wanted to make Aliyah to the Land of

Israel. I was surprised by the large number of Jews in Budapest who were interested in staying in Hungary."

"Did you help them too?"

"Them too… that is, until I left my position at the Eretz Israel office."

"Why did you leave?"

"It wasn't my choice, but I used the time I suddenly had available to support the effort to bring the Nazi war criminals to justice."

"In Hungary?"

"All over Europe. I wasn't allowed to testify firsthand in other countries, but a large portion of those criminals came to Hungary in 1944 after they finished their murder campaigns in other countries, and I could testify about some of them. I knew that the other leaders of Hungarian Jewry were in continuous contact with the Nazis during the war years, and I trusted that their testimony would be even more incriminating."

"Who, for example?"

"I heard Kastner's reference to the subject in 1944, and it seemed that he too had gotten on board."

"What did he say?"

Kraus searched through the binder until he found one of the relevant documents. "Here, I quote: 'Kurt Becher took me under his wing, ultimately, to establish an alibi for himself,' said Kastner, and, regarding Wisliceny, he added: 'He kept me alive and made some concessions in the campaign against the Jews so that I could be a defense witness for him when he and his organization would be called to judgement for their atrocities' – end quote. Kastner had eventually figured out that he had been led astray, and I was happy to hear that he was declaring his intention to mobilize for the hour of revenge."

"So what about testifying in Hungary?"

"Since the Nazis were put on trial in Nuremberg, the Hungarian authorities' main action was to prosecute Hungarian war criminals. They contacted me because they knew about my contacts with the previous government during the war, and I readily agreed. The authorities asked me for all the written material in my possession and, in return, they agreed to give me copies of all the material they would receive from the Nuremberg trials. The Hungarians assisted the new German government and summoned Edmund Wiesenmeier, the former German ambassador, to testify in Budapest."

"To testify? He wasn't prosecuted?"

"Unfortunately, he was not considered a defendant. He was summoned to help locate Hungarian war criminals."

"Weeks after the Wiesenmeier investigation, I received a shocking piece of news. As part of the materials from Nuremberg that the Hungarians gave me, I received a statement that Yisrael Kastner wrote about Kurt Becher. Kastner wrote," Kraus flipped through the binder, pulled out a paper and read: "'Kurt Becher was one of the few SS leaders who had the courage to oppose the plan to exterminate the Jews and to try to save their lives.'"

"Who did he give that statement to?"

"He gave it to the Americans who conducted the Nuremberg trials, and they were surprised by how the witness for the prosecution, Kastner, had changed his tune. Kastner, with his own hands, saved Kurt Becher, the criminal who commanded the unit that murdered at least 15,000 Jews in Russia."

"That's shocking."

"But that's not all. He signed the affidavits as 'Official of the Jewish Agency in Geneva.'"

"He represented them?"

"He didn't ask anyone... I hope. But not just Becher. He also testified on behalf of Hermann Krumey and saved him from death, and Dieter Wisliceny."

"Wisliceny?!"

"Yes. Kastner tried to make sure that the torturer was not handed over to the Slovaks, where he was expected to be given a death sentence."

"Are you sure? But why?"

Kraus went back to the binder and read: "Kastner wrote, and I quote: 'It would be more appropriate for the Americans to prosecute the case against him, since Germany's satellites themselves were too involved in operations against the Jews and, as a result, they may be unable to conduct such a trial impartially.'"

"Why? Why for the biggest villains in particular?"

"Not just for them... Here I have here a comment from Robert Kempner, a senior figure in the Nuremberg trials. Quote: 'Kastner ran around Nuremberg looking for Nazis he could save.'"

"And it worked?"

"Wisliceny was hanged by the Slovaks, but all the others were saved, to a great extent thanks to Kastner's efforts. I went wild, and so did Vrba."

"Vrba... were you two in contact at that time?"

"Somewhat at that time, but much more in the fifties. He himself continued to testify in Nazi trials for many more years. Remember Graf?"

"Who?"

"Otto Graf, from the Canada Commando."

"Oh yes. The one who almost prevented Vrba from entering the hideout... he gave him a Greek cigarette."

"Exactly. It was only in 1971 that he was prosecuted in Austria, and Rudy Vrba, of course, was there."

"So there were some successes. Like Eichmann, for example," I showed off my knowledge.

"Yes... Eichmann," he sighed and went on. "Many fled and disappeared, but many were caught and tried. What is more important is for every trial like that to be publicized all over the world, revealing the dimensions of the horror, and preventing the fugitives from having even one more peaceful night's sleep."

"And what about the official activity of the Jewish Agency? Of the Eretz Israel offices in the various capitals?"

"I tried to skip over that. It's a particularly painful chapter in my life... but you're a sharp-eyed hunter. Let's take a short break," he said and went out to the balcony to smoke. While he was gone, Gusta came into the room.

"How are you, Uri?" She stood next to me.

"You mean yesterday? I'm fine. It's over."

"Sima told me last night that Rutha really wanted to talk to you. Do you want me to ask for her phone number?"

"What, does she have a phone in the kibbutz?"

"Not her own, but there is a phone in the secretary's office."

"No... it's not necessary, thanks."

"Who are you talking about?" Kraus asked from the balcony.

Gusta answered him in German or Hungarian, I wasn't sure which, and he put out his cigarette and came back to his seat.

"Okay, then let's go back to my farewell to the Eretz Israel office. On the 4th of May 1945, Yoel Palgi sent a letter to the Jewish Agency, allegedly on behalf of all the Zionist organizations in Budapest, requesting that I be released from my position."

"Palgi?" I was amazed. "Even though you arranged refuge and certificates for him?"

"Yes, Palgi. Three weeks later I was released from my position by Chaim Barlas without any reason given. Palgi apologized to me and said 'it was an order from above' that he could not go against. They claimed that the census of the communities, on which my appointment had been based, was taken before the war and was no longer representative. We conducted a new census which yielded the same results in terms of the distribution of the various movements. But they refused to acknowledge the results."

"So what did they do?"

"They made personal accusations against me. Barlas, who understood that Hungarian Jews were angered by the actions taken against me, appointed a committee to look into the accusations, and gave it a month to do so. The committee delayed, meanwhile proposing a compromise arrangement where there would be two general managers of the office. I tried to live that way for two months, but came to realize that all my powers had, in fact, been taken from me. The committee was reprimanded and eight months later all the charges against me were dropped… but they had already achieved their goal. Mapai took over the office."

"That's so frustrating. And then you gave up?"

"No. I prepared all the material for the Zionist Congress, which convened in Basel in 1946. I filed a suit against Kastner for misuse of funds. I was called to testify, and then I learned that Kastner was counter-suing me for libel. From the content of his complaint, I understood that all the material that I had passed on had been handed over to him.

"I spent a whole day testifying against Kastner but, the next day, I was told not to come back because the hearing on my complaint had been halted. Four different entities," Kraus raised his voice, "four of them investigated my complaints, but not a single one of them merited a real investigation, until the Kastner trial."

My heart went out to this impressive old man who had been so wronged. He didn't look at me. Instead, his face was turned towards the yard, engraved with the pain in his soul. I refrained from breaking the silence that filled the room.

"At least one good thing came out of that Congress," he said in a low voice before he brought his attention back to me. "Carl Lutz was honored. He was inscribed in the Jewish National Fund's Golden Book.[48] He is the only Gentile, with the exception of Churchill, to have received this honor. David Remez, a member of the Congress presidium, gave a speech in which he explained what led to the award. He concluded his speech by saying that 50,000

---

48. The Golden Books are a series of books of honor established by the Jewish National Fund. In part they recognize donors but, since they were started in the early 1900s, they preserve the memory of ruined communities and the names of Israeli and diaspora leaders, of Jewish Zionist families, of those who fought for Israeli freedom and of people who just wanted to take part in the building of the Jewish state. Almost all of those whose names are inscribed in the books are Jews.

Jews were saved by virtue of the rescue documents. I believe that there are not enough words to express what I feel and what the Jewish people will always feel, the gratitude for the humane act of one of the Righteous of the Nations."

"And you were not mentioned, Mr. Kraus?"

"Three speakers heaped praises on the operation but ignored my existence. Lutz had tried earlier to include me in the ceremony. He wrote to Dov Yosef from the Zionist Agency on the 15th of June." He pulled out a page from the binder and waved it in front of me before beginning to read it: "'I think it is my duty to report to you the priceless service performed by my dedicated assistant, Mr. Miklós Kraus, in those dark days when our hope of saving those same 200,000 Budapest Jews had almost entirely disappeared. Mr. Kraus somehow never wavered, never lost his nerve, constantly found new ways to gain time to avoid the impending catastrophe. In the midst of a populace in a state of panic, Kraus was infused with humanity. He stood his ground when armed gangs were already spreading destruction among the Jews in the streets and airplanes were dropping their deathly loads over the city. As an eyewitness, I would like to state that because of Mr. Kraus's unwavering courage, thousands survived Szálasi's terror and the siege of Budapest. I know there will never be a better opportunity to thank Mr. Kraus than the upcoming Zionist Congress. When my name is frequently mentioned in the press in this regard, I would like to make it clear that, without the help of Mr. Kraus, my efforts would have been of little avail. I am confident that the upcoming Congress will seriously consider publicly thanking a man who fought bravely on the front line and won the battle.' End of quote." Kraus finished reading and looked at me.

"Wow, the things he said about you! I'm so proud! And did they invite you?"

"No. Carl Lutz gave me words of appreciation from the stage and earned applause. Among the pages of the report, prepared for the Zionist Federation administration at the congress, my work was referred to by the Jewish Agency management for the first time, and also the last time. I made a copy of the document for you. Authorized testimony from a Zionist entity," he said, handing me the photocopy.

I read proudly out loud: "One of the Eretz Israel offices which existed throughout the years of the war and played a valuable role in Aliyah and rescue was the office in Budapest. Even when Hungary was swept into the system of the Nazi occupation, the Eretz Israel office did not cease its operations, through 'rescue certificates' sent to them by the Jewish Agency in Istanbul to save the olim[49] from deportation to Poland. From the time the German troops entered Budapest in March 1944 and the persecutions and deportations against the Jews in Hungary began, the Eretz Israel office, under the direction of Mr. M. Kraus, became a rescue institution for many olim who gathered under the protection of the Swiss consulate, and the right to Aliyah certificates protected them from deportation to Poland. About 40,000 of Hungary's Jews were saved from death in this way."

---

49. Jews who are immigrating to Israel (lit. trans.: "people who are ascending").

I returned the document to him with a beaming smile of pride. "So you got recognition anyway."

"Yes, except that only a few people have seen this report, Uri. I walked around Basel as an outcast in the eyes of most of the emissaries, sadly following Kastner who was strutting around there like a peacock, sought out by crowds of people. Take this, Uri. Keep this paper."

I picked up the paper and folded it in half with a sense of awe, glancing at Kraus and obtaining his approval. "I'll take care of it, Mr. Kraus."

"Well... after that, I continued to travel around Europe for a few years. I helped in Nazi trials and in organizing illegal Aliyah. With the establishment of the State of Israel, the gates of Aliyah opened, but even these waves subsided at the end of the 1940s. So I sent Gusta to Israel in the early fifties while I tried to find a way to make a living in Israel. The unofficial 'boycott' against me closed all doors. I turned to my friend from the Mizrahi movement, Minister Yosef Burg, and Knesset member Yitzhak Raphael, but to no avail."

"But they are from Mafdal,[50] not from Mapai."

"That's right, and they also really tried, but their power was limited... and they didn't ..."

"Didn't what? Please go on."

"They tried. They did help me get reimbursement from the Jewish Agency for the shipment of furniture I sent to Israel, and they tried without success to help me get the Jewish Agency apartment promised me in Yad Eliyahu, but nothing more than that... and the closed doors became locked from the moment the defamation trial

---

50. The National Religious Party, formed in 1956.

against Malchiel Gruenwald began, or as it was known then, the 'Kastner trial.'"

"What did they sue this Gruenwald for?"

"He publicly stated that Kastner had rescued his own relatives and helped the Nazis send hundreds of thousands to the extermination camps without resistance. Gruenwald even accused Kastner of receiving money from the Nazis for his services, including his testimony in their favor after the war."

"And why did this trial close the doors of employment to you?"

"Because I assisted the defense with a lot of information, and also gave testimony, while Mapai was busy making any witnesses disappear who could have helped testify against Kastner, and who might have spotlighted the role and dysfunction of the Yishuv[51] leadership during the war years."

"Make them disappear? What do you mean? Eliminate them?"

"No, you don't need to go that far. Not at first… I mean, for example, George Mantello, remember?"

"Yes. The one who distributed the Auschwitz report throughout the world."

"Nice, Uri. He came to Israel to testify, but Moshe Sharett, the prime minister at that time, approached him and asked him not to shake up Israel's fledgling system of government. In the morning, before it was time for him to testify, Mantello boarded a plane and left Israel. Isaac Sternbuch, who had worked from Switzerland to save Hungarian Jews, flew to Israel to testify but then also left

---

51. Lit. Settlement. Refers to the Jews living in pre-state Israel.

before testifying, claiming that his wife was ill. Bandi Grosz, a key messenger of the rescue committees in Budapest and Istanbul, received $15,000 from Teddy Kollek on the condition that he would leave Israel without testifying."[52]

"Literally all the senior government officials joined the campaign."

"Yes. All of them. Yoel Brand, Kastner's partner, reported that days before his testimony documents were stolen from him relating to the fact that Moshe Sharett had turned him over to the British. He had been unemployed for five years and bitterly resented the authorities.

"Attorney Tamir, who led Gruenwald's defense, claimed that Brand's life was in danger and that he was being pressured to evade testifying. Indeed, before the trial, a job was arranged for him on the ship 'Shoham' and he sailed out of the country on that ship."

"So why weren't you offered anything?"

"Oh, they made offers, of course they did. At first, they sent me my friend, Michai Shlamon, and then Dr. Judah Spiegel, and when those two came back with a negative response from me, Prime Minister Sharett approached me and offered to arrange employment for me."

"And you refused?"

"The offer was very tempting. They offered me the position of deputy ambassador in whatever Israeli embassy in the world I chose, provided that I disappeared from the country... and I refused, Uri. Yes, I refused. During that same period, they also broke into my apartment in Hadar Yosef and stole documents from me."

---

52. From Ayala Nedivi, *Between Kraus and Kastner* (Heb.), Carmel Publishing, Jerusalem, 2015, pp. 436 (coll. 18 January 1955, gimmel"mem 009/657)

"I remember. This was also the event that caused the attorney Shmuel Tamir to warn you not to walk near the edge of the sidewalk. If they were so worried about the trial, why did they sue that Gruenwald for libel?"

"Arrogance. A mistake that came from a lack of boundaries. They felt that all systems were operating and would continue to operate at the Movement's command. This feeling was a consequence of years of rule that dominated all aspects of life in the young country, and of decades of running the Yishuv before the War of Independence."

Kraus got up and brought three thick binders from the bookshelf bearing the title 'The Kastner Trial' in black marker, along with a book in English called *Perfidy* by Ben Hecht. "I'd rather read to you from the court records, together with Ben Hecht's perceptive descriptions," said Kraus, returning to his seat as I nodded curiously.

"I was a key witness on behalf of Malchiel Gruenwald and, of course, I was present for all the hearings. At the beginning of the trial, the atmosphere of governmental arrogance pervaded the courtroom. Kastner and the prosecutor, full of confidence, described their glorious work during the Holocaust, presenting it as a symbol of courage and honor. And thus he testified:

"'At the end of April 1944, the German military agents informed us that the deportation had already been finally decided upon, and an agreement had been reached between Hungary and Slovakia for the passage of the deportation trains from Hungary to Auschwitz. There was also notification from Auschwitz itself that they were preparing to receive Hungarian Jews...'"

"This happened after he revealed the Vrba-Wetzler report to the Nazis."

Kraus took off his reading glasses, scratched his right cheek and looked at me. "That's right, Uri but, of course, he didn't describe that in his testimony. I'll continue with a quote from Ben Hecht's book: 'In the last meeting with Krumey I demanded to speak urgently with Wisliceny. I wanted to try and get an immediate intervention in the situation through him. Krumey told me that Wisliceny was in Cluj and I demanded that he allow me to travel to Cluj. He agreed, on the condition that we pay the million pengős that we still owed. Wisliceny did not give me all the details about the dirty job he had done, but it was clear that he would not engage in rescuing Jews now, that instead he was there to destroy Jews, as one of the leaders of the annihilation.' This is a quote from Kastner's words."

"And even though he heard it in Cluj, and even though it was after he read Vrba's report, Kastner didn't warn the Jews of Cluj," I said.

"No. He didn't warn them. He misled them and kept order and, in his testimony at this point, he stood tall, proud and confident. Listen to this: 'The German de-Nazification court invited me to appear at the trial of Kurt Becher. I didn't go. I had no desire to appear there before the Germans. I had enough of them during the war. However, I agreed to give a statement regarding Becher. It is not true that I helped him in Nuremberg to escape his punishment. In Nuremberg I gave no formal testimony in his favor. I did not testify or give a sworn statement.' At this point there was a sense of victory in Kastner's legal camp. The judge suggested to Tamir that his client, Gruenwald, plead guilty. Tamir, who had recognized the lies in Kastner's testimony, pretended to consider the offer and consulted with his client who, of course, refused. And this is where Tamir's cross-investigation began."

"It's really a thriller."

"Indeed, it's a thriller built in stages. Tamir released his ammunition slowly. The first day was a day of exploration, after which Tamir chose the 'Kurt Becher' incident as the main issue for breaking through the wall of lies. I will read you the dialogue between the two:

"Tamir: 'Perhaps you have a copy of the sworn statement regarding Becher?'

Kastner: 'I don't know if I have a copy.'

Tamir: 'You brought a whole briefcase full of documents here, including insignificant ones. How is it that you did not preserve a document of such historical importance?'

Kastner: 'I don't have to keep every single paper.'

Tamir: 'Perhaps you remember, Mr. Kastner, how many pages there were in that sworn statement?'

Kastner: 'No. I don't remember, but it was short.'

Tamir: 'Was the statement in favor of Becher or against him?'

Kastner: 'I didn't give a statement either in his favor or against him. I meant to tell the truth, neither to benefit him nor to harm him.'

Tamir: 'Is it true that you had no personal or Jewish-national interest to take an initiative in favor of Becher?'

Kastner: 'That's right.'

Tamir: 'And when you were asked about him, you only told the truth.'

Kastner: 'When I was asked, I testified only the truth.'"

"He's setting a trap for him!" I exclaimed.

"That's right. I'll continue:

Tamir: 'Your testimony in Nuremberg did not influence his release?'

Kastner: 'I don't know if my testimony influenced his release.'

Then Tamir pounced on him:

Tamir: 'And I tell you that Becher was released from Nuremberg thanks to your personal intervention.'

Kastner (shouting): 'That's a blatant lie!'

Tamir: 'I request Exhibit 22.'

"Understand, Uri, Exhibit 22 was a document that Kastner himself submitted to the court. It was a long letter that Kastner wrote to Eliezer Kaplan, a board member of the Jewish Agency, in 1948. Tamir reads from the letter:

'Kurt Becher was a former colonel in the SS and served as liaison officer between Himmler and me during our rescue efforts. He was released from his imprisonment in Nuremberg by the Allied occupation authorities thanks to my personal intervention.' Is that what you wrote?

Kastner: 'Yes.'

Tamir: 'Now choose one of the two answers. Well, which one do you choose?'

"Kastner didn't sound so confident any more. He squirmed for a while between the two contradictory claims until he finally made a choice: 'It is a lie that Becher was released due to my personal intervention.'

"Now Tamir asked him again for a copy of the testimony he had given, and Kastner again claimed that he did not have it.

Tamir: 'Did you insert a recommendation at the end of the statement?'

Kastner: 'I do not remember. I think there was no recommendation.'

Tamir: 'Would you agree with me, Dr. Kastner, that personal intervention in favor of an SS officer, including Kurt Becher, constitutes a crime against the nation?'

Kastner: 'I answer in the affirmative: it constitutes a crime against the nation.'

"Fear of Holocaust survivors' outrage led the senior Mapai officials to decide to replace the prosecutor and turn over the management of the case to Chaim Cohen, the Attorney General. Tamir understood that his life would become more difficult, but he continued his attack in the next session of the trial:

Tamir: 'On page 108 of your testimony you said: When I was in Nuremberg the first and second times, I did not give any testimony regarding Becher. Did you say that?'

Kastner: 'I do not remember.' (looking at his testimony papers) 'Yes, I did say that.'

Tamir: 'When I asked you, on page 291, whether, from your point of view, personal intervention in favor of an SS officer, including Becher, constituted a crime against the nation, you testified that this constituted a crime against the nation. Is that correct?'

Kastner: 'That is right.'

Tamir: 'Now, sir, this is the sworn statement you gave,' (hands him the document that Kastner claimed he did not have. Kastner looks at the document for a long time.) 'Is it so difficult to identify?'

Kastner: 'I'm checking it.'

Tamir: 'Look at the back, it's certified by a notary public. Is it hard for you to remember? Well, is that it?'

Kastner: 'As far as I remember.'

Tamir: 'Now I'll read to you the end of your sworn statement: There can be no doubt that Becher was one of those very few SS leaders with the courage to oppose the plan to exterminate the Jews and to try to save human lives.'

And so, Tamir continued reading until he came to the final words of the document: 'I am making this statement not only in my own name, but in the name of the Jewish Agency and the World Jewish Congress. Signed by Rudolf Kastner, Jewish Agency official in Geneva.'

Judge Halevi addresses Kastner: 'Who gave you the authority to make this statement on behalf of the Jewish Agency?'

Kastner: 'Dobkin and Barlas empowered me to speak on behalf of the Jewish Agency.'"

"Those were the two who ousted you after the war!" I exclaimed.

"Indeed, those are the two, but let's go on. Kastner claimed that he understood from his conversations with them that he was authorized: 'And, within this framework, I am permitted to make the statement,' he said. Then came the knockout.

Tamir: 'When you told this honorable court that you did not give any testimony or sworn statement at Nuremberg, neither before the International Court nor before any of its subsidiaries, you knowingly lied to this court!'

Kastner (shouting): 'I deny this. What you are doing is a national crime.'

Pandemonium broke out in the courtroom, followed by screaming newspaper headlines. There was testimony from that Nazi prosecutor, Taylor, whom Kastner had boasted about inviting, and testimony from his deputy, Walter Rapp, who said: 'Until Kastner arrived, there was a greater chance that Becher would be tried by us. Becher's final release was solely a result of Kastner's arguments and pleas, and from the content of his sworn statement.'

"Chaim Cohen interrogated Kastner again.

Cohen: 'If you had to give this statement today, would you give it or not?'

Kastner: 'Yes, but without the last sentence. That is, I would not give this statement on behalf of the Jewish Agency.'

"What do you think, Uri?"

"I don't understand why, from the bottom of the hole he had dug himself into, he changed that sentence in particular. It seems to me that this Chaim Cohen was more concerned about the Jewish Agency than about Kastner... but... but why did Kastner cooperate with this?" I asked.

"He was terrified of the regime. But he continued to proudly claim that his human duty was to support Kurt Becher."

"But that contradicts his sworn statement in the Israeli court."

"At this point, it was already clear to everyone that he was a liar. Now he was trying to save the remains of his honor. But Tamir wouldn't let him:

Tamir: 'Do you know that the Waffen-SS used to handle the clothes and belongings of the exterminated Jews?'

Kastner (angrily): 'I have never heard of that! It is absolutely not true that they did this systematically.'

Tamir: 'Is it true that the Economic Department extracted the gold teeth of the murdered Jews?'

Kastner: 'You are a complete ignoramus! That is a lie!'

"Tamir did not need to continue listening to Kastner's denials, shouting and insults. He had achieved his goal. In the next stage, Tamir brought in about 20 survivor-witnesses from Cluj who told their stories from the witness stand."

"Those that Kastner never told what he knew about the destination they were being sent to?"

"Yes, Uri, and he may have prevented the bedlam that would have ensued if they had heard about it. One of them, named Freifeld, testified:

'After the first transport left the ghetto, the residents of the ghetto gathered in the community yard, and Kohani,' (one of the Kastner group) 'climbed on a crate and read a letter to them saying that the first group had arrived in 'Kenier Mezo,' that the families there live together, the elderly look after the children, the young go to work, there are proper places to sleep, proper places to work. I asked Hillel Danzig what this letter was based on. And he replied that it had a basis and that I should try to get organized and leave early, since we know very well from our experience that whoever arrives first gets a better place.'

Tamir: 'Were you transported to Auschwitz?'

Freifeld: 'Yes.'

Tamir: 'Did Hillel Danzig also go there?'

Freifeld: 'God forbid.'

"You understand, Uri. Danzig left on the Kastner train and, at the time of the trial, he was an important journalist at the newspaper 'Davar,' the newspaper of Mapai. He was also called to testify and, under Tamir's interrogation, he was forced to admit that he knew in advance that he was going to be taken to a 'safe place.' Danzig testified that Kastner did not tell him that the Cluj masses were about to be sent to the gas chambers at Auschwitz. And so, after Freifeld, more and more witnesses came forward and told the stories of the deception that had been sold to them and that had caused them to walk in orderly fashion to the trains and to Auschwitz. Joseph Katz testified that it was only a short distance to the Romanian border. 'It was very easy to cover that distance, only no one knew what the danger was.'

"From here, Tamir went on to interrogate Kastner:

Tamir: 'Is it true that during the entire time that the list of the 388 to be rescued was being compiled, deportation from Cluj continued at a rapid pace?'

Kastner: 'That is correct.'

Tamir: 'I tell you that your "rescue committee" in Cluj never advised the Jews to resist, either with arms or passively.'

Kastner: 'I have never heard that people would advise the Jews to resist.'

Tamir: 'At that time, did you know the significance of the expected deportation to Auschwitz?'

Kastner: 'Yes.'

Tamir: 'When you spoke to your father-in-law, Dr. Fischer, the leader of the Cluj Jewish Council, did you advise him to organize resistance?'

Kastner: 'I did not advise him that.'

Tamir: 'How do you explain that in Cluj there were more Jews on the rescue train than in any other city?'

Kastner: 'It was not up to me.'

Tamir: 'So it was just a coincidence that Eichmann preferred Cluj over the other provincial towns, and it had nothing to do with the fact that Cluj is your hometown and where you had relatives and friends?'

Kastner: 'It was just a coincidence.'

Tamir: 'And I'm telling you that you specifically asked Eichmann for that. It's natural. Why don't you admit it?'

Kastner: 'That's right, I specifically requested it.'

"Tamir questioned Kastner about warnings he had passed on to other provincial towns, and Kastner was forced to admit that he had not done so due to lack of time. Then Tamir called Hanna Szenes' mother to the stand, and she explained how Kastner had avoided meeting with her many times when she knocked on his door, and how his assistant, Grossman, had convinced her not to hire a lawyer."

"Very thorough work," I marveled. "He completely undermined Kastner."

"Not only Kastner. Tamir later systematically attacked the lack of reaction by the Yishuv leadership in Israel, including pointing an accusing finger at verified decisions by David Ben-Gurion. According to Tamir, during the Holocaust of Hungarian Jews, Mapai's newspaper 'Davar' covered the terror of the Irgun[53] and Lehi[54] more than Nazi terror.

"The trial, as I described to you, Uri, was transformed from a libel trial of Gruenwald to a prosecution of Kastner. Gruenwald was acquitted of the libel charge, but was fined one lira because he could not prove that Kastner

---

53. Trans.: organization. A Zionist paramilitary organization that operated in Mandatory Palestine between 1931 and 1948. Its official name was the National Military Organization in the Land of Israel, abbreviated in Hebrew as Etzel, which was the other name by which the organization was known.

54. An acronym that stands for Fighters for the Freedom of Israel. It was a militant paramilitary organization founded in 1940, pejoratively known as the Stern Gang after the founder Avraham Stern.

received money from his Nazi collaborators in exchange for the assistance he gave them. The court ordered the Israeli government to pay Malchiel Gruenwald's legal costs."

"If they did not prove that he received money, why did Kastner assist the Nazis after the war?" I asked.

"The fact that they did not prove it doesn't mean that it did not happen. It just means that they did not find evidence. There are opinions that say that the Nazis blackmailed him and threatened to reveal his collaboration during the war, or the fact that some of the money collected by the Jews to pay a Nazi ransom remained in his pocket. I have no proof, but I cannot explain the special effort that Kastner made."

"What effort?"

"The American prosecutor testified that Kastner ran around Nuremberg looking for Nazis who were seeking protection. He contacted families of SS men who were on trial. He offered to send food parcels to the wife of the villain Krumey. How do you explain that?"

"I don't know. I'm waiting for your testimony."

"Okay, Uri. So, of course, I was one of Gruenwald's defense witnesses, and a source of information for Attorney Tamir, but the biggest compliment I received was from my opponent, Chaim Cohen. Cohen tried to clear Kastner of bad intentions and attribute his bad deeds to something like good faith... and said: 'I claim that one should not believe that this damned Eichmann is capable of making a promise and keeping it, but this clear and bitter fact has nothing to do with Brand's and Kastner's good faith and purity of intention. Apparently, there was only one Jew in all of Hungary wise enough not to believe this, and that was the witness Kraus.' These are the words of the Attorney General, Chaim Cohen. But this did not convince the court, which ruled: 'Kastner sold his soul to the Devil.'"

"So you both won compliments and finally got a platform for a fair trial."

"I hoped that the ruling party would change its conduct in the wake of the trial, but that was not the case. That same night, an appeal was filed with the Supreme Court. And a few years later, it ruled, not unanimously mind you, that Gruenwald had slandered Kastner. Three of the five judges ruled that Kastner did not collaborate with the Nazis during the war. All five agreed that Kastner acted 'criminally and fraudulently' in rescuing the war criminal Becher after the war 'without justification.' Do you understand that, Uri? And so, people claim today that Kastner was acquitted by the Supreme Court." Kraus paused and looked at me for a few seconds. "But that's not true," he said hoarsely. "It's simply not true."

I looked at him, focusing on his unlined face, wondering how a man of his age, who had been through so much in his life, could have such a smooth complexion. Kraus, who caught my gaze, looked straight at me and continued:

"But even before the appeal, Mapai senior officials began to prepare for the expected developments. Ben-Gurion was very afraid of what would happen in the appeal. There were rumors that Tamir had a suitcase full of new evidence against Kastner, and against others. The government feared that Kastner would break again in the face of the new evidence. Kastner himself also felt at that time that the leaders' feelings toward him had cooled. He wanted to believe that the Ben-Gurion government, with all its strength after the glorious victory in the Sinai campaign, would be able to rescue him. But what was decisive here, Uri, was the irony of fate – at midnight, one night in March 1957, a few months before the Supreme Court appeal opened and two months after the security guard that had been assigned to Kastner after the trial was removed, he drove home alone in his car and crossed the sidewalk to the entrance of his house when a man approached him from the shadows and asked if he was Dr. Kastner. When he answered in the affirmative, the young man fired shots at him. Kastner tried to escape, but two bullets struck him, one in his body and one in his head. He was taken by ambulance to the hospital. After surgery, he began to recover his senses but, ten days later, on the 15th of the month, he was found dead in his bed."

"Were you happy to hear about that?"

"No, Uri. I was really looking forward to the Supreme Court trial, and I'm never happy about a person's death, even someone with whom I was in conflict. The whole murder case was very strange to me. The murderers were arrested and sentenced to life imprisonment. Strangely, four years later, they were pardoned and released. The gunman himself, Ze'ev Eckstein, was a secret agent of the Shin Bet until two months before the murder."

"So you think the Shin Bet murdered Kastner?"

"I'm not saying that, but I suspect that it knowingly did not prevent the murder."

"Wow. That's explosive. And the police didn't look into it?"

"All the government institutions breathed a sigh of relief and buried the affair, until today," he said, closing all the open binders on the table and getting up to put them back in their places.

"Mr. Kraus, thank you. It was a fascinating morning. And thank you for everything in general."

"Thank you, Uri. Take this book," he said, handing me Ben Hecht's book *Perfidy*. "It's in English, but I've already seen your impressive abilities. Keep it with the page I gave you."

"Certainly. I'll keep them. I mean, I'll read them and keep them, Mr. Kraus. Are we done?"

"Absolutely. Unless you want to hear a summary of the Eichmann trial."

"Is it as long as the Kastner trial?"

"It was very long, but we'll cut it short." He looked at his watch. "I'll have to finish in fifteen minutes anyway," he said, and went to the telephone in the hallway.

I took advantage of the break to stretch and go the bathroom. Gusta, who was moving around quietly in the kitchen, approached me on my way back to the living room.

"Mrs. Tsipora told me you are leaving tomorrow evening. When will you visit us again?"

"I don't know exactly. Probably during the holidays, Mrs. Gusta. For sure at Passover."

"I'll be happy to see you. You've brought Miklós a lot of joy. I usually don't let him talk about those times; he gets very angry, and his heart isn't that strong. But with you it's different."

"Why is it different?"

"It's different because..." Kraus cut her off with his entrance to the room, and she seemed to be grateful for the interruption.

"Let's continue, Uri."

"So what was your life like after the trial? And why, in fact, didn't you testify at the Eichmann trial?"

"Well, Uri," Kraus sighed. "Look. My life after the testimony I gave at the Gruenwald trial wasn't easy. My ability to find work was severely affected. I managed to find positions in the Welfare Ministry when the Mafdal ministers were in power, and in the Youth Aliya[55] Swedish village, but I didn't manage to find satisfaction or an adequate livelihood in my professional life. I had high expectations of the Eichmann trial. For me, he was the symbol of evil, the one primarily responsible for millions of murders." As he spoke, he got up and brought a new binder from the shelves.

"At night I dreamed of the day when I would face him on the witness stand and settle the score. Almost a year passed from the day of his capture until the opening of the trial. During these months I sorted through the thousands of documents I had, and added hundreds more that were sent to me from Hungary. Vrba was also filled with excitement. At that time he was in London, but he intended to come to Israel for the trial. Six months after Eichmann's capture, Vrba called me, very agitated, and asked if I had seen the recent issue of 'Life' magazine. He told me that, in anticipation of the trial, the magazine had published the transcript of interviews with Adolf Eichmann by the Dutch Nazi journalist Willem Sassen. 'There Eichmann admits to all his crimes and even boasts about them,' Vrba told me in agitation. 'And there is even more sensation-

---

55. An organization that rescued thousands of Jewish children from the Nazis during the Third Reich. Youth Aliyah arranged for their resettlement in Palestine/Israel in kibbutzim and youth villages.

al news there,' he continued. 'Eichmann describes the aid and cooperation he received from Jewish leaders in Hungary.'" Here Kraus stopped and looked at me.

"So that's good, isn't it?" I asked.

"It could have been good. A real disinfection of terrible wounds but, from my experience in the Kastner trial, I knew that there was explosive material here that the Israeli government would be afraid to make public."

"Why?"

"First, there was Eichmann's description of Kastner. I quote:

Eichmann: 'I now concentrated on negotiations with the Jewish activists in Budapest... among them Dr. Rudolf Kastner, the authorized representative of the Zionist movement. Dr. Kastner was a young man, my age, an attorney who was cold as ice, a fanatical Zionist. He agreed to help persuade the Jews not to show opposition to the deportations – and even to maintain order at the collection camps – if I would close my eyes and allow a few hundred or a few thousand young Jews to immigrate illegally to the Land of Israel... "You can take the others," he would tell me, "but give me this group." That was the gentleman's agreement between me and Kastner.'

"Do you understand what Ben-Gurion was afraid of?"

"I understand."

"But there was another big fear. The interview mentioned senior Nazis who, in the early 1960s, were at the top of the government of the 'new Germany.' The German Chancellor, Adenauer, and Ben-Gurion had a close relationship in those years, and this revelation embarrassed them."

"So what happened with this testimony at the trial?"

"The testimonies for the trial were carefully selected to suit the government. Despite my numerous appeals, and meetings that were held with me, I was not allowed to testify in court. Vrba was also rejected. What the prosecutors did agree to was a written statement from Rudy Vrba."

"Why was that better for them?"

"Because a written statement cannot spring any surprises on the witness stand. Ben-Gurion was very afraid of a situation in which the Eichmann trial would also serve as an indictment against the Zionist leadership's conduct in Israel during the war. For the same reason, they also refused to bring a 'walking hazard' like me to the stand. What we gained from the ban on Vrba's testimony was a series of interviews he conducted with the English newspaper 'The Daily Herald.' Three years later, he sat down again with the same journalist, Alan Bastic, and published his book, *I Cannot Forgive*."

"That's the book we read."

"Yes."

"And what happened at the trial with Eichmann's interviews with Sassen?"

"The prosecutor managed to obtain the original draft, with Eichmann's handwritten notes and corrections. The court allowed only the sentences in his handwriting to be used and ignored the dozens of printed pages with Eichmann's notes on them, which could, in fact, serve as his 'signature' approving the content that wasn't marked."

"So if Ben-Gurion was so afraid of the trial, why did he embark on the complicated operation to capture him?"

"Good question, Uri. Good question."

"Miklós, I'm sorry to bother you, but we have to go,"

Gusta interrupted our conversation. She said this in Hebrew, directing a broad smile at me.

"We've just finished, my dear," Kraus said and stood up. I stood up too, very close to Kraus. Silence fell in the room. I put my hands in my pockets, seeking a solution and relief for the embarrassment that had descended on both of us. Gusta took another step and placed her hands on both of our shoulders.

"Dear Uri, it was a great pleasure to host you in our home."

"I'm so grateful to both of you… I wasn't expecting such an experience," I raised my eyes from the carpet and noticed that Kraus's eyes were moist. He took half a step and raised his hands, making me think he was going to hug me. I raised my hands too, but he turned towards Ben Hecht's book on the table and said: "Don't forget it, Uri. You'll need it."

"What will I need it for?"

"For your project, you'll see." He gave me a hug from afar, his outstretched hands on my shoulders, keeping the distance between us. Gusta joined the circle and added a kiss on each of my cheeks. I picked up the book, the document, the tape recorder, and the notebooks. I took one last look at the room that had filled so many hours of my life in the past week, without imagining the role it would still play in my life 50 years later.

Chapter 14

Tel Aviv, June 2022

After I finished reading the last notebook, I got caught up in my business and travelling again. Two weeks later, in a taxi coming home from the airport, I got a scolding call from Rona. The conversation quickly shifted from welcoming me back to Israel to complaints that I was keeping her friend Ruthy hanging.

"Have you two already gone through the tapes you took from Tel Aviv? And the notebooks?"

"Well, Dad, sure. What do you think? It's been about three weeks. Ruthy has to submit an outline for her thesis by the end of the semester, and I'm starting to finalize plans for the summer. We talked about July in Budapest."

"We talked, Rona'leh? You talked about it."

"Ruthy sent a summary of the Supreme Court story on WhatsApp, did you see? It's in the group that I opened for the three of us."

"No."

"Do you want to hear it? Are you free?"

"Yes. I'm stuck in traffic on the Ayalon highway."

"I'm reading it to you:

"'Ze'ev Eckstein, Yosef Menkes and Dan Shachar – former members of the Lehi underground – were convicted of murder and sentenced to life imprisonment. They were pardoned in 1963. During the trial, it emerged that Eckstein was an agent of the Shin Bet, in the underground group that later committed the murder. Many years later, Eckstein confirmed the Shin Bet's claim that he had cut off contact with his operators and had become part of the group. In 2015, it was claimed that the Shin Bet knew about the murder in advance and therefore removed the security it had provided to Kastner.'

"And Ruthy later adds: 'Answer to question 7 from Uri's notebook. Reminds me of the handling of the Champagne case[56] surrounding the Rabin assassination.' What do you say?"

"I see it now. I owe Ruth an apology, I'll write to her."

"I think a phone call would be more appropriate," my daughter lectured me.

A few hours after I got home, I called Ruthy Shor. I was glad to hear her calm voice, free of anger. "Everything's fine, Uri. If it doesn't work for you, let's forget it. I enjoyed the materials you brought anyway."

"No, no, Ruthy. I'm clearing the next few weeks. Are you in Jerusalem? I'm planning to come up this week."

"This week is too busy for me but, if you come up to Jerusalem, maybe you'll meet Ze'ev Maor, who's mentioned in your notebook. He has the entire Kraus family tree. He lives in the Har Nof neighborhood. I'll send you

---

[56]. After Prime Minister Yitzhak Rabin's murder, it was revealed that Avishai Raviv, a well known right-wing extremist at the time, was in fact a Shin Bet agent-informer code-named Champagne. Raviv was later acquitted in court of charges that he failed to prevent the assassination. The court ruled there was no evidence that Raviv knew assassin Yigal Amir was plotting to kill Rabin.

his contact information to the group. We'll talk later, I have to go."

"Thank you, Ruthy. I'll call him this evening."

As if the signals I received weren't enough to spur me on, that same week I was surprised to discover that Channel 11 was broadcasting a film about Eichmann's lost tapes. From my conversations with Kraus, I recognized the printed content of the interviews that Sassen conducted with Eichmann in Argentina. Most of them were not admitted as evidence due to unjustified doubts about their authenticity. The film featured the recorded interrogations in the voice of the fiend. The interviews also brought to the surface Ben-Gurion's network of connections with the German government, as well as the Israeli's government's need to remove the spotlight from the Nazi figures who continued to hold positions in the government. The specific references in Sassen's tapes to Eichmann's connections with Kastner, and the latter's positions, were abhorrent to the Israeli government at the time of the Eichmann trial.

An important name that emerged around Eichmann's capture was Fritz Bauer. Bauer was a German jurist of Jewish origin who, in the late 1950s, became the Attorney General of the State of Essen in Germany. In September of 1957, he received information that Adolf Eichmann was living in Buenos Aires. Bauer tried several times to convince the German federal government and Chancellor Konrad Adenauer to ask Argentina to extradite Eichmann. All of his attempts were rejected. When he realized that Adenauer was not interested in extradition, Bauer quickly passed the information on to the Israeli Mossad. In November of 1957, Shlomo Cohen Abarbanel of the Mossad visited Bauer and received all the material. To Bauer's disappointment, Isser Harel[57] decided to close the case. Bauer did not give up and, at the end of 1959, he arrived in Jerusalem with all the detailed material and threatened the head of the Mossad and Attorney General Chaim Cohen that if they did not act on the material he had disclosed to them, he would release it to the Israeli press. The pressure bore fruit, and two and a half years after being exposed to the precise information, the Mossad began planning the operation to capture Eichmann.

I was upset by this information, and I found myself sharing it on WhatsApp with Rona and Ruthy Shor. Ruthy's response was brief: "Congratulations. You also got an answer to question number 8!"

As a continuation to that week, in which I felt that the universe was sending me signals, Mickey called me from Greece.

"Uri!" he said with glee.

"What's up, Mickey? Where are you?"

"You won't believe it, Uri. I'm sitting on a balcony in the Peloponnese right now with Uri Even. Do you remember him?"

"Of course. We met at your place on Independence Day."

"Right. So I'm telling him about your Hungarian stories, and what do I find out?"

"What?"

"No, you won't believe me. Rudolf Vrba... he... are you sitting down? He's his 'Uncle Rudy.'"

"Stop it. No way. Wow, Mickey. Now that I think about

---

57. Director of the Mossad from 1952-1963.

it, Kraus did mention in one of the recordings some relative of Vrba's in Israel, and he noted that he was my age and had the same name as me."

"So that's him! Want to talk to him?" Without waiting for my response, Mickey handed the phone to Uri Even. We arranged to meet in Israel two weeks later.

• • •

The meeting with Uri Even, which I had been eagerly awaiting, took place at Mickey's house in Afeka.[58] Uri had conducted extensive research with his older cousin beforehand, and had also brought with him Jonathan Freedland's new book on Vrba, which had just been published in England.

After two hours in which I described my meetings with Moshe Kraus, Uri Even began Vrba's family history, calling him 'Uncle Rudy,' moving back and forth between reading from his notebook and quoting from Freedland's book.

"Uncle Rudy, of course, was outraged when the distribution of the Auschwitz report was delayed. In mid-1944, when it was finally distributed throughout the world by Kraus and Mantello, Rudy felt that his first mission was completed and he returned to the region where he grew up. He was surprised to discover that his mother was still alive."

"He didn't try to contact her earlier?" I asked.

"Apparently he couldn't have. The Nazis were also looking for him in Trnava, and he assumed that his moth-

---

58. A neighborhood of Tel Aviv.

er's house was under surveillance. So he looked for alternative ways to contact her. When he arrived in the city, he asked a friend to make his apartment available for a meeting with his mother. With hugs and tears, they fell into each other's arms. Rudy told her about the horrors of Auschwitz, and she told him how she was saved from deportation to there."

"It's really amazing that she survived – most of the Jews of Trnava were murdered in 1942," I said.

"That's right. His mother told him that shortly after his departure in 1942, she had met a new partner, her future husband. Her partner was protected from deportation due to his profession, and was entitled to choose another relative to be included under his own protection. He wavered for a long time between his beloved sister and Ilona, his future wife. He chose Ilona, and the couple married a few days later. His sister was arrested and deported in the next transport, and when he later found out from Uncle Rudy that she had probably perished, he went to the authorities in Trnava and asked to be deported. Rudy described it as a 'suicide by deportation,' and experienced for the first time how his report could also end a life."

"That was traumatic."

"Very much so. Uncle Rudy avoided talking about it. I first learned about it from Freedland's book. After this encounter, he moved to Bratislava where he joined the Slovakian partisans and, after a short training period, he went on his first operational mission. He experienced victories and retreats, recognition and comrades-in-arms, and also the loss of comrades along the way, but nothing could compare to the sense of satisfaction he felt after eliminating Nazi soldiers."

"Is that what he told you?" I asked.

"Again, I remind you that I was a child during Uncle Rudy's visits to Israel. My older cousin mentioned this fact. In any case, Rudy Vrba's unit caused great damage to the German forces, and he was one of the bravest heroes in the unit, and also one of the only survivors, as the unit was gradually depleted. During the Russians' liberation of Slovakia, he found himself in a military hospital; apparently he was wounded in battle. For his achievements and heroism, he was awarded three decorations: the Czechoslovakian Medal of Valor, the Slovakian Uprising Order, and the Czechoslovakian Partisan Medal of Honor. These medals came together with membership in the Communist Party."

"So far, nothing surprises me," I said. "Even from his behavior in the Auschwitz camp and his escape from it, you can already see the image of a hero who does not flee from danger. A role model and someone to be admired."

"Definitely not by everyone," said Uri Even.

"Well, at least for me, and at least from the stories I've heard about him. I suppose many envied him. Maybe that's what's behind the cover-up of Vrba's story all these years. Just like Kraus's story."

"There's a grain of truth in that, but Uncle Rudy's image is much more complex and complicated. His experiences left deep scars on his psyche, making him a controversial figure."

I raised a curious eyebrow, and he continued:

"Beyond his heroic deeds, Uncle Rudy was also one of the smartest people I've ever known and, as you know, he had a phenomenal memory. After the war he joined a special school for military veterans and, in five months, he managed to complete all the high school studies he had missed. He left Bratislava and continued his studies in chemistry at the University of Prague. After his bachelor's, he went directly to his doctorate in biochemistry."

"And all this in communist Czechoslovakia?" asked Mickey as he approached bearing a tray with three glasses of fresh lemonade.

"Yes. He liked the different message that Communism offered as a contrast to Nazi fascism, and the Party also embraced him warmly on the basis of his daring actions. In 1948, the Communist Party appointed him to the position of a 'non-political member of the Action Committee,' which effectively controlled the university. A few weeks after his appointment, he was asked to identify 'negative elements' among the students, expel them from the institution, and fill the ranks with party supporters. Rudy Vrba refused. He refused to cooperate and paid the price. Thus, although he received his doctorate in 1951, he quickly discovered that, in his new status as a 'refusenik,' he could not find research positions or a decent job."

"That's the other side of heroism," I said.

"And of integrity," added Even. "Fortunately, a friend secretly arranged a job for him in a basement laboratory, where he delved into the biochemistry of the brain. An article that he published in a leading Russian scientific journal raised his professional profile and enabled him to participate in professional seminars, first in countries behind the Iron Curtain and later in Western countries. But the atmosphere of terror in Prague only grew stronger, and his friends disappeared overnight. The climax for him came when 14 senior officials were arrested on charges of ideological heresy. Ten of them, Jews, were also accused of Zionism and hanged. Vrba felt that he was trapped again, this time behind human barbed wire. By this time he already had a family with a wife and children."

"Interesting. Kraus did not mention this side of Vrba."

"It may have been Kraus' personal choice," said Uri. "Vrba met his wife, Greta, that summer of 1944, even before the reunion with his mother. A passionate romance developed between the two and he shared with her the full contents of the Auschwitz report. When the Germans invaded Slovakia, their ally, in August 1944, and the Gestapo arrested Greta and her mother, Greta realized that the Auschwitz report had one meaning, and that she had to escape. She and Uncle Rudy were reunited at Prague University after the war, when Greta was a medical student. They were married on April 16, 1949."

"Were you at the wedding?"

"Hello!!! 1949? That's years before I was born."

"Oh, right..." I buried my head in my hands.

"The four Auschwitz escapees were reunited under the wedding canopy: Alfréd Wetzler was a witness, Ernst Rosin was a best man, and Władysław Mordowicz was a happy guest. The alcohol that was poured in large quantities synergized the four, but left Greta outside the circle. It was a sign of things to come. The loneliness grew deeper with the years of marriage. Each of the spouses immersed themselves in their work and research and, even their two daughters, Helena and Zuzana, were unable to bridge the gap that grew until the couple finally separated. Thus, in 1958, Uncle Rudy found himself in a hostile environment, both family-wise and nationally, and decided that it was time for another escape."

"A serial escapee," I said.

"John Freedland calls him the 'escape artist.'"

"In planning and executing a truly complex escape, all of his strengths come to light," said Mickey.

"Reminds me a lot of your father," I commented, "of Ervinka."

"That's right," confirmed Uri Even, who had known Erwin well. "I also see a lot of similarities. In any case, Uncle Rudy's opportunity arose when he received an invitation to participate in two seminars on consecutive dates, in Strasbourg and Vienna. Vrba decided to take advantage of the timing. He met with Greta and gave her back all the girls' things that he had in his possession on the pretext that, after the seminars, he was going to spend a sabbatical year teaching in Moscow. Greta was suspicious of the story, especially since none of her acquaintances at the university had heard of his sabbatical plans. Indeed, he did not return to Prague. Once in Vienna, he bought a one-way plane ticket and landed in Israel, leaving his family behind, unaware of Greta's own plans."

"Wow. He left his daughters behind... that's beyond bravery... and how did Greta respond?" I asked.

"There's an amazing coincidence here. Greta was also fed up with her life in communist Prague and was planning to defect to Britain. At the time, she was having a passionate affair with a British scientist who visited Czechoslovakia frequently. Vrba's expected defection, which she didn't know about, would certainly have blocked any possibility of her going to seminars in the West. As fate would have it, Greta's planned defection day was the same as Vrba's. Her plan was much more complex and complicated, since she, unlike him, was not willing to leave the girls behind. The seminar she was invited to was held in Poland. She had been given a visa that included permission to return from Poland to Prague by plane via any neighboring country. She planned to return from Poland by bus and go by foot to Prague to pick up little Helena and Zuzana, return to Poland by car and on foot and, using forged documents for the girls, take advantage of her visa to fly to Copenhagen."

"She was quite brave, too," I said.

"Greta? An iron woman, as I described, and had a much more complicated and dangerous escape plan than Vrba's. With fateful timing, Greta and the girls boarded the flight to Copenhagen before the Czechoslovak authorities noticed that Vrba had not shown up for his return flight from Vienna to Prague."

"Sounds like a story from a thriller novel," I said.

"It certainly does. He landed in Israel, unaware that his ex-wife and daughters had also escaped from Czechoslovakia. His attempts to obtain a senior research position at the Weizmann Institute, as well as his applications to American institutions, were rejected due to his communist background. He finally found a position in the chemistry department of the Veterinary Institute in Beit Dagan.[59]

"He was very excited to be reunited with us, his relatives living in Israel. He visited us often at our home in Ramat Gan. The sadness of parting with his daughters weighed on him, and he tended to make up for it by playing games and showering affection on me, the little one, and by having long conversations with my older cousin."

---

59. A small town near Tel Aviv.

"This was the period when he met Kraus face to face in Israel."

"I assume they shared their resentment of the Zionist institutions. Although Uncle Rudy arrived after Kastner's murder, he never forgave the man. He saw him as the main culprit in the failure to disseminate the Auschwitz report in May and June of 1944, when hundreds of thousands of Jews from the provincial towns were murdered. Vrba claimed that Kastner was the one who informed Eichmann of the report's existence, and that an arrest warrant was issued for him and Wetzler as a result. He also claimed that in addition to the blackmail the Nazis exerted on Kastner through his relatives trapped on the train, they also knew about the money he had taken during the war and, because of this, and in return for additional payments, they received his favorable testimony after the war."

"Do you or your cousin have any written documents regarding this?"

"No. Rudy Vrba did not present any evidence or concrete information to support his accusations. His encounter in Israel with the heads of Slovakian Jewry brought his anger to the boiling point. These were the two Slovakian Jewish leaders who had interrogated him after he escaped from Auschwitz, and who had received the full report from him. Now, in the late 1950s, they were government officials in the young Israeli state under the wings of Mapai.

"Only two years after landing in Israel did he learn that his ex-wife and daughters were in London and then, after seeing that he had little to look for here, he left Israel and moved to Britain."

"Again a combination of an unpleasant political environment and a fraught family situation," I muttered as if to myself.

"Yes. In England he found a job at the Institute for Medical Research in Carshalton, a half-hour drive from London. The physical proximity and family connection did not bear the desired fruit, and the quarrels with Greta picked up again where they had left off in Prague, until Greta managed to obtain full custody of the girls."

"What year was this?" I asked.

"1960. The following year the Eichmann trial opened in Jerusalem, which also attracted great interest in the English capital, and Uncle Rudy received a lot of press, even though he was not invited to testify at the trial. The journalist Alan Bestic interviewed him for a series of articles he wrote for the Daily Herald. Three years later, the two of them sat down together again and, within three weeks, they had published the book *I Cannot Forgive*, the same book you say you read in 1972 at Kraus's house. The world thought Vrba was accusing the Nazi murderers, but we knew he was accusing those who had denied the victims the knowledge that would have allowed them to rise up and resist these crimes.

"Following the deterioration of his relationship with Greta, Uncle Rudy also managed to arouse opposition from his employers and found himself on a new journey, which eventually landed him at the University of British Columbia in Vancouver."

"The Wandering Jew," I commented. "According to Kraus, that's where he settled."

"Yes, that was his home base from then until his death. That's where he also set up a home with Robin Lipson, a 24-year-old woman who fell in love with the handsome

50-year-old professor. The young Robin managed to free Vrba from the grip of the demons of the past."

"And his connections with the girls?"

"Helena, the older of the two, ended her own life at the age of 30. Uncle Rudy kept in touch with the younger Zuzana, nicknamed Zuza, until the day he died."

"Oh. What a disaster. What a disaster."

"Yes," said Uri. "He went through a very difficult time."

"And besides his wife and Zuza, was there anyone who supported him? Did he keep in touch with anyone from the past?"

"Uncle Rudy didn't talk. The only one he opened up to was his escape partner, Alfréd Wetzler, but communication with Czechoslovakia before the fall of the Soviet bloc was difficult."

"And after the fall of the Iron Curtain?" I asked.

"Alfréd Wetzler died in 1988, two years after Kraus and a year before the fall of the communist regime. He, too, like Uncle Rudy, died forgotten and bitter."

"Vrba, Kraus and Wetzler, three heroes without laurels," I mused aloud.

"Exactly. After his partners in memory died, Vrba was left alone in the world in his attempts to break through the veil of denial and oblivion that had overshadowed him and Wetzler in the State of Israel. His books were never translated into Hebrew and were blocked by historians of the previous generation, most notably Yehuda Bauer, who claimed that Vrba's hatred of the Zionist leadership blinded him and impaired his judgment.

"Fortunately, new hope arose in the late 1990s. Professor Ruth Linn brought to light the story of the Auschwitz escapees and their direct contribution to saving the lives of hundreds of thousands of Hungarian Jews. Professor Lin researched and published Uncle Rudy's extraordinary story, made sure to bring it to public awareness in Israel and, thanks to her, he was awarded an honorary doctorate from the University of Haifa in 1998. His book, the same book you read in English as a teenager, was then translated into Hebrew by Yehoshua Weiss Ben Ami and Shlomit Kedem, and is called in Hebrew *I Escaped Auschwitz*."

"At least justice was done while he was still alive," I declared. "It's a shame that Kraus was denied this. I hope that this gave his tortured soul some rest."

"The following years did bring comfort to Uncle Rudy. He died in March 2006, and was buried in a modest ceremony conducted by his widow and his daughter, Zuza, but without the presence of a Jewish minyan[60] that would have allowed for public prayers to be said." Uri Even closed Freedland's book and leaned back on the couch.

Mickey lit a cigarette and said, "It's amazing how for both Vrba and Kraus there is such a gap between their heroic deeds and the picture that was painted in the collective memory."

"Even for me, despite being exposed to 'the truth' at a young age, there is a big difference between the characters that were engraved into my consciousness in childhood and the way I see them today," I said.

"Sight is deceptive," Mickey said. "Light brings the colors and lines to the eye, but it is the brain that puts together the picture and constructs the memory."

---

60. A prayer quorum of 10 men, required in order to chant certain prayers.

Chapter 15

Tel Aviv, July 2022

I left my meeting with Mickey and Uri Even feeling dejected. The gloomy picture of Vrba's life that I had just heard contrasted sharply with the confident, all-powerful image Kraus had painted for me. I started the car, turned on the music channel and, to the strains of tranquil classical melodies, drove away slowly, wrapped in thought.

When I was already close to home, I called Ruthy Shor and told her about the meeting.

"The truth is that I received answers to the first three questions," I told her.

"Well, go on," Ruthy urged me.

I told her everything I had heard, processing things as I spoke.

"Well, regarding the first question, there's not much new in what you heard beyond what Kraus already knew or suspected," she declared. "Regarding Vrba's book in Hebrew, I was just about to tell you that I also found it in the meantime… and I even read it!"

"Amazing, Ruthy… When did you find the time?"

"While you were on your travels. And as for the question of why Vrba didn't stay in Israel, or return to it, I understand the course of events but still find his choice illogical, especially after the upheaval of 1977."[61]

I found myself coming to Vrba's defense and, in the process, unfolding to her the entire story of his life, including the hidden aspects of his personality and tragic family life. "Wow, Uri," Ruthy said, "this is the first time I've heard you so upset. I understand that encountering this material again wasn't easy."

"The truth is, you're right, I left with a heavy heart. It surprised me too."

"Every hero has his own Little Bela, Uri," she said perceptively, and I nodded as if she could see.

"Oh, listen, Ze'ev Maor, the guy you put me in touch with, sent me the location of Kraus's grave. I think I'll go up to Jerusalem later this week to visit it."

"Where is it?"

"On Har Hamenuchot,[62] Har Tamir. He sent me directions to get there."

"I think I'll come too. I can do it on Wednesday. I have a meeting scheduled with Rona, but I'm sure she'd be happy to join us."

"Great, I'd be happy too, so I'll schedule my trip for Wednesday."

"Send us the location of the plot and we'll meet at the gravesite," Ruthy concluded.

---

61. In elections of that year, the Mapai party lost their control of the government.

62. Trans. "Mount of Burial," the largest cemetery in Jerusalem, built on the side of a mountain.

• • •

On Wednesday at nine in the morning I got on the Hashalom interchange and merged onto Highway 1. The first week of summer vacation had calmed the traffic somewhat which, together with the extra time I had allowed as a safety margin, allowed for a peaceful trip. As I passed Sha'ar Hagai, Rona sent a WhatsApp message to the group informing us that she would not make it to the cemetery, but that she would meet us at Ruthy's apartment in the afternoon.

The closer I got to Jerusalem, the more my thoughts turned to that summer vacation 50 years earlier, when Moshe Krauss's great story was placed on my young shoulders. I reflected on the fact that, at that time, he was same age I was today. I tried to imagine what my meeting today with a 14-year-old boy would be like. I tried, without success, to pick out one such person from the collection of teenagers with whom I am on speaking terms. The only one who fell within the age range was Pierre, the neighbor's son; our conversations in Hebrew spiced with beginners' French usually don't exceed the three minutes that we spend waiting for the elevator. Still, I could recognize in my feelings towards him the curiosity and hope that are stirred by contemplating the promise of an unknown future.

As I drove into Har Hamenuchot, I tried to follow Zeev Maor's instructions. After fifteen minutes of wandering around the mountain, I gave up and pulled over next to a yeshiva student standing by the side of the road. He called over another yarmulka-wearing Jew who was standing by a parked car and, together, they managed to identify the bloc and the plot of Moshe Krauss's gravesite, using some app I was not familiar with.

To spare me the trouble of finding the location myself, the two yeshiva students, Yehuda and Aharon, invited me to follow them. When we parked our cars, they walked with me to the gravesite itself. We stood in front of the tombstone and read:

Moshe (Miklós) Kraus,
son of the late R. Shmuel Halevi
28th Menachem Av 5746.

May his soul be bound up in the bond of eternal life.
Director of the Eretz Israel office, whose initiative saved thousands of Jews in Budapest in the Holocaust, 1944, under the auspices of the Swiss consul, Carl Lutz.

I told them with the pride of a son about Kraus's exploits during the war years, and they suggested that we recite Kaddish[63] together for the repose of the righteous man's soul. When we finished, I paid them generously for their help and said goodbye. I sent a WhatsApp message with my exact location to Ruthy, who thanked me and wrote that she would be there in 20 minutes. I straightened up and looked around. The bright sun beat down on my head and shimmered before my eyes, reflecting off the marble tombstones around me.

In front of me, a group of people gathered by a gravesite 20 meters away. As the last women in the group passed by

---

63. A prayer said for a person who has died.

me, one of them made her companion swear, "You're not bringing this up with them today."

I turned my gaze to the right and focused on Gusta's grave:

> Here lies **Gusta Kraus**,
> daughter of the late Nessa and Frida Stahl
> She made Aliyah from Budapest,
> died in Jerusalem on 13 Tishrei 5760.
> May her soul be bound up in the bond of eternal life

"September 23, 1999," I muttered to myself, looking at the Google translation of the date. Thirteen years after Kraus's burial, and yet his tombstone looked newer. Two pebbles lay on Kraus's tombstone, a sign that someone still visited the grave. I guessed that the same person had also recently renovated it and replaced the slabs covering it. Troubled by the marital symmetry that had been violated, my heart went out to Gusta. I placed my right hand on my head[64] and said the Mourner's Kaddish[65] in her memory.

"Hey, friend," a voice was directed at me from the group clustered around the grave in front of me.

"Could you complete the minyan for us?" I walked towards them and received a warm welcome. I joined in the Sephardic-style Kaddish, silently protesting against the sectarianism that insists on accompanying us even in our death. When we finished, one of the men said: "Let's

---

64. The intention is that he covered his head with his hand out of respect as he said the prayer, since he did not normally wear a yarmulka to cover his head.

65. The prayer said for a deceased person at the funeral, every day for 11 months after the death, and then annually on the anniversary of the death, traditionally by the deceased's son or sons.

join this dear man and say Kaddish at the grave of his parents too." I decided to go with the flow. The men of the group and I walked together to the Krauses' plot and I recited Kaddish while they all responded "Amen." When we finished, the elder of the group said to me:

"It's a great mitzvah[66] for the souls of the dead."

"Rather than prayers, the souls of the dead would prefer that you have peace at home and brotherly love."

The men stared at me, mouths agape. "You're right, you're right," they said as they moved away from me towards the nearest exit. I looked in their direction, happy to see a wide-brimmed hat striding briskly across the entrance and approaching me, with Ruthy's smiling face beneath it.

"I don't get it, you organized a minyan here?!"

I told her with a smile about the events of the last few minutes.

"Aah. Now I understand who they were talking about."

"What did they say?" I asked.

Ruthy glanced at me with a big smile and said, "They said: 'This man channeled our quarrel from the souls of the deceased.' You've become Baba Uri."[67]

"The truth is, I'm the one who got a big lesson here."

"I guess someone had a hard time financing the renovation of both plots," Ruthy pointed to Gusta's tombstone.

"So you noticed too. I'll check it out with Ze'ev Maor, we arranged to meet up."

"Excellent," Ruthy said, opening her bag and taking out

---

66. Literally "a commandment" but in this case the meaning is "a good deed."

67. A play on the name "Baba Sali," a well-known kabbalistic rabbi.

a visor. "You need to protect your beautiful bald head, and drink too," she added, pulling out a thermos and pouring some cool water from it.

"Thank you, what other rabbits do you have in your hat? It's been a while since I've been pampered like this," I laughed. I looked at her admiringly. Red nail polish adorned her fingernails and the nails of her big toes peeking out from flat-heeled sandals. Peach-colored shorts, mostly covered by a white T-shirt, highlighted her tanned legs.

"You're dressed warmly," she said when she caught my glance.

"Last time I was in the area, it was freezing."

"I wanted to give you something I read." Her face grew serious as she pulled two books out of her bag.

"Is there no bottom to this bag?" I asked.

"It really did tear my shoulder muscle," she laughed.

I looked at the Hebrew book. *Between Kraus and Kastner: The Struggle to Rescue the Jews of Hungary*, by historian Ayala Nedivi. "Let's sit there, in the shade," Ruthy said, leading me to the stone fence next to the entrance.

"This is a giant historical work. It's really groundbreaking. You have to read it, you'll get endless support for Kraus's story here."

"Great, how did you find it? But doesn't it, in fact, make your thesis redundant?" I asked in disappointment.

"The book covers the events surrounding the Holocaust of Hungarian Jewry, up until the early 1960s, in depth. We're missing coverage of Kraus's personal and family side, both during his life in Hungary and in his years until his death in Israel. It is a real puzzle, and that is exactly what you should investigate."

"You've surprised me. I did not expect... "

"It is not easy. Compared to the historical wealth surrounding his actions and work, there are almost no traces left of his personal and social life. Most of his contemporaries have already passed away, and he and Gusta left no successors... But there is no need to give up. I know that his sister Rivka's two daughters are still alive. I am trying to arrange a meeting for us with one of them, Shoshi Roth. She lives in Kfar Saba."

"Wow, Ruthy! Well done," I marveled. "But let's think about it for a moment. I didn't even think about the personal-family aspect. Who said that's necessary? I'm not sure Kraus himself would have liked that direction; he guarded his privacy zealously."

"That's up to you; think about it. I don't have a firm opinion about that direction, but I will complete the historical work anyway."

"Yes, I need to think about it. And what is the book in English?" I pointed to the second book she had taken out of her bag.

"It's Jonathan Freedland's new book, *The Escape Artist*, about Rudolf Vrba. Most of it won't tell you anything new, but the last part has some personal details."

"Yes. Uri Even, Vrba's nephew that I told you I met, showed me the book. I ordered it from Amazon."

"So take this one, we'll save you the wait."

"Thanks. How do you feel about the materials you read? Is it similar to what we already know?"

"I don't remember exactly what you knew before... What is certain is that I discovered new angles I didn't know – about the political conduct of the various Zionist movements in the Yishuv and in the Diaspora... and, on second thought," she continued, "I think it's worthwhile for you to delve into his personal story."

"I'll do it, I'm just not sure it will be included in the commemoration project," I said.

"That could be. In any case, you'll get reinforcement when you read Ayala Nedivi's book. I was filled with admiration for his work and his choices, but I finished reading with the feeling of missed opportunities and the pain of his years in Israel."

"I've been feeling this pain in recent months."

"You know..." Ruthy spoke softly, as if talking to herself. "Kraus lived in greatness when the entire dark world around him wanted to escape the uncertainty of the period... and, at the end of his days, when he supposedly lived in an environment full of light, his life was reduced to the hope that his memory would be rescued from the absolute certainty of his small existence."

• • •

We sat silently in the car in the cemetery parking lot listening to the hum of the air conditioner, enjoying the waves of cool air slowly filling the interior of the car. Ruthy finally broke the silence. "So you're sure you're ready to dedicate yourself to this project?"

"With your help and Rona's... yes. Besides, with all the coincidences that the universe has been throwing at me lately, it seems I have no choice."

I was cut off by the ringing of a phone. I heard Ruthy say: "We're still at the cemetery," before she got out of the car and walked away for a private conversation.

"Okay, listen," Ruthy came back and closed the car door. "The next stop is Rehavia. I have a surprise for you. Maybe we'll meet Dina there. It'll be interesting for you," she said with a mischievous glance, noticing that she had aroused my curiosity.

"Let's go…" I muttered, a bit stunned. "But give me directions."

"So go ahead, put on Waze and I'll tell you about it on the way. I sent Rona a WhatsApp that we're on our way." I nosed the car down the slope that connected us to the cemetery's main road and drove on toward the center of Rehavia. Ruthy waited a moment and examined me before continuing.

"Dina told me that many of Kraus's family members were sent to Auschwitz in those few weeks of May-June 1944."

"I know," I said, "that's in my tapes."

"Yes. But it really is a tragic story, Uri. There is Kastner, who saved all his relatives from Cluj and abandoned hundreds of thousands… and there is Kraus, who saved tens of thousands but lost his family to his own detriment."

"Yes. He was busy saving the community," I said. "And who do you think was happier?"

"Are you seriously asking that? I don't think any of them were happy, although Kraus at least got to die among friends in the middle of a game of bridge."

"Cold comfort."

"Yes. Many Holocaust survivors get vitality and a new lease on life from their children and grandchildren, but he didn't get that either. Gusta told Sima who told Dina…" she smiled, "that, at some point, after the German invasion in 1944, a beloved child joined their family in Budapest, but he didn't survive the war."

"Well, she must have meant Little Bela, I told you about him."

"Tragedy after tragedy," said Ruthy, "although it's still unclear why Kraus and Gusta didn't have any descendants of their own. Dina realized that Miklós's brothers also died childless and wondered if there was a genetic issue there or a human choice in the spirit of the terrible times. Kraus didn't tell you anything about it?"

"No. He just talked at length about Little Bela, who was supposed to be not only the beloved son, but also the torchbearer of the entire destroyed Mezőladány community," I said.

"And you, Uri, according to Dina, were Kraus's hope to carry the torch of his life's work for future generations."

"Now you're telling me that?"

"I didn't want to put this burden on your shoulders, but today I see that you're up to the task."

"So you think that's why he chose to talk to me of all people, because I was a young boy?"

"You were a young boy but with good eyes. So different from the nefarious eyes that surrounded him."

"Nefarious from shame, I think."

"That too. You said that he had completely given up on the historians of his time. You have to remember that in those years, Holocaust survivors in general did not receive the support and embrace that they get in our day; most of them also collapsed in the face of the feelings of guilt and the questioning looks they got. You, on the other hand, according to Dina, came as a blank slate, with innocence and curiosity, integrity and intelligence, and you won his heart. Your young and unthreatening age was a bridge for him that he did not find in his own realm. And, of course, you touched him first of all as a boy, drawing from him his unfulfilled love for children."

"Okay. So I think we've checked off a few more items. What do we have left, the riddle fairy?"

Ruthy took the smartphone and looked at her screenshot of the page with questions.

"Question 9: Why were there detectives in the garden?"

"Well, I already figured that out myself. The guy that Rutha met at the demonstration, Udi Adiv, was not just a Matzpen member. He was later arrested and charged with spying for Syria and his connections to a terrorist cell. I assume the Shin Bet did not recommend releasing him after three years," I added sarcastically.

"No. But he was released after twelve-and-a-half years. But question 10 is more interesting: 'Should I call Ruthy?'"

"We've already talked about it. You said you would have behaved like I did."

"Maybe it's because I'm as screwed up as you, but you've had 50 years to dig into the issue, search on Facebook, Google... you were never tempted?"

"As I saw it, as a teenager, as a child, I experienced unrequited love. It was really traumatic as a first love, or a first crush, I don't know. I guess that later I feared another rejection, and then it was already too late, too much time had passed."

"And maybe, like Kraus, you also needed a young bridge," said Ruthy.

A red light stopped us on Ben Zvi Boulevard on our way

to Rechavia. I looked at her inquisitively, admiring her initiative.

"I'm getting off here," she said suddenly as we passed the square on Ben Maimon Boulevard. "I have to go to the grocery store, my refrigerator is completely empty. Take the key to my apartment. Do you remember where it is?" she asked with a smile. "Go in and turn on the air conditioners, okay? I'll be there in ten minutes."

I couldn't keep up with her. I saw her enter Reuven's grocery store, and I veered to the right toward the parking lot. I parked the car and picked up my backpack and her apartment key, which was lying on the seat next to me. I locked the car and walked to the yard of Kraus's building.

"Uri." A voice that sounded vaguely familiar called my name. I took a step back and looked to the right toward the top of the road, trying to identify the figure behind the voice. "Uri. Over here." I saw a waving hand that was already quite close to me.

"Rutha Shorin…? Ruthy?"

"Yes, silly. Still Ruthy to you," she said, and a beloved smile crinkled beautiful blue eyes set under a crown of white curls. "Ruthy… the young one… will return in an hour. That way you'll have time to get to know the editor of your book." She burst out laughing at my shocked expression, took my hand in hers and led me to the stairwell.

Acknowledgments

First of all, thanks to Dr. Nadav Kaplan who got me started on my way when he connected me to the story of Vrba's and Wetzler's escape from Auschwitz and the Budapest Jewish leadership's suppression of the report they wrote.

I am grateful to Dr. Ayala Nedivi, whose doctoral thesis first exposed the work of Moshe (Miklós) Kraus, and whose excellent book *Between Kraus and Kastner* includes thousands of documents that aided me in writing this book. Ayala accompanied me throughout the writing of the book, connected me to additional sources, and reviewed the manuscript as it emerged.

Ze'ev Maor, whose father was saved by Moshe Kraus, and who introduced me to the magnificent Kraus family tree and genealogy, also connected me with other acquaintances and family members whose stories allowed me to draw the lines of Kraus's character as reflected in this book. I also thank Shoshi Roth, Moshe Kraus' niece, who generously gave of her time.

Israel Igra, who received English lessons from Gusta Kraus in his youth, formed the basis for the encounters between Uri, the narrator boy, and Moshe Kraus.

Thanks to my friend Mickey Ber, Arbinka's son, who accompanied me throughout the writing of the book and who connected me with Uri Steinmetz, who shared with us his childhood experiences with "Uncle Rudy" – Rudolf Vrba.

To my friend Miki Haran, who was completely unaware of the heroic deeds of Moshe Kraus, her elderly and beloved neighbor from her childhood. Beyond the description of the couple Gusta and Moshe Kraus, Miki also connected me with the owner of the apartment where the couple once lived, thus allowing me to visit it and absorb the atmosphere and aromas of its surroundings.

I greatly appreciate Timea Tarjani, who guided me between Kraus's stops in Budapest and helped me with my visits to Miskolc and Mezőladány.

Thanks to Dov Eichenwald, owner of Yedioth Books Publishing, who has been pushing me for years to write and opened the doors of the publishing house to me.

Michal Heruti, the book's editor, deserves special mention. Michal has held my hand for the past several years, criticizing, helping, and improving my first two books, and has wisely and sensitively edited this current book. Beyond the editing work, Michal's sensitivity is also reflected in the design of the book's characters, and also in the image of me as I am today after finishing it.

I thank you, my readers, for becoming partners in the effort to correct a historical injustice, to bring Moshe (Miklós) Kraus to center stage as a hero, much to the displeasure and reluctance of all those eyes, evil with shame, who pushed him out of his rightful place.

Notes on the Characters in the Book

The vast majority of the characters presented in the book are based on real people who participated in documented historical events. In addition to the fictional narrator Uri (and his family members and acquaintances, including the two Ruthies), the following fictional characters have been added:

Big Bela and Little Bela – represent the Jewish community of Mezőladány, Moshe Kraus's hometown, most of which perished in the Holocaust.

István Kovacs – represents the Hungarian collaborators, some of whom surpassed their Nazi operators in their cruelty.

Dieter Koch – represents the officials and representatives of the Nazi civilian government who enabled the killing machine to operate, most of whom were spared prosecution at the end of the war.

SOURCES FOR THE BOOK

Hebrew books

Ber, Mickey (editor), *With his Left Finger* (Hebrew), Tel Aviv, self-published, 2010.

Hartman, Yehuda, *Patriots without a Homeland* (Hebrew), Open University, 2020.

Hecht, Ben, *Perfidy* (Hebrew), Israel Press, 1971 (original published in English in 1961 in New York by Julian Messner, Inc.).

Kaplan, Nadav, *Supreme Oblivion* (Hebrew), PhD Thesis, Haifa University, 2010.

Landau, Yehudit, *Fateful Decisions: Jewish Leadership in Hungary and Slovakia 1939-1945* (Hebrew) PhD Thesis, Tel Aviv University, 2020.

Nedivi, Ayala, *Between Krausz and Kasztner: The Struggle for the Rescue of the Hungarian Jews* (Hebrew), Jerusalem: Carmel Publishing House, 2014.

Vámos, György, 1944, *The Glass House Memorial Room*, the Carl Lutz Foundation, Budapest, 2005.

Wetzler, Alfréd, *Escape from Hell* (Hebrew), Yad Vashem, Jerusalem, 2013.

English books

Braham, Randolph L., and Miller, Scott, *The Nazis' Last Victims*, Wayne State University Press, Detroit, MI, 2002.

Freedland, Jonathan, *The Escape Artist*, John Murray (publishers), London, 2022.

Linn, Ruth, *Escaping Auschwitz*, Cornell University Press, Ithaca and London, 2004.

Pecsi, Tibor, *Miklós Krausz and Otto Komoly*, Translation from Hungarian by Timea Tarajani, Budapest, 2022.

Vagi, Zoltan, Csosz, Laszlo, and Kadar Gabor, *The Holocaust in Hungary*, AltaMira Press, Maryland, 2013.

Vámos, György, *Carl Lutz (1895-1975)*, Infolio editions, Geneva, 2013.

Vrba, Rudolf, *I Cannot Forgive*, Regent College Publishing, Vancouver, 1997.

Vrba, Rudolf, *I Escaped from Auschwitz*. London: Robson Books, 2002.

Vrbova, Gerta, *Trust and Deceit*, Vallentine-Mitchell, Chicago, IL, 2006.

Zimring, Nikola, *The Men Who Knew Too Much*, Master's degree thesis in Jewish History, Tel Aviv University, Tel Aviv

Interviews

Igra, Israel, **Miklós and Gusta, 1970s Jerusalem, Jerusalem,** 14 November 2021.

Maor, Ze'ev, **Kraus family tree, rescue stories**, Jerusalem, 8 November 2021

Nedivi, Ayala, **Moshe Kraus's life in Israel and contacts**, 31 August 2021.

Roth, Shoshana, Moshe Kraus's niece, **Moshe and Gusta Kraus's history in Israel**, Kfar Saba, 28 November 2021.

On-site visits

Glass House in Budapest, 29 Vadas Street, visited 8 June 2022.

Budapest community building, 12 Ship Street, visited 8 June 2022.

Old synagogue, Miskolc, visited 9 June 2022.

Jewish cemetery, Mezőladány, visited 9 June 2022.

Synagogue, Kisvárda, visited 10 June 2022.

Archives

Kraus, Moshe, **Rescue Operation in Budapest 1944**, Testimony House Archive, Moshav Nir Galim.

Kraus, Moshe, **Letters, pages of reminiscences, and documents** – Files 1-10, Religious Zionist Archive, Bar Ilan University.

Kraus family, **Pages of testimony – to grant memorial citizenship to victims of the Holocaust**, Yad Vashem, Jerusalem.

Printed in Dunstable, United Kingdom